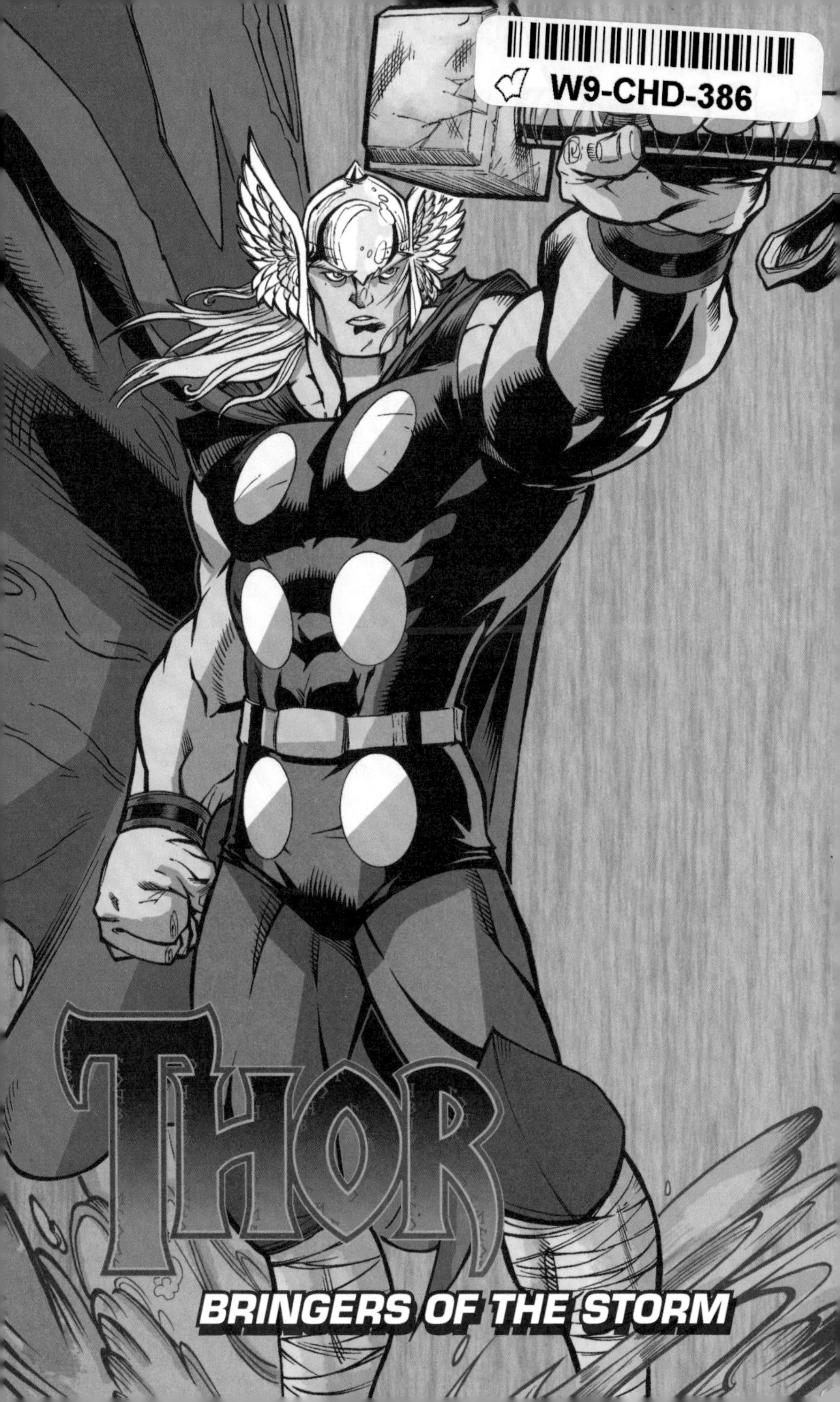
THOR
BRINGERS OF THE STORM

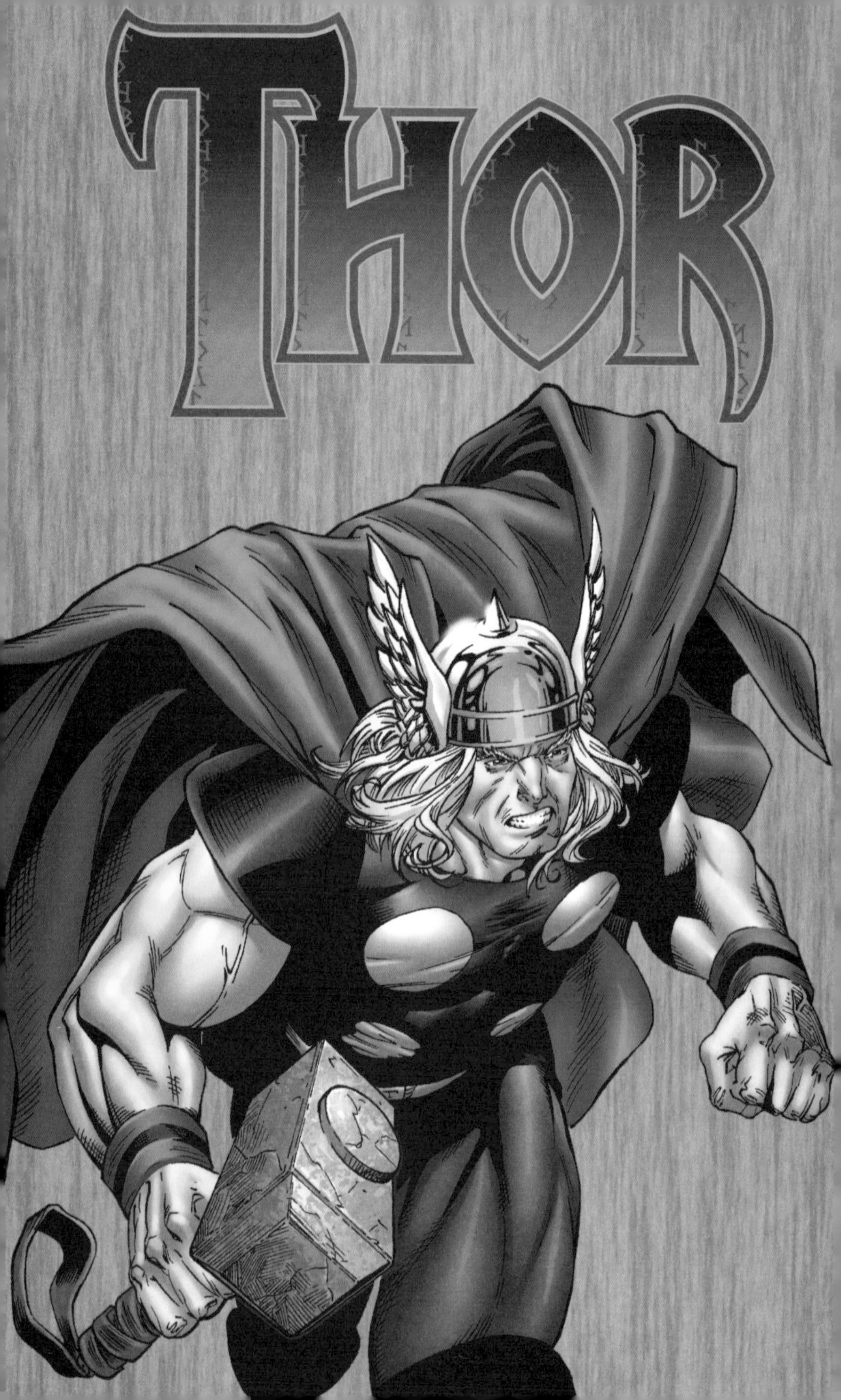
THOR

BRINGERS OF THE STORM

Writers: *Tony Bedard, Jeff Parker & Louise Simonson*
Pencilers: *Shannon Gallant, CAFU,*
Rodney Buchemi & Jon Buran
Inkers: *John Stanisci, Terry Pallot,*
Rodney Buchemi & Jeremy Freeman
Colorists: *Gotham Studios, Val Staples,*
Guru eFX & Sotocolor
Letterer: *Dave Sharpe*
Cover Artists: *Sean Chen, Sandu Florea & Guru eFX;*
Leonard Kirk, Terry Pallot & Chris Sotomayor;
Salvador Espin, Karl Kesel & Pete Pantazis;
and Tom Grummett & Guillem Mari
Assistant Editor: *Jordan D. White*
Editors: *Nathan Cosby & Mark Paniccia*
Consulting Editor: *Ralph Macchio*

Captain America created by Joe Simon and Jack Kirby

Collection Editor: *Cory Levine*
Editorial Assistants: *James Emmett & Joe Hochstein*
Assistant Editors: *Matt Masdeu, Alex Starbuck*
& Nelson Ribeiro
Editors, Special Projects: *Jennifer Grünwald*
& Mark D. Beazley
Senior Editor, Special Projects: *Jeff Youngquist*
Senior Vice President of Sales: *David Gabriel*

Editor in Chief: *Axel Alonso*
Chief Creative Officer: *Joe Quesada*
Publisher: *Dan Buckley*
Executive Producer: *Alan Fine*

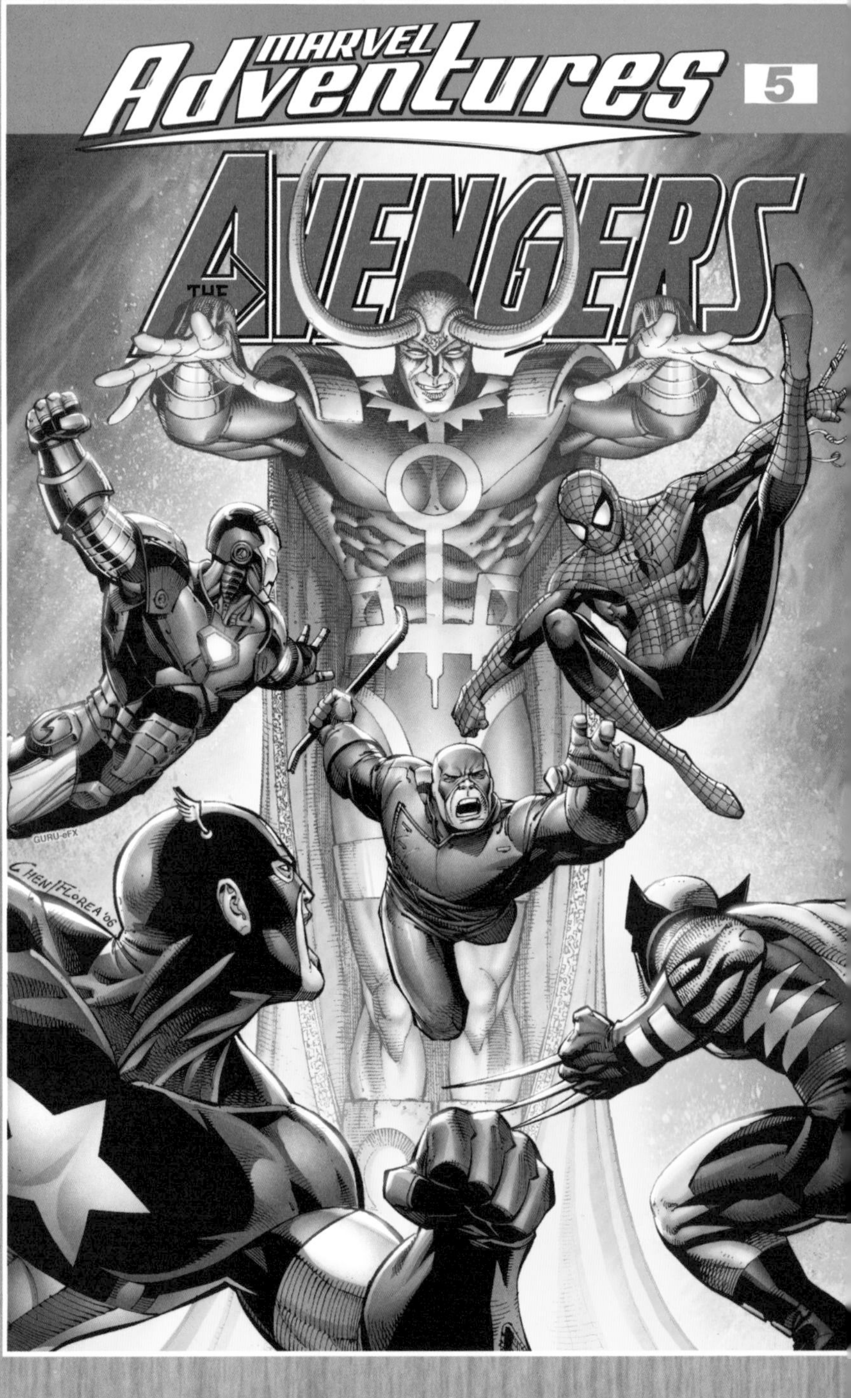
MARVEL Adventures
5
THE AVENGERS
GURU-eFX
CHEN/FLOREA '06

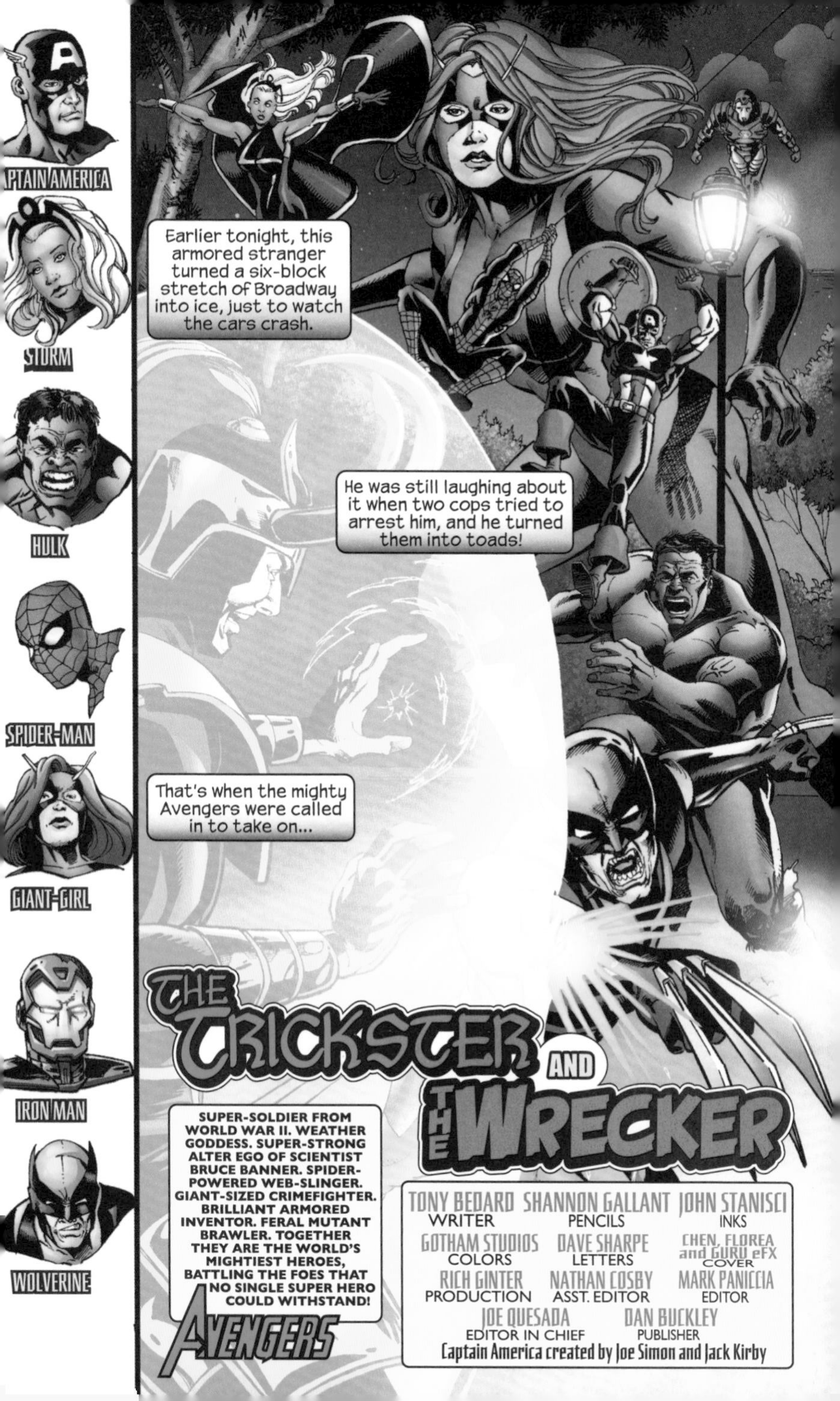
PTAIN AMERICA
STORM
HULK
SPIDER-MAN
GIANT-GIRL
IRON MAN
WOLVERINE
Earlier tonight, this armored stranger turned a six-block stretch of Broadway into ice, just to watch the cars crash.
He was still laughing about it when two cops tried to arrest him, and he turned them into toads!
That's when the mighty Avengers were called in to take on...
THE TRICKSTER AND THE WRECKER
SUPER-SOLDIER FROM WORLD WAR II. WEATHER GODDESS. SUPER-STRONG ALTER EGO OF SCIENTIST BRUCE BANNER. SPIDER-POWERED WEB-SLINGER. GIANT-SIZED CRIMEFIGHTER. BRILLIANT ARMORED INVENTOR. FERAL MUTANT BRAWLER. TOGETHER THEY ARE THE WORLD'S MIGHTIEST HEROES, BATTLING THE FOES THAT NO SINGLE SUPER HERO COULD WITHSTAND!
AVENGERS
TONY BEDARD WRITER
SHANNON GALLANT PENCILS
JOHN STANISCI INKS
GOTHAM STUDIOS COLORS
DAVE SHARPE LETTERS
CHEN, FLOREA and GURU eFX COVER
RICH GINTER PRODUCTION
NATHAN COSBY ASST. EDITOR
MARK PANICCIA EDITOR
JOE QUESADA EDITOR IN CHIEF
DAN BUCKLEY PUBLISHER
Captain America created by Joe Simon and Jack Kirby

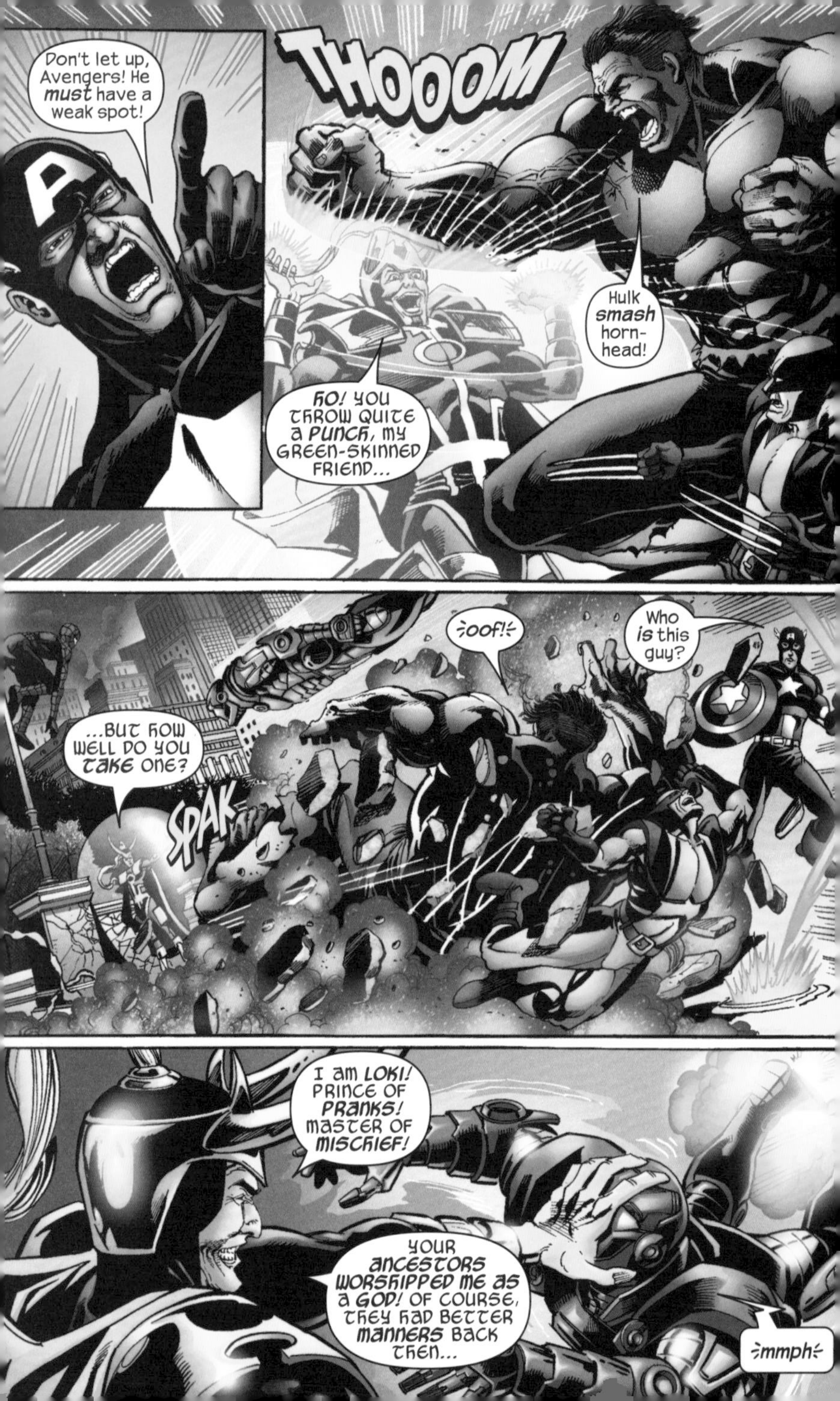
Don't let up, Avengers! He must have a weak spot!
THOOOM
Hulk smash horn-head!
HO! YOU THROW QUITE A PUNCH, MY GREEN-SKINNED FRIEND...
...BUT HOW WELL DO YOU TAKE ONE?
SPAK
oof!
Who is this guy?
I AM LOKI! PRINCE OF PRANKS! MASTER OF MISCHIEF!
YOUR ANCESTORS WORSHIPPED ME AS A GOD! OF COURSE, THEY HAD BETTER MANNERS BACK THEN...
mmph

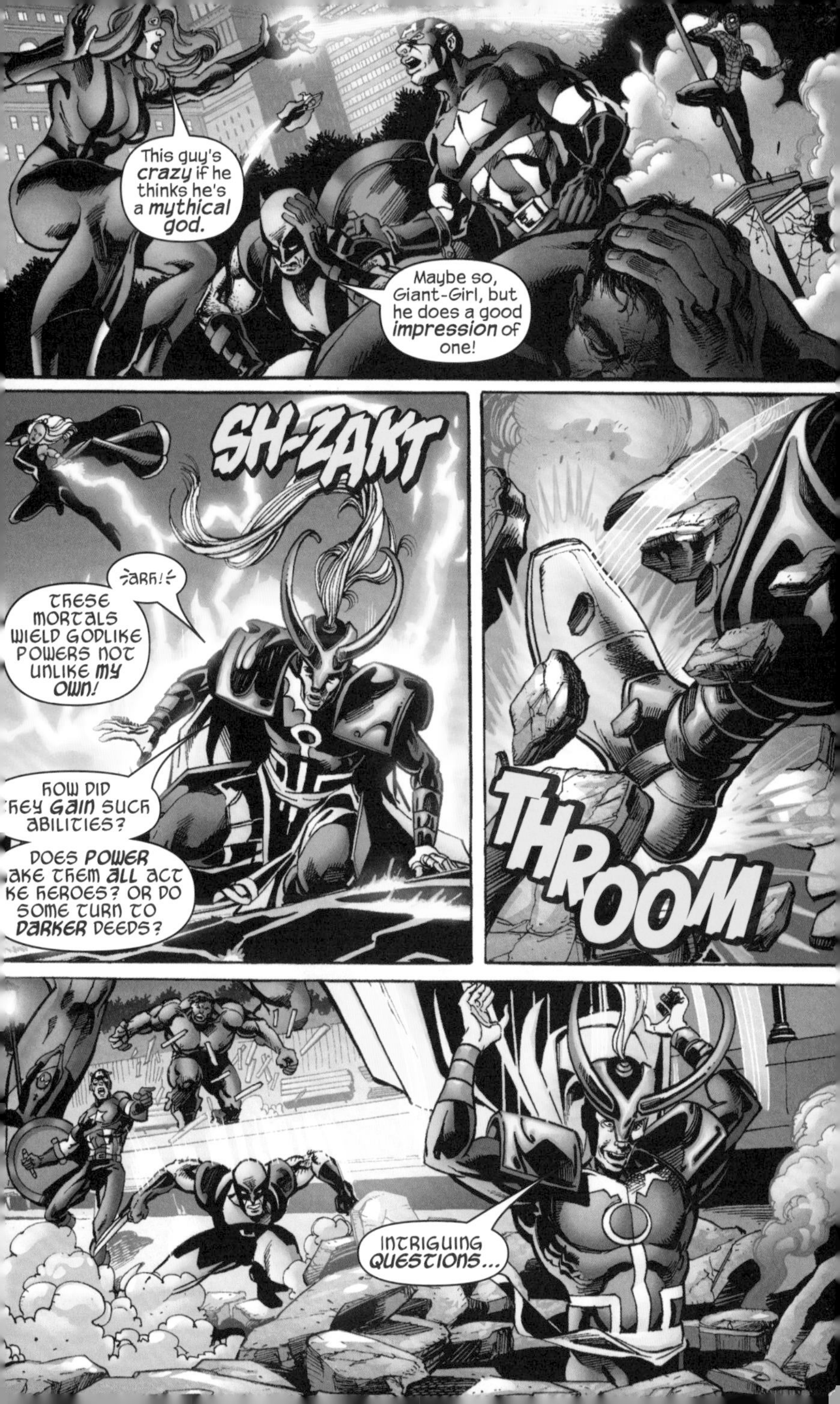

This guy's crazy if he thinks he's a mythical god.
Maybe so, Giant-Girl, but he does a good impression of one!
SH-ZAKT
ARH!
THESE MORTALS WIELD GODLIKE POWERS NOT UNLIKE MY OWN!
HOW DID HEY GAIN SUCH ABILITIES?
DOES POWER AKE THEM ALL ACT KE HEROES? OR DO SOME TURN TO DARKER DEEDS?
THROOM
INTRIGUING QUESTIONS...

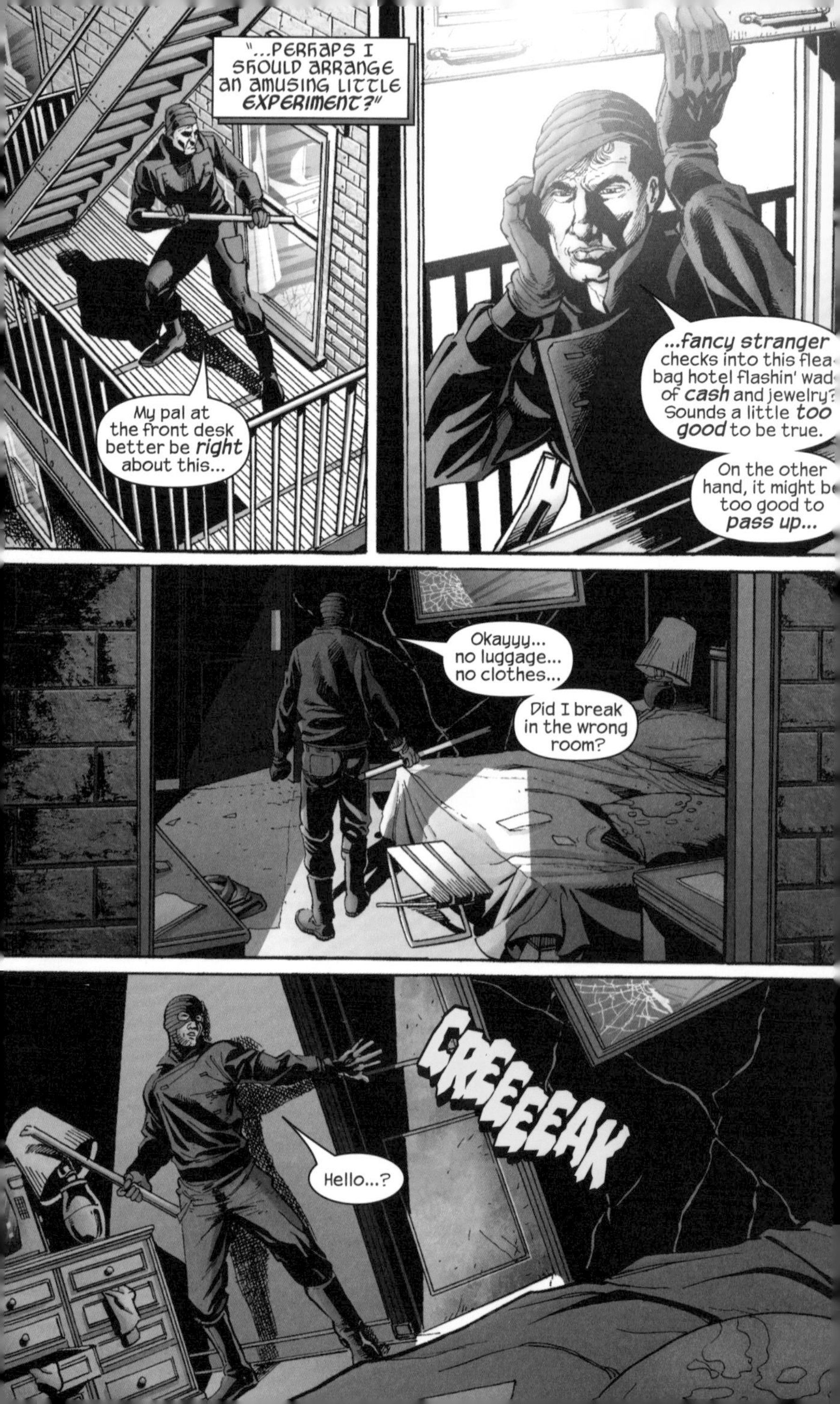
"...PERHAPS I SHOULD ARRANGE AN AMUSING LITTLE EXPERIMENT?"
My pal at the front desk better be right about this...
...fancy stranger checks into this flea-bag hotel flashin' wad of cash and jewelry? Sounds a little too good to be true.
On the other hand, it might be too good to pass up...
Okayyy... no luggage... no clothes...
Did I break in the wrong room?
CREEEEAK
Hello...?

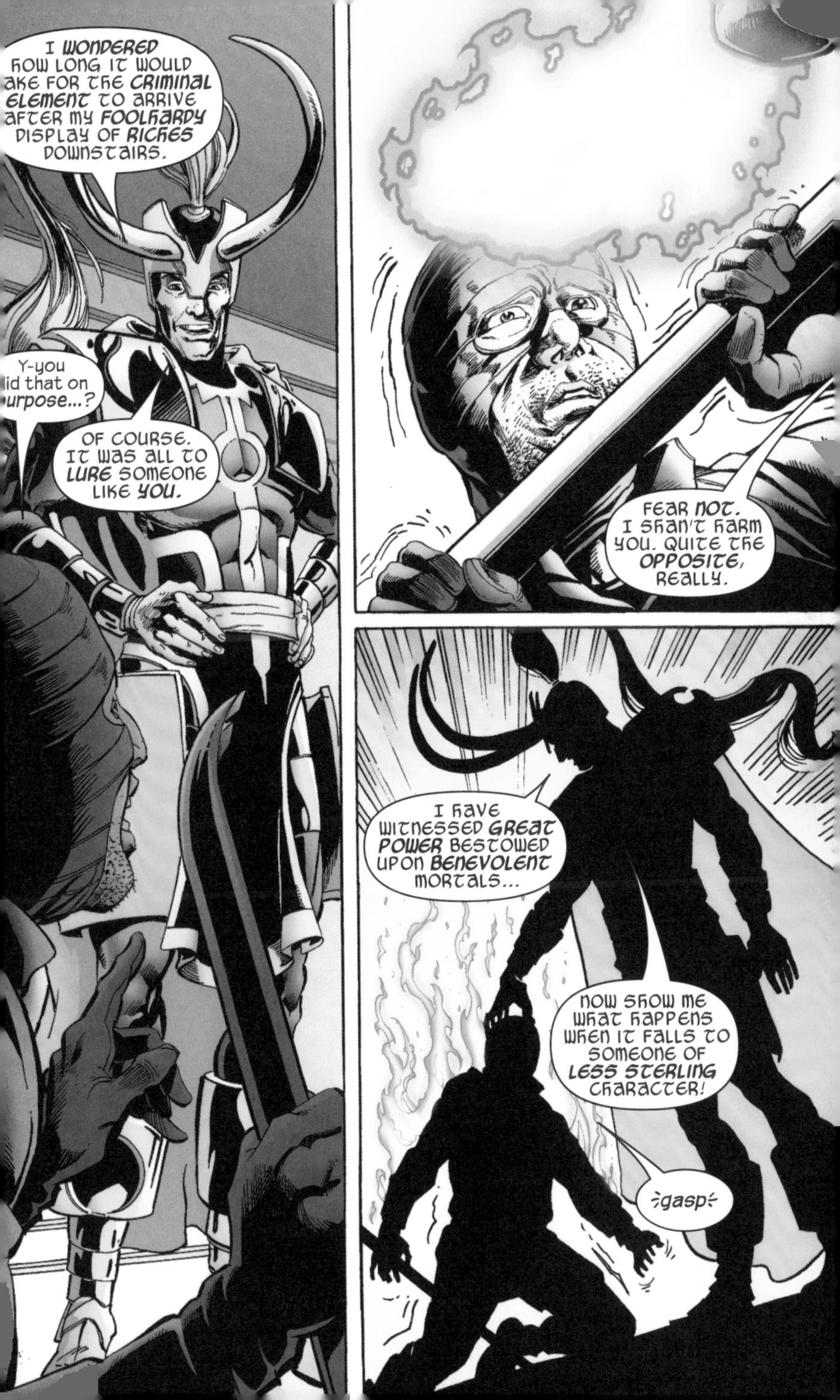
I WONDERED HOW LONG IT WOULD AKE FOR THE CRIMINAL ELEMENT TO ARRIVE AFTER MY FOOLHARDY DISPLAY OF RICHES DOWNSTAIRS.
Y-YOU ID THAT ON URPOSE...?
OF COURSE. IT WAS ALL TO LURE SOMEONE LIKE YOU.
FEAR NOT. I SHAN'T HARM YOU. QUITE THE OPPOSITE, REALLY.
I HAVE WITNESSED GREAT POWER BESTOWED UPON BENEVOLENT MORTALS...
NOW SHOW ME WHAT HAPPENS WHEN IT FALLS TO SOMEONE OF LESS STERLING CHARACTER!
gasp

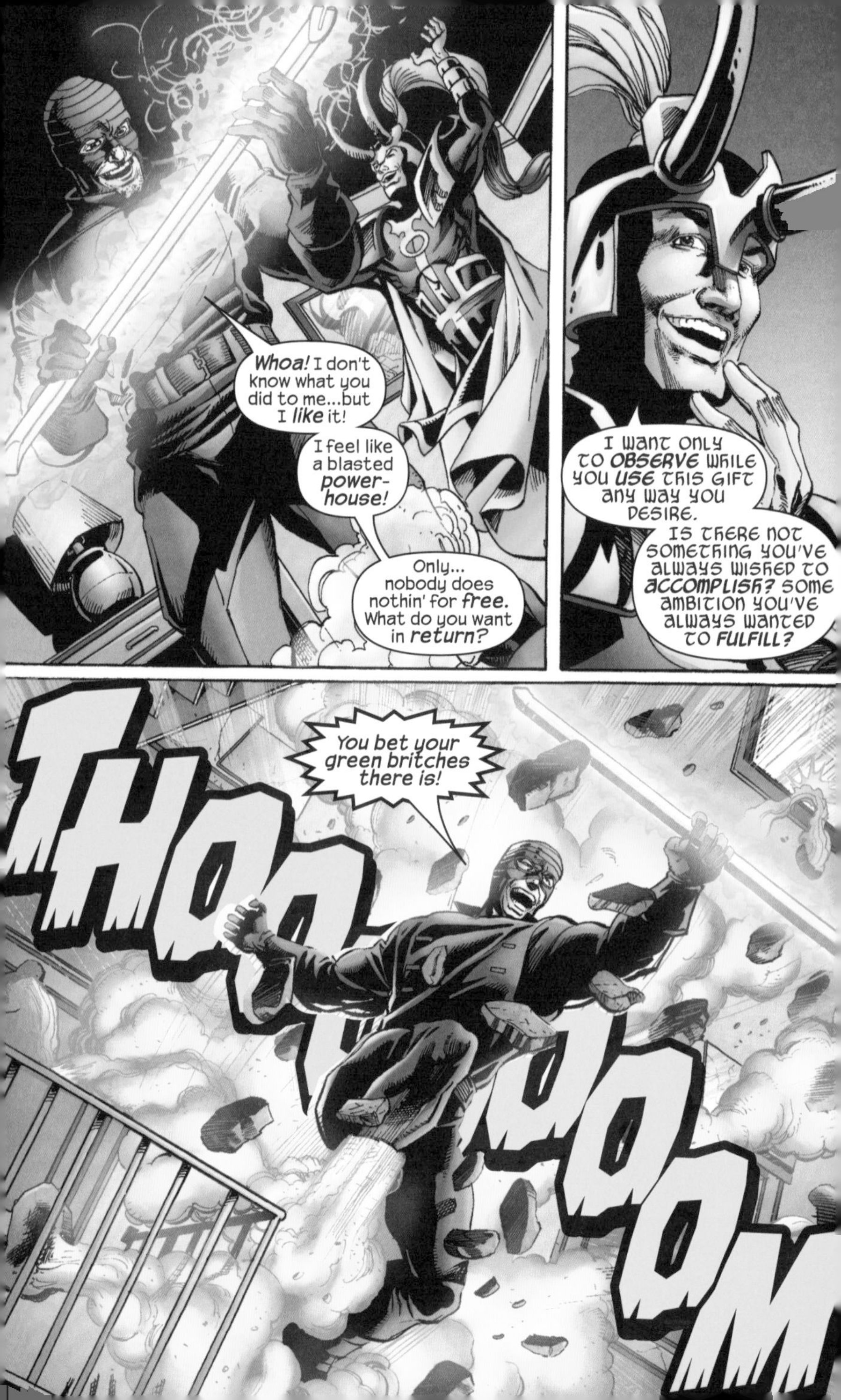

Whoa! I don't know what you did to me...but I like it!
I feel like a blasted power-house!
Only... nobody does nothin' for free. What do you want in return?
I want only to observe while you use this gift any way you desire.
Is there not something you've always wished to accomplish? Some ambition you've always wanted to fulfill?
You bet your green britches there is!
THOOOOOOM

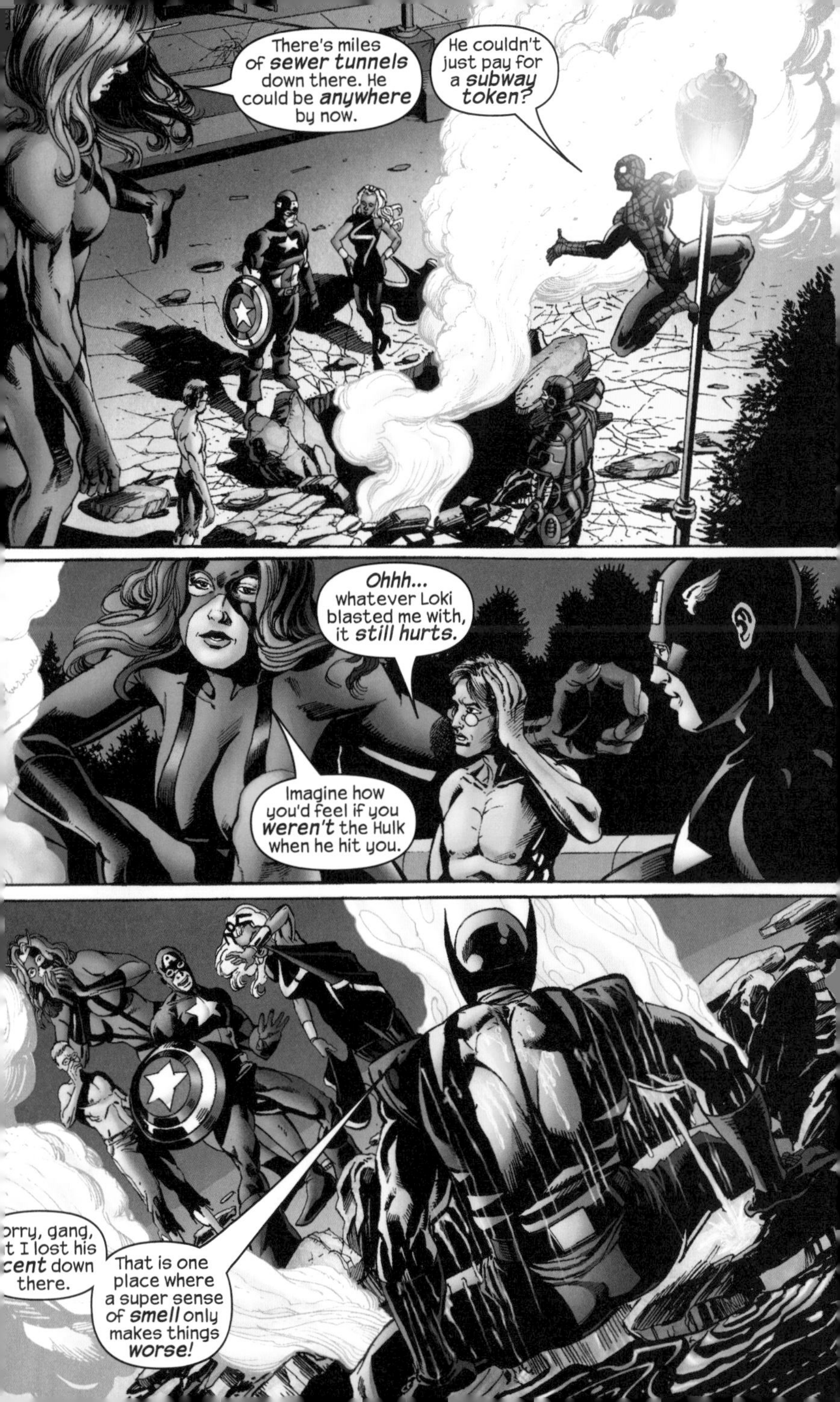
There's miles of sewer tunnels down there. He could be anywhere by now.
He couldn't just pay for a subway token?
Ohhh... whatever Loki blasted me with, it still hurts.
Imagine how you'd feel if you weren't the Hulk when he hit you.
orry, gang, t I lost his cent down there.
That is one place where a super sense of smell only makes things worse!

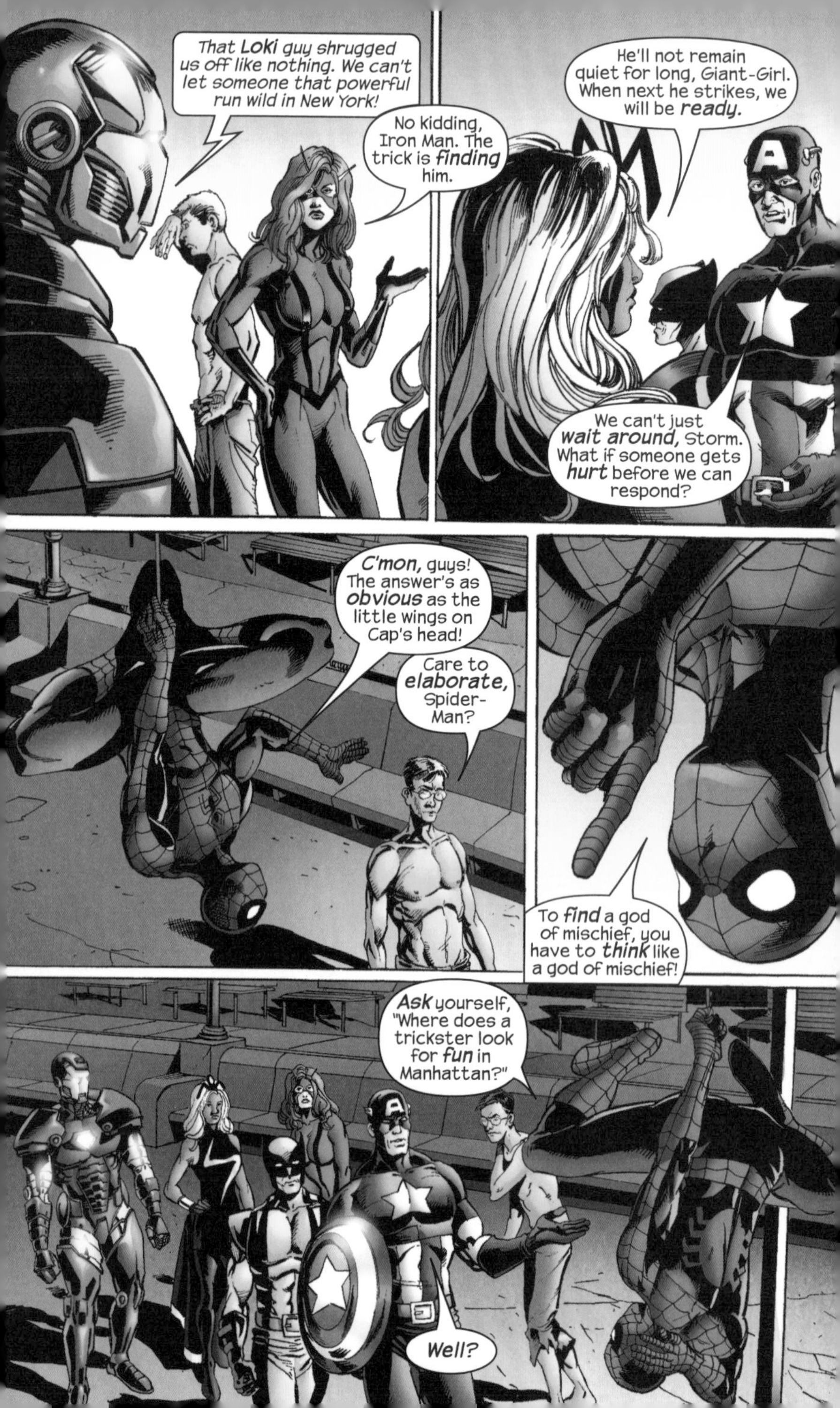
That Loki guy shrugged us off like nothing. We can't let someone that powerful run wild in New York!
No kidding, Iron Man. The trick is finding him.
He'll not remain quiet for long, Giant-Girl. When next he strikes, we will be ready.
We can't just wait around, Storm. What if someone gets hurt before we can respond?
C'mon, guys! The answer's as obvious as the little wings on Cap's head!
Care to elaborate, Spider-Man?
To find a god of mischief, you have to think like a god of mischief!
Ask yourself, "Where does a trickster look for fun in Manhattan?"
Well?

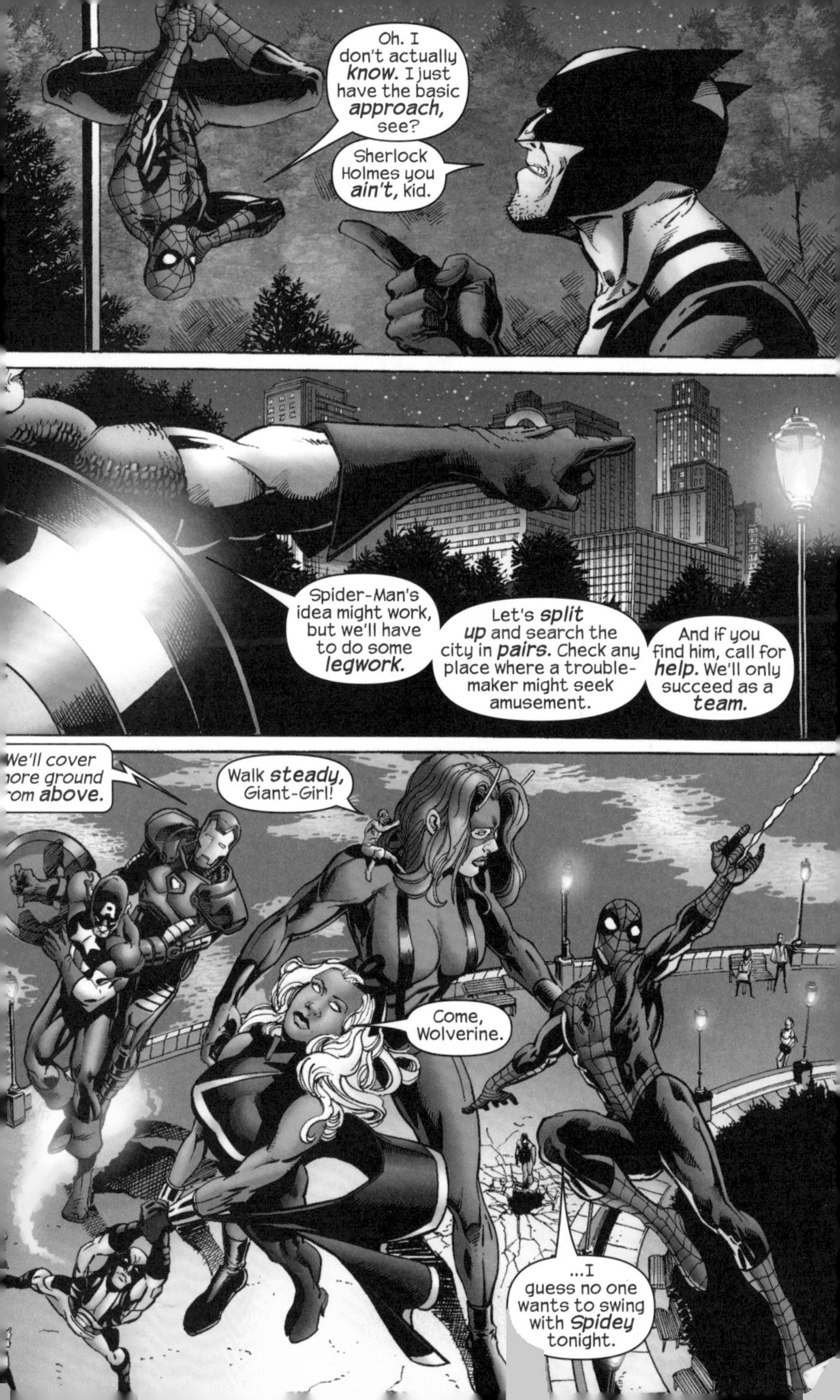

Oh. I don't actually **know**. I just have the basic **approach**, see?
Sherlock Holmes you **ain't**, kid.
Spider-Man's idea might work, but we'll have to do some **legwork**.
Let's **split up** and search the city in **pairs**. Check any place where a trouble-maker might seek amusement.
And if you find him, call for **help**. We'll only succeed as a **team**.
We'll cover
ore ground
om **above**.
Walk **steady**, Giant-Girl!
Come, Wolverine.
...I guess no one wants to swing with **Spidey** tonight.

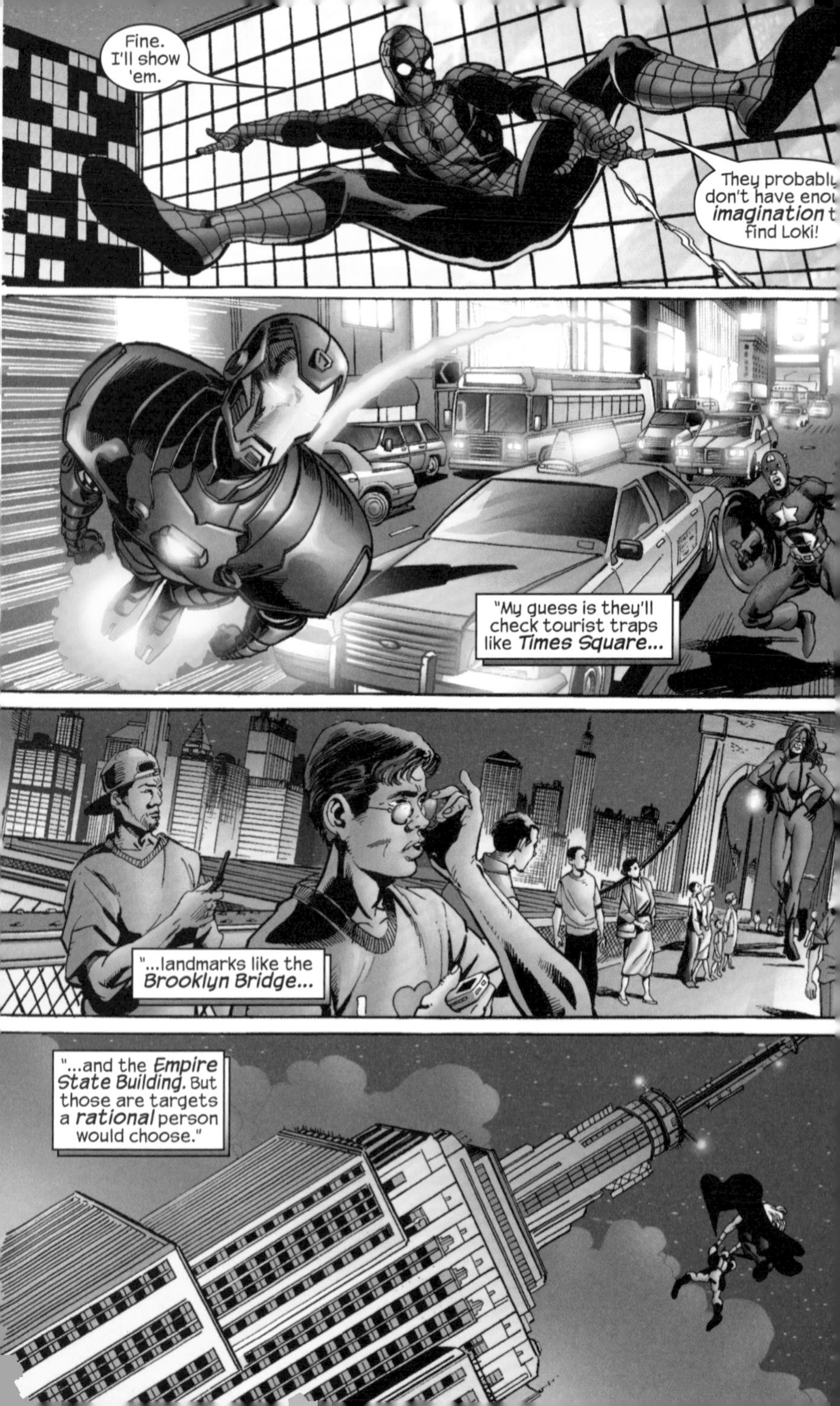

Fine. I'll show 'em.
They probably don't have enou imagination t find Loki!
"My guess is they'll check tourist traps like *Times Square*...
"...landmarks like the *Brooklyn Bridge*...
"...and the *Empire State Building*. But those are targets a *rational* person would choose."

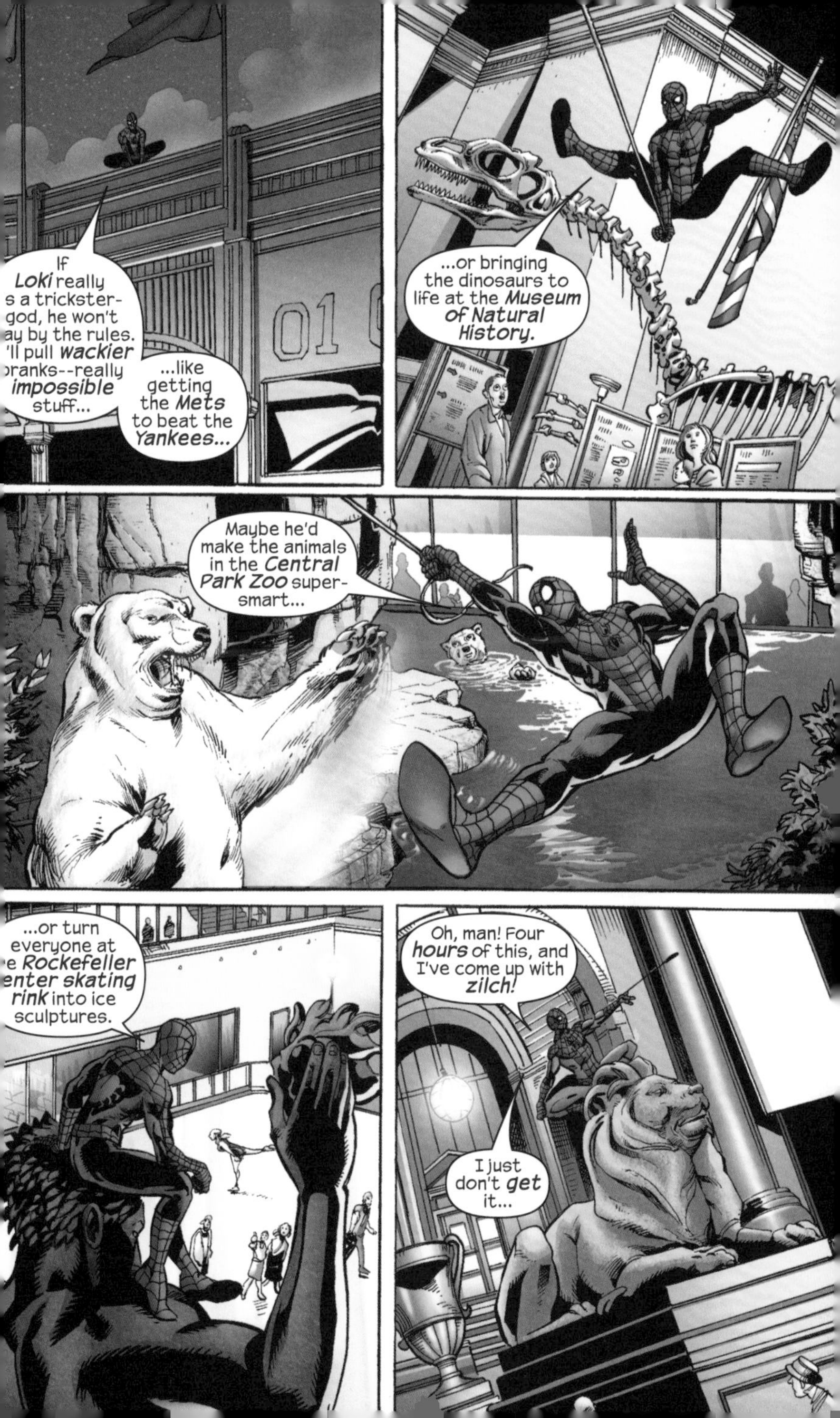
If Loki really s a trickster-god, he won't ay by the rules. 'll pull wackier ranks--really impossible stuff...
...like getting the Mets to beat the Yankees...
...or bringing the dinosaurs to life at the Museum of Natural History.
Maybe he'd make the animals in the Central Park Zoo super-smart...
...or turn everyone at e Rockefeller enter skating rink into ice sculptures.
Oh, man! Four hours of this, and I've come up with zilch!
I just don't get it...

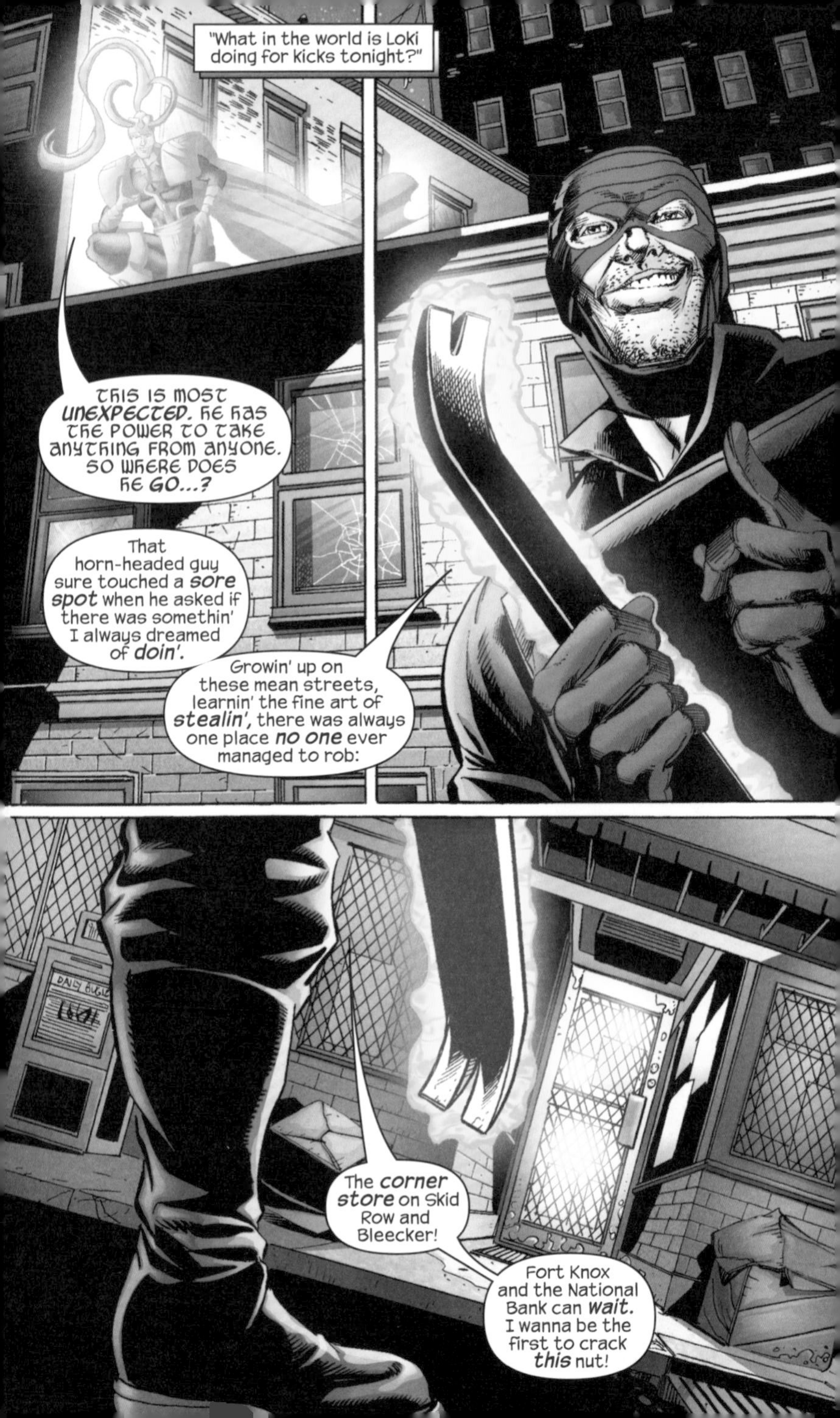

"What in the world is Loki doing for kicks tonight?"
THIS IS MOST UNEXPECTED. HE HAS THE POWER TO TAKE ANYTHING FROM ANYONE. SO WHERE DOES HE GO...?
That horn-headed guy sure touched a sore spot when he asked if there was somethin' I always dreamed of doin'.
Growin' up on these mean streets, learnin' the fine art of stealin', there was always one place no one ever managed to rob:
The corner store on Skid Row and Bleecker!
Fort Knox and the National Bank can wait. I wanna be the first to crack this nut!

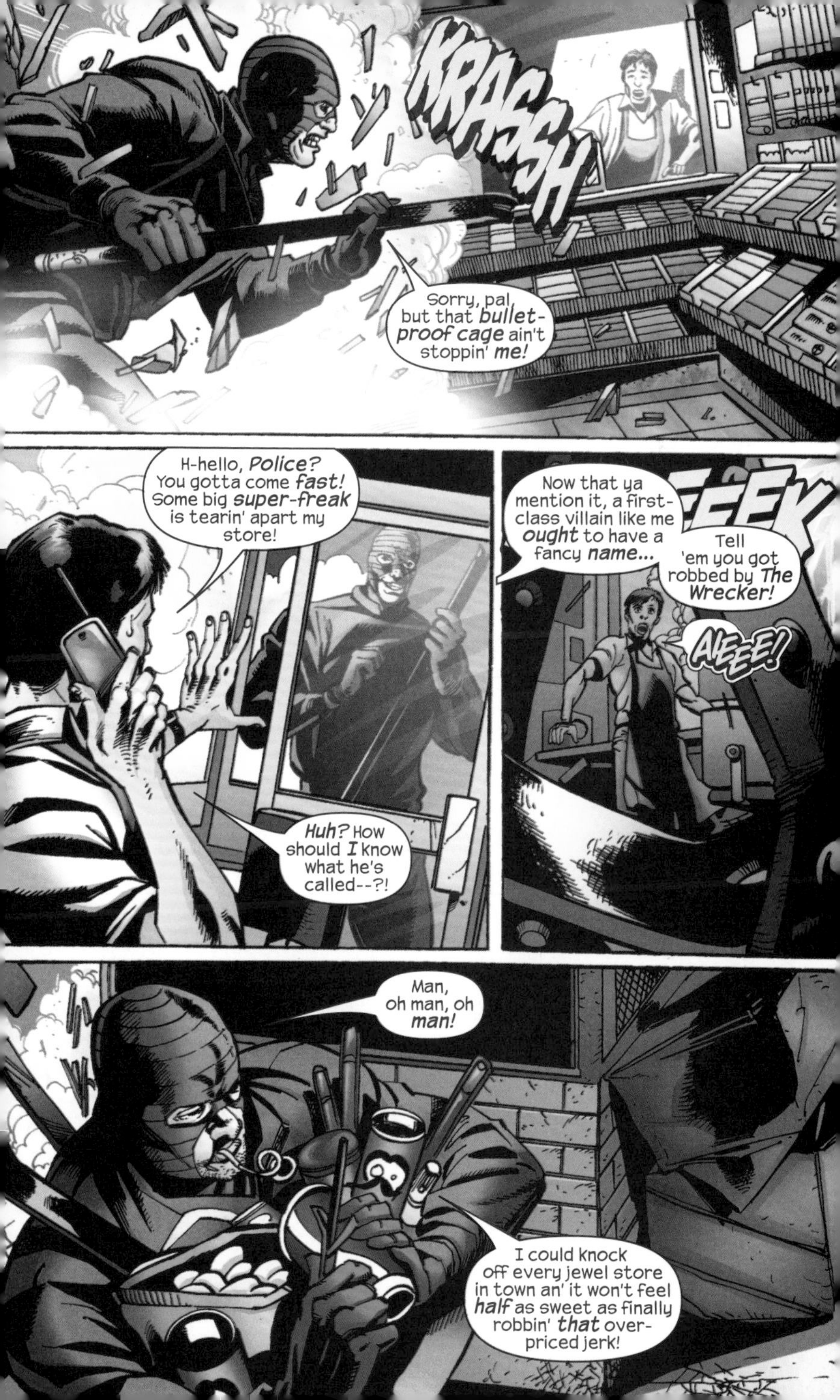
KRASSH
Sorry, pal, but that bullet-proof cage ain't stoppin' me!
H-hello, Police? You gotta come fast! Some big super-freak is tearin' apart my store!
Huh? How should I know what he's called--?!
Now that ya mention it, a first-class villain like me ought to have a fancy name...
Tell 'em you got robbed by The Wrecker!
AIEEE!
Man, oh man, oh man!
I could knock off every jewel store in town an' it won't feel half as sweet as finally robbin' that over-priced jerk!

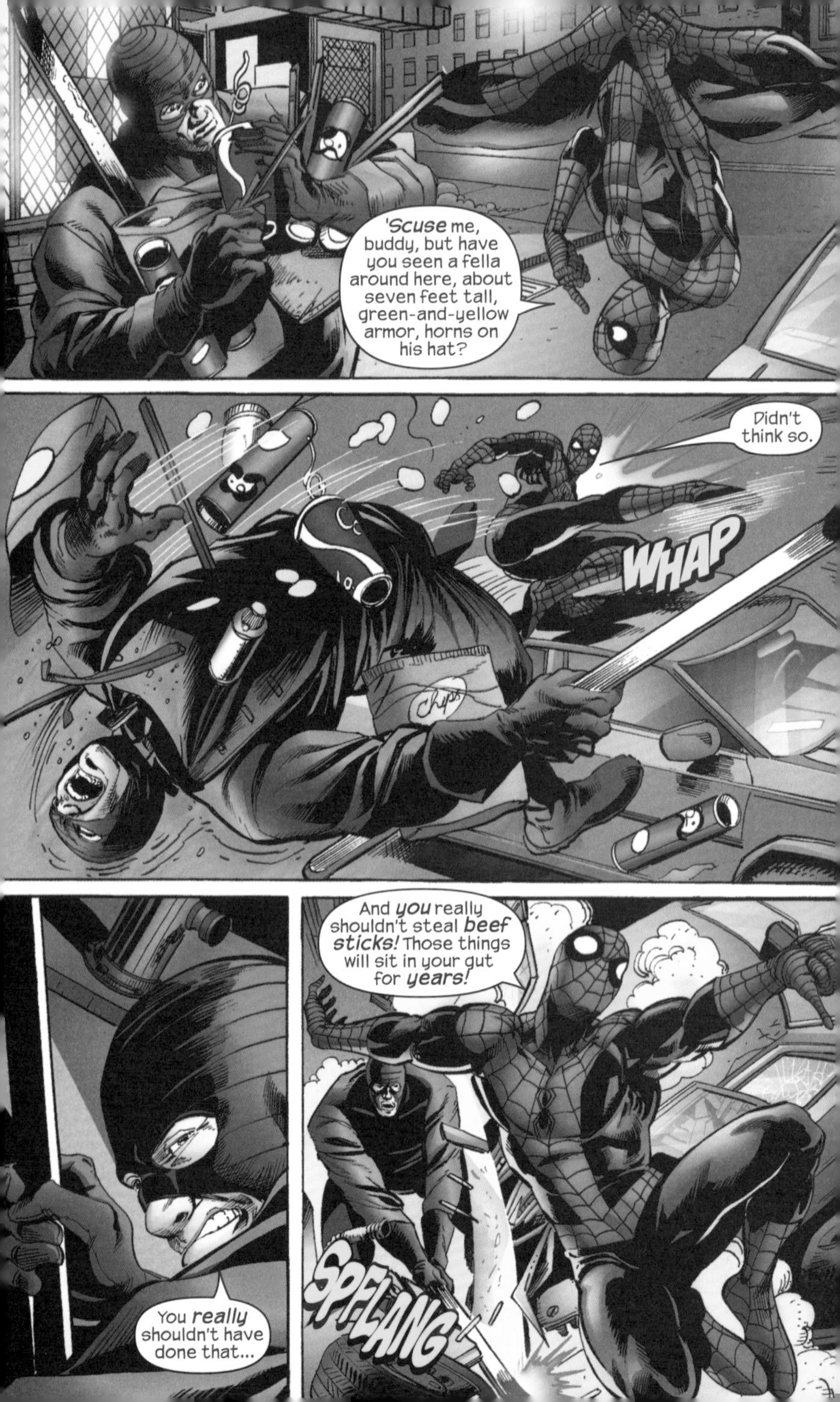
'Scuse me, buddy, but have you seen a fella around here, about seven feet tall, green-and-yellow armor, horns on his hat?
Didn't think so.
WHAP
You really shouldn't have done that...
And you really shouldn't steal beef sticks! Those things will sit in your gut for years!
SPFLANG

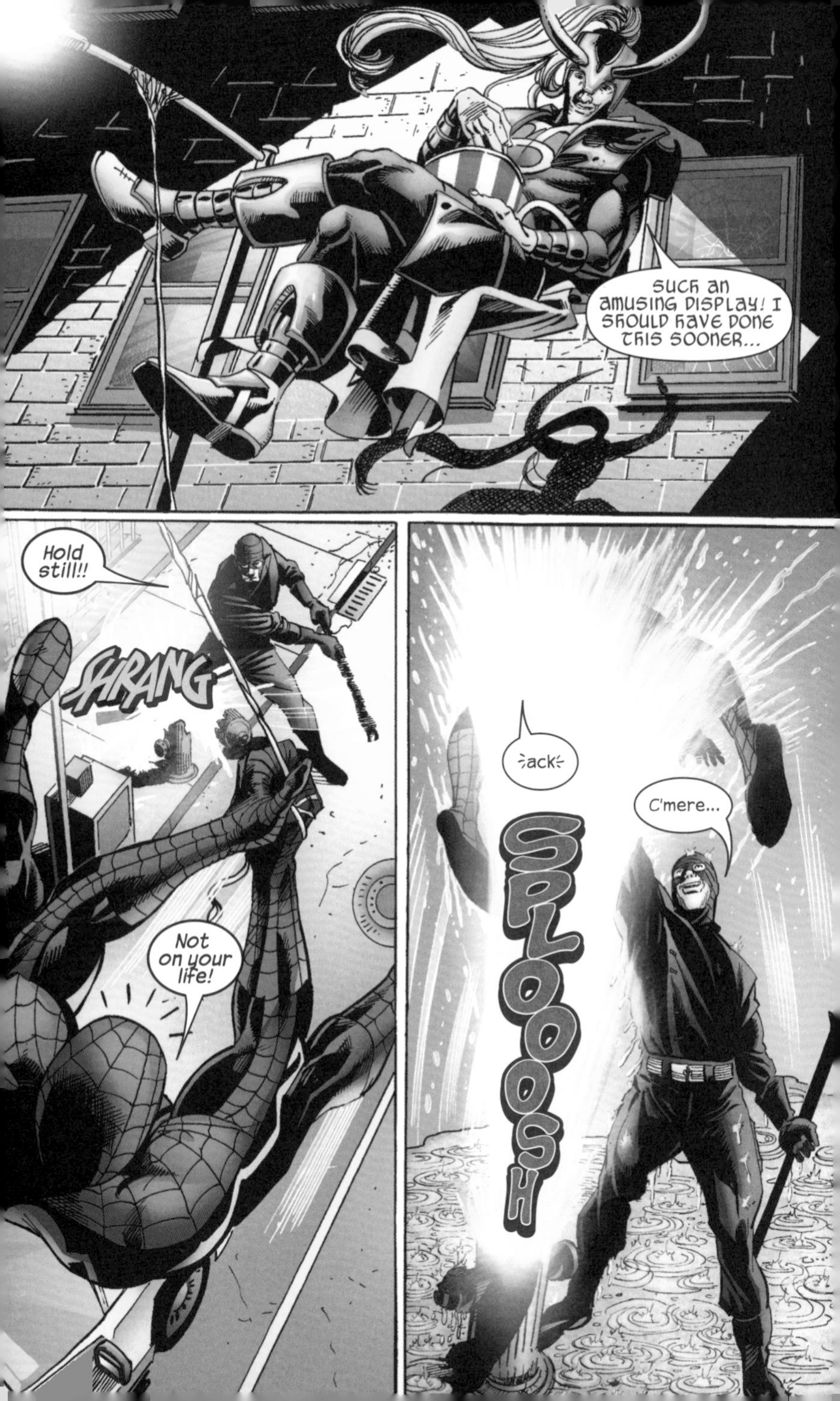
SUCH AN AMUSING DISPLAY! I SHOULD HAVE DONE THIS SOONER...
Hold still!!
SHRANG
Not on your life!
ack
SPLOOOOSH
C'mere...

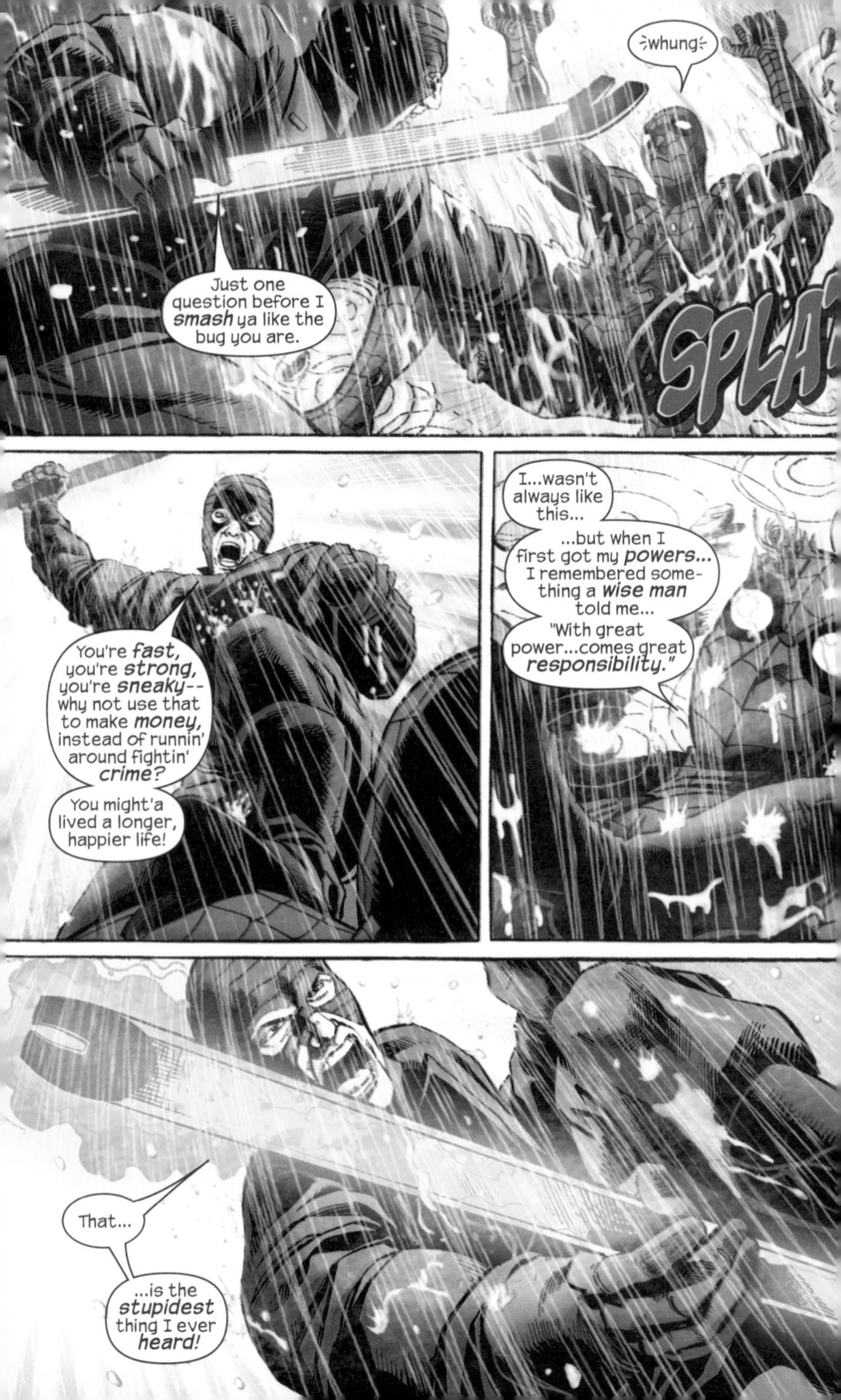

whung
Just one question before I smash ya like the bug you are.
SPLAT
You're fast, you're strong, you're sneaky--why not use that to make money, instead of runnin' around fightin' crime?
You might'a lived a longer, happier life!
I...wasn't always like this...
...but when I first got my powers... I remembered something a wise man told me...
"With great power...comes great responsibility."
That...
...is the stupidest thing I ever heard!

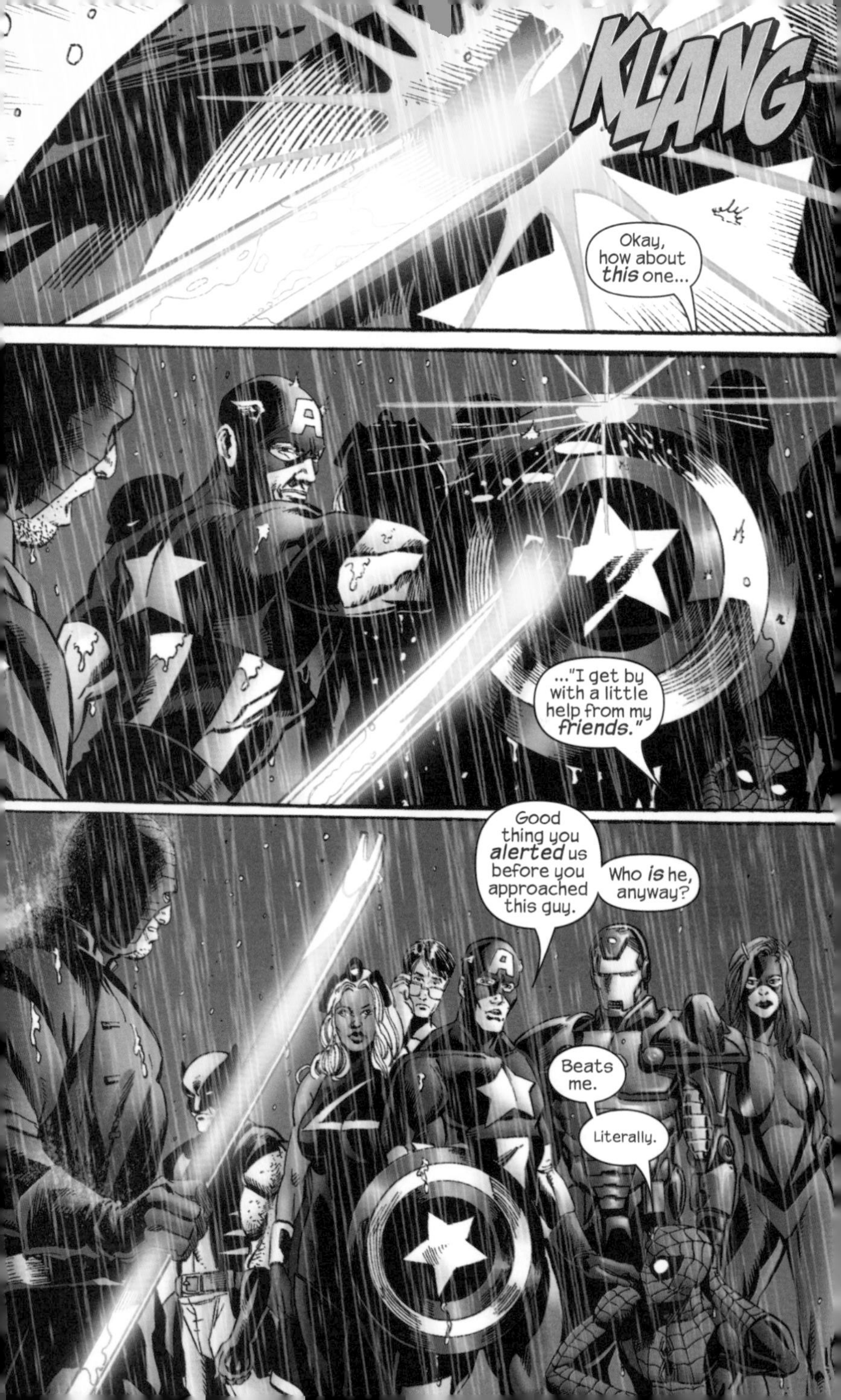
KLANG
Okay, how about *this* one...
..."I get by with a little help from my *friends.*"
Good thing you *alerted* us before you approached this guy.
Who *is* he, anyway?
Beats me.
Literally.

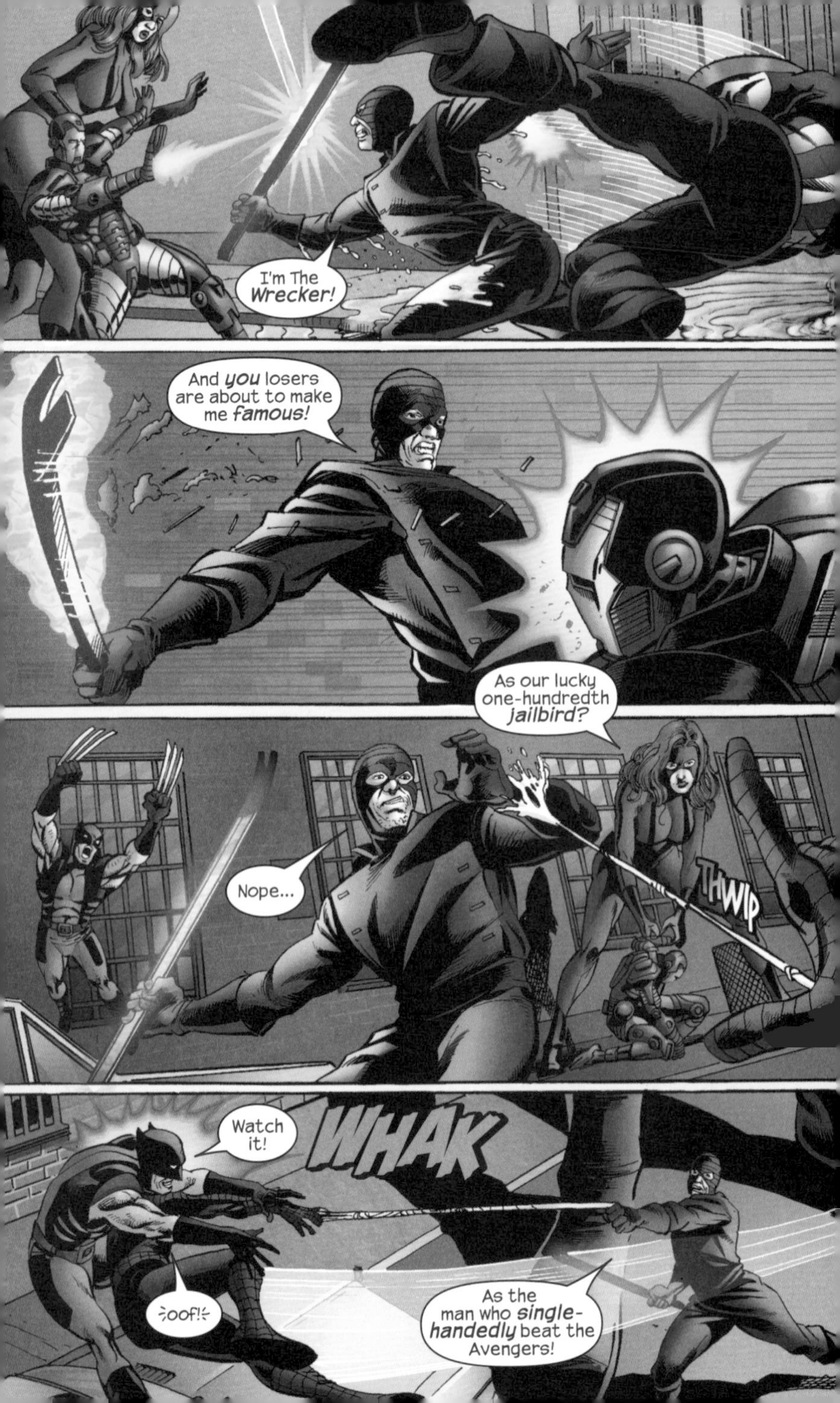
I'm The Wrecker!
And you losers are about to make me famous!
As our lucky one-hundredth jailbird?
Nope...
THWIP
Watch it!
WHAK
oof!
As the man who single-handedly beat the Avengers!

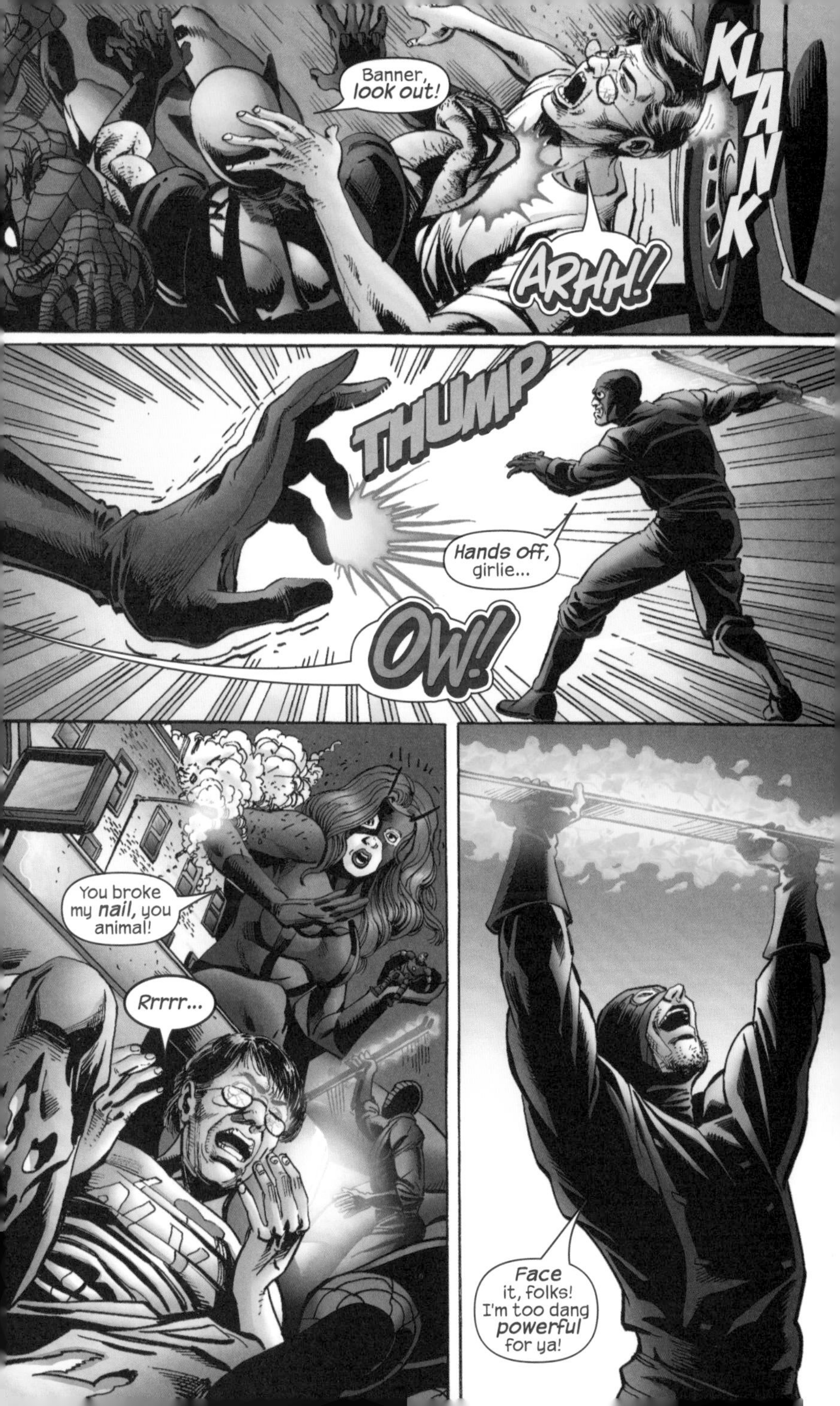
Banner, *look out!*
KLANK
ARHH!
THUMP
Hands off, girlie...
OW!
You broke my *nail,* you animal!
Rrrrr...
Face it, folks! I'm too dang *powerful* for ya!

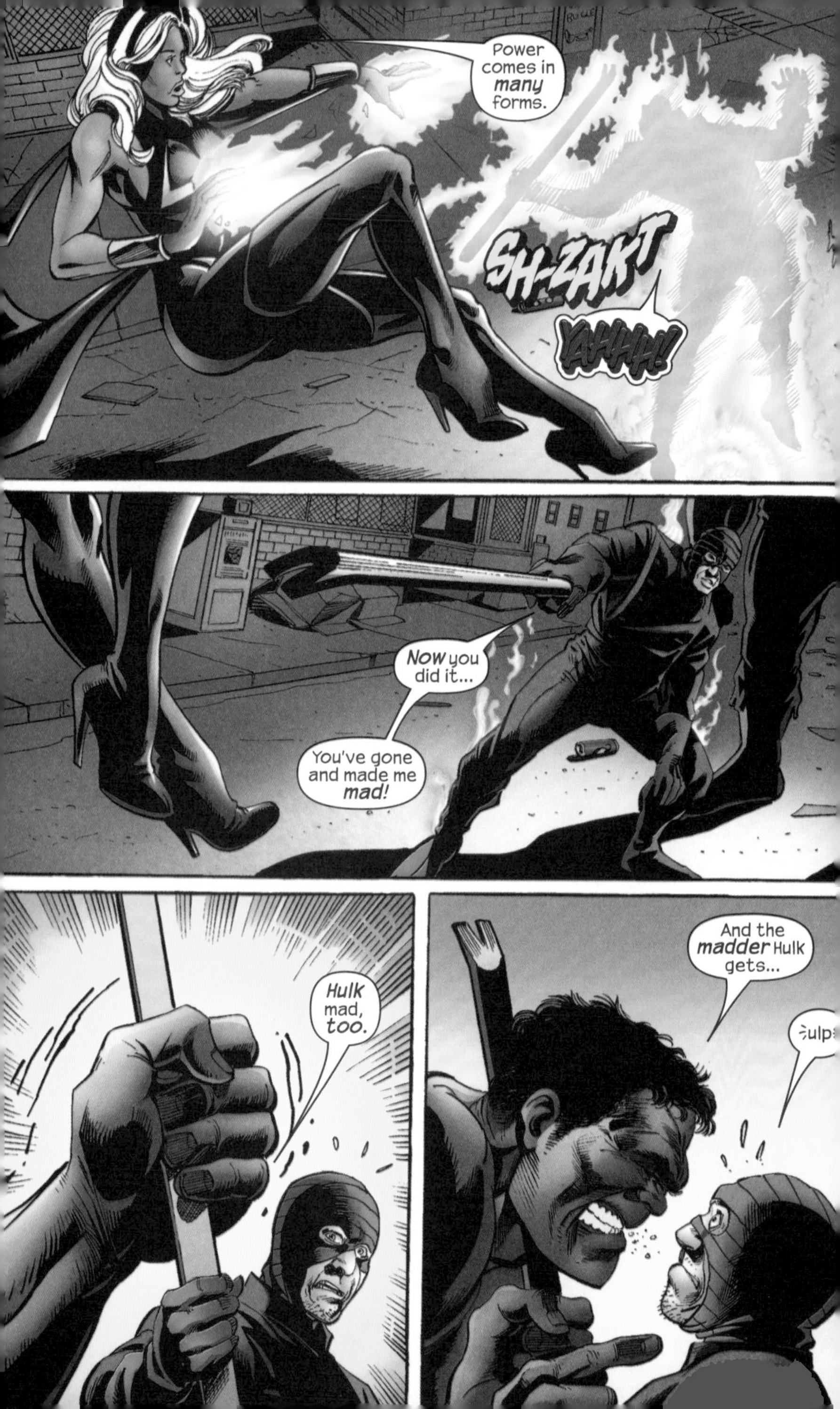
Power comes in *many* forms.
SH-ZAKT
YAHHH!
NOW you did it...
You've gone and made me *mad!*
Hulk mad, *too.*
And the *madder* Hulk gets...
ulp

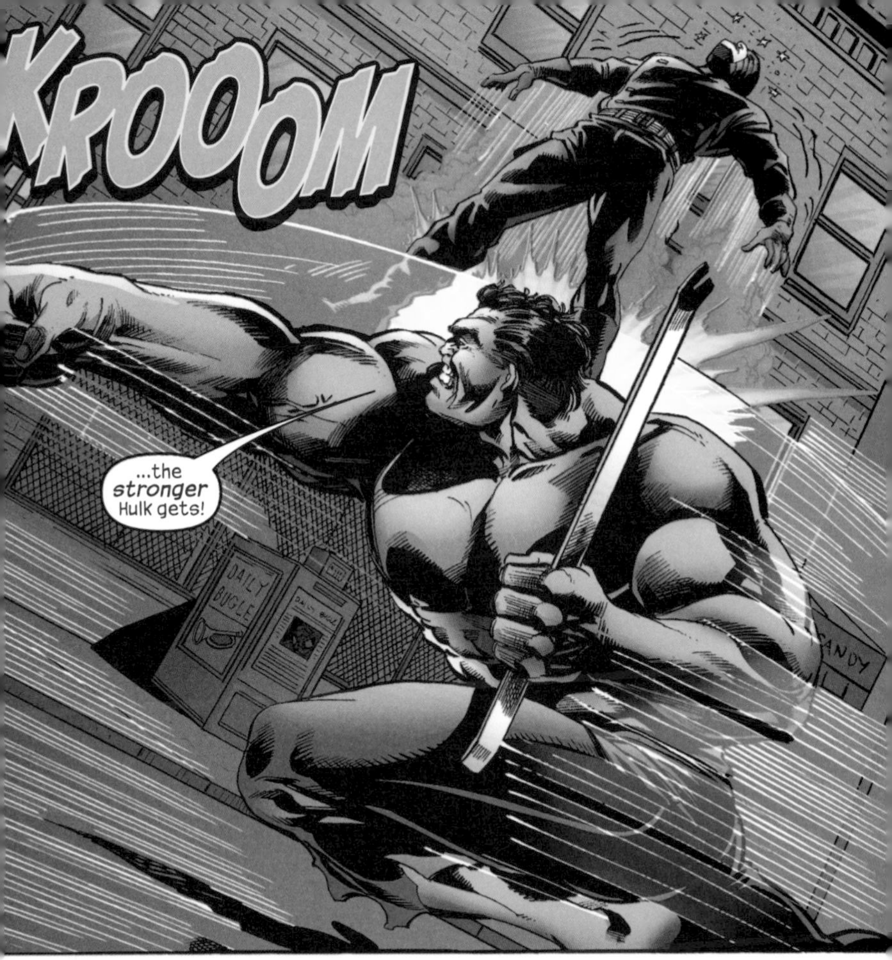
KROOOOM
...the stronger Hulk gets!
DAILY BUGLE

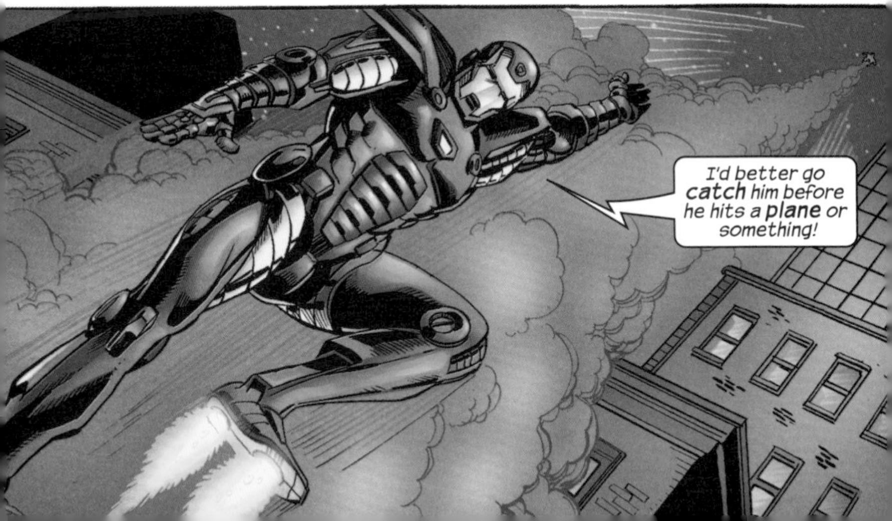
I'd better go catch him before he hits a plane or something!

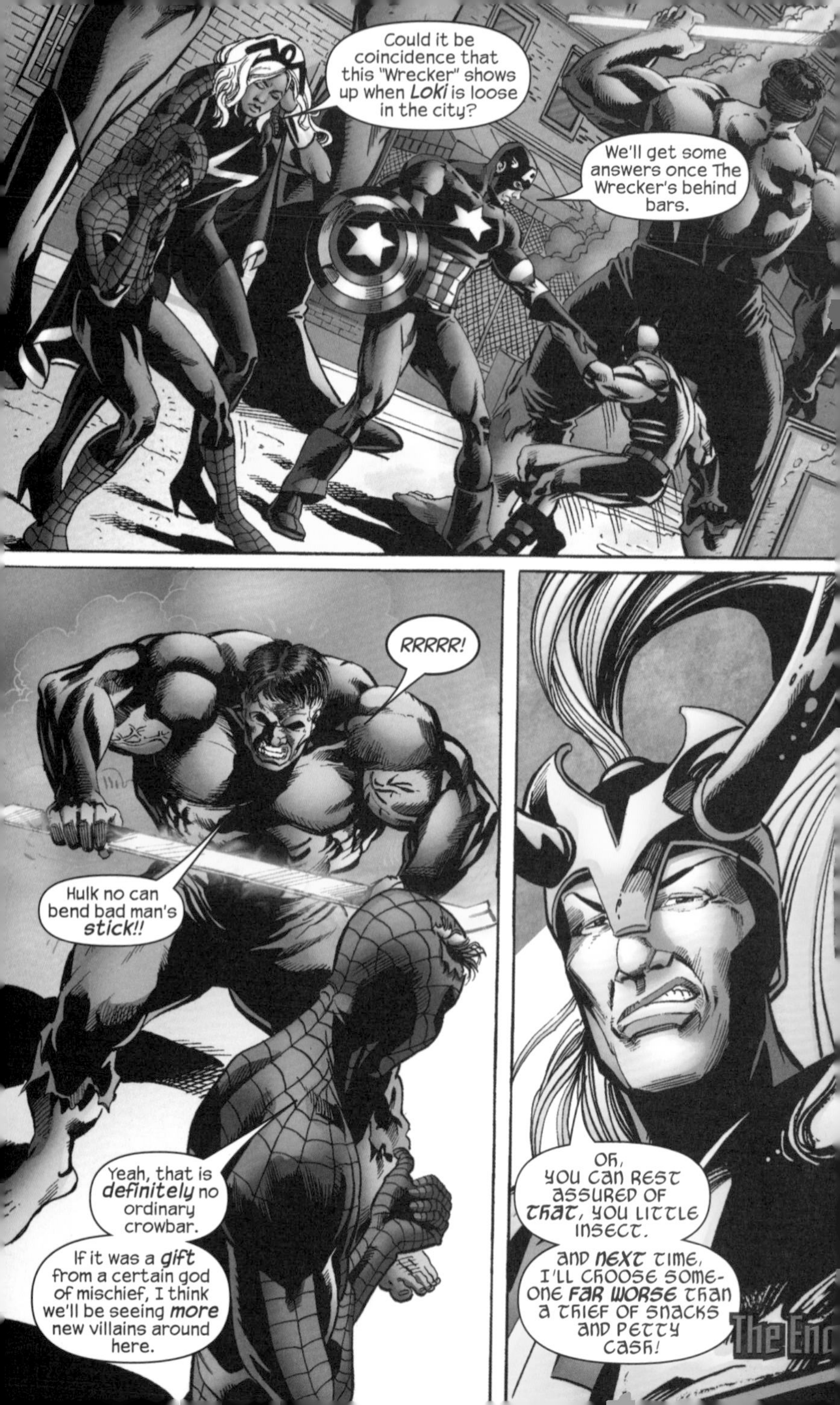

Could it be coincidence that this "Wrecker" shows up when Loki is loose in the city?
We'll get some answers once The Wrecker's behind bars.
RRRRR!
Hulk no can bend bad man's stick!!
Yeah, that is definitely no ordinary crowbar.
If it was a gift from a certain god of mischief, I think we'll be seeing more new villains around here.
Oh, you can rest assured of that, you little insect.
And next time, I'll choose some-one far worse than a thief of snacks and petty cash!
The End

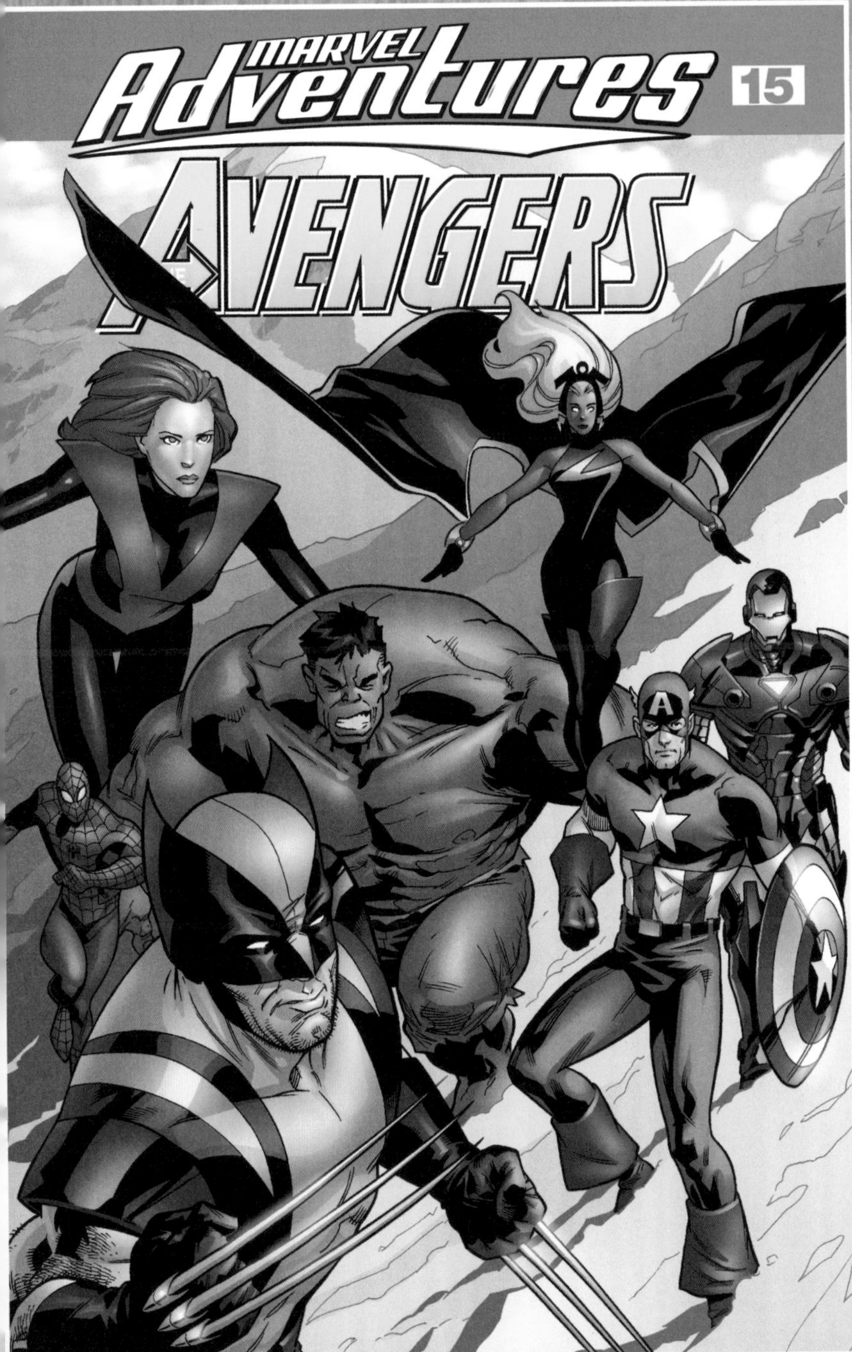
MARVEL
Adventures
15
AVENGERS

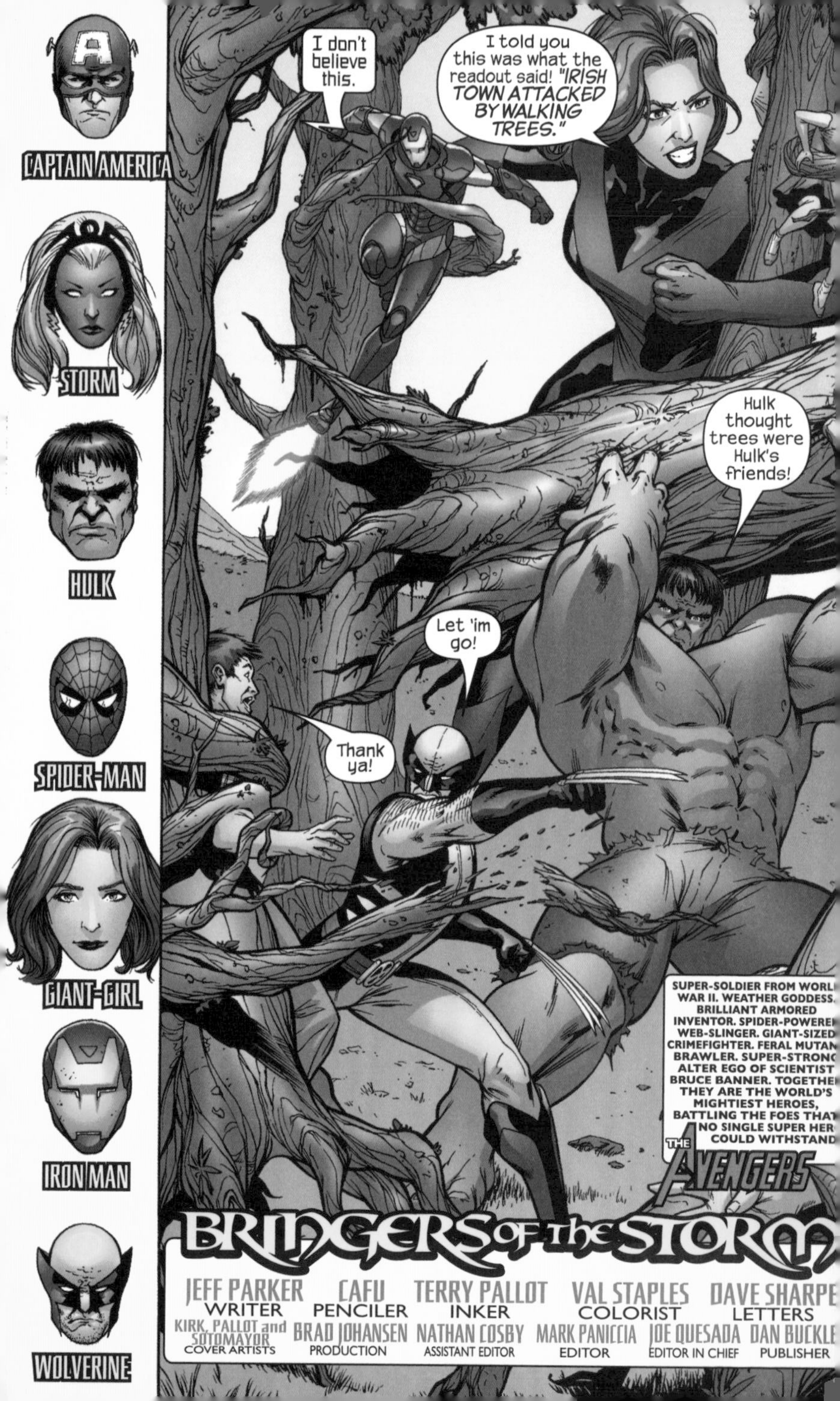
CAPTAIN AMERICA
STORM
HULK
SPIDER-MAN
GIANT-GIRL
IRON MAN
WOLVERINE
I don't believe this.
I told you this was what the readout said! "IRISH TOWN ATTACKED BY WALKING TREES."
Hulk thought trees were Hulk's friends!
Let 'im go!
Thank ya!
SUPER-SOLDIER FROM WORL WAR II. WEATHER GODDESS. BRILLIANT ARMORED INVENTOR. SPIDER-POWERE WEB-SLINGER. GIANT-SIZED CRIMEFIGHTER. FERAL MUTAN BRAWLER. SUPER-STRONG ALTER EGO OF SCIENTIST BRUCE BANNER. TOGETHE THEY ARE THE WORLD'S MIGHTIEST HEROES, BATTLING THE FOES THAT NO SINGLE SUPER HER COULD WITHSTAND
THE AVENGERS
BRINGERS OF THE STORM
JEFF PARKER WRITER
CAFU PENCILER
TERRY PALLOT INKER
VAL STAPLES COLORIST
DAVE SHARPE LETTERS
KIRK, PALLOT and SOTOMAYOR COVER ARTISTS
BRAD JOHANSEN PRODUCTION
NATHAN COSBY ASSISTANT EDITOR
MARK PANICCIA EDITOR
JOE QUESADA EDITOR IN CHIEF
DAN BUCKLE PUBLISHER

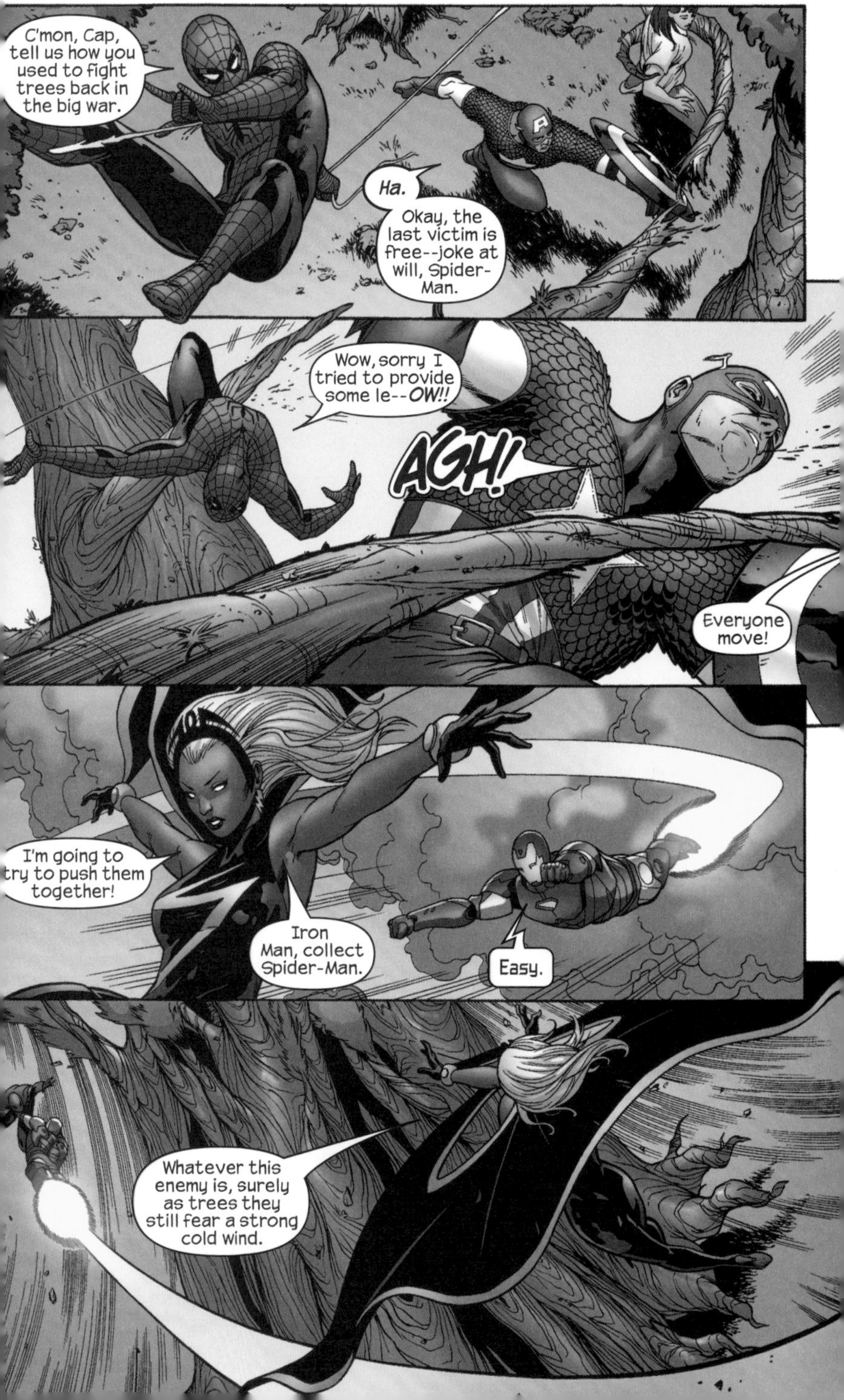
C'mon, Cap, tell us how you used to fight trees back in the big war.
Ha.
Okay, the last victim is free--joke at will, Spider-Man.
Wow, sorry I tried to provide some le--OW!!
AGH!
Everyone move!
I'm going to try to push them together!
Iron Man, collect Spider-Man.
Easy.
Whatever this enemy is, surely as trees they still fear a strong cold wind.

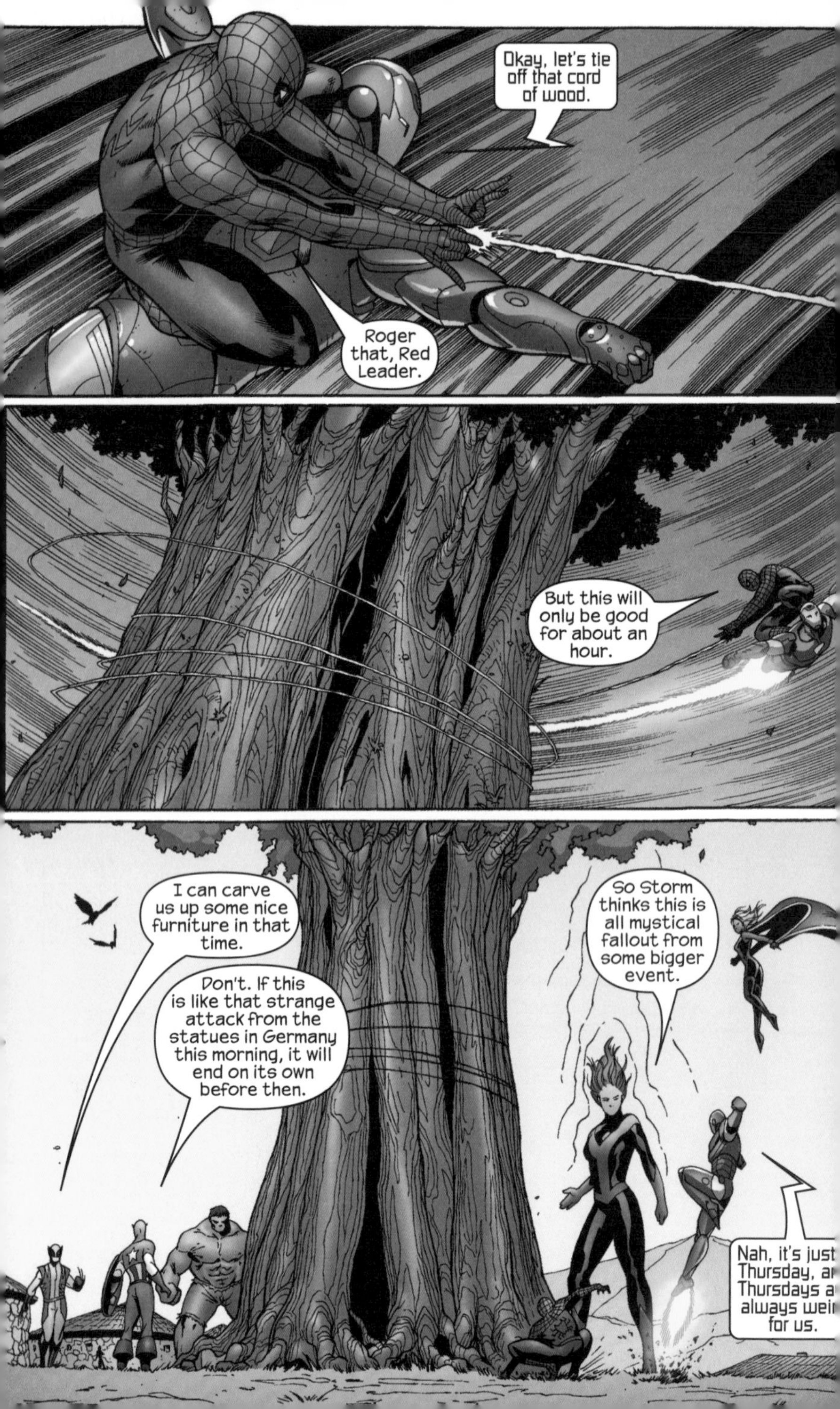
Okay, let's tie off that cord of wood.
Roger that, Red Leader.
But this will only be good for about an hour.
I can carve us up some nice furniture in that time.
Don't. If this is like that strange attack from the statues in Germany this morning, it will end on its own before then.
So Storm thinks this is all mystical fallout from some bigger event.
Nah, it's just Thursday, a
Thursdays a
always wei
for us.

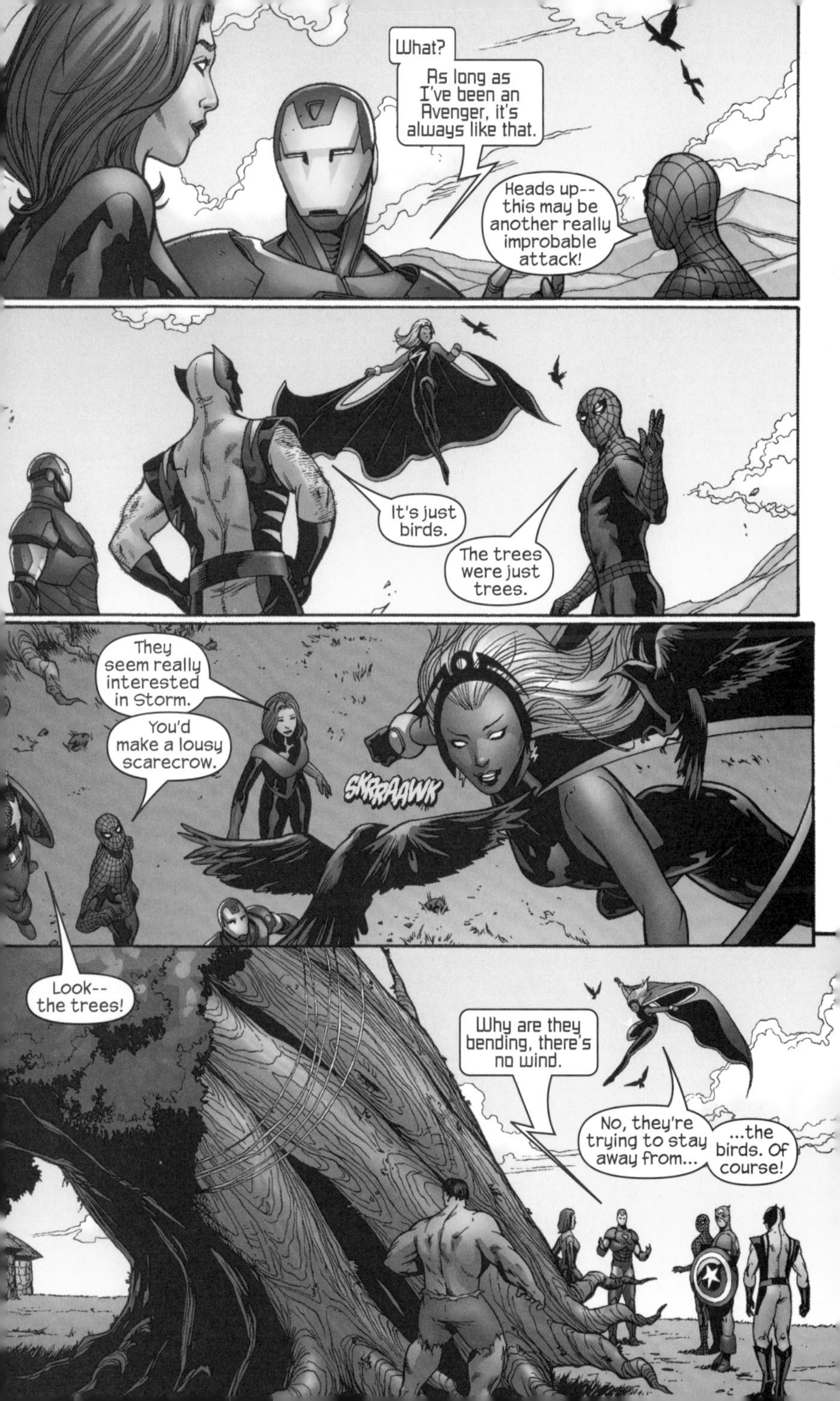
What?
As long as I've been an Avenger, it's always like that.
Heads up-- this may be another really improbable attack!
It's just birds.
The trees were just trees.
They seem really interested in Storm.
You'd make a lousy scarecrow.
SKRRAAWK
Look-- the trees!
Why are they bending, there's no wind.
No, they're trying to stay away from...
...the birds. Of course!

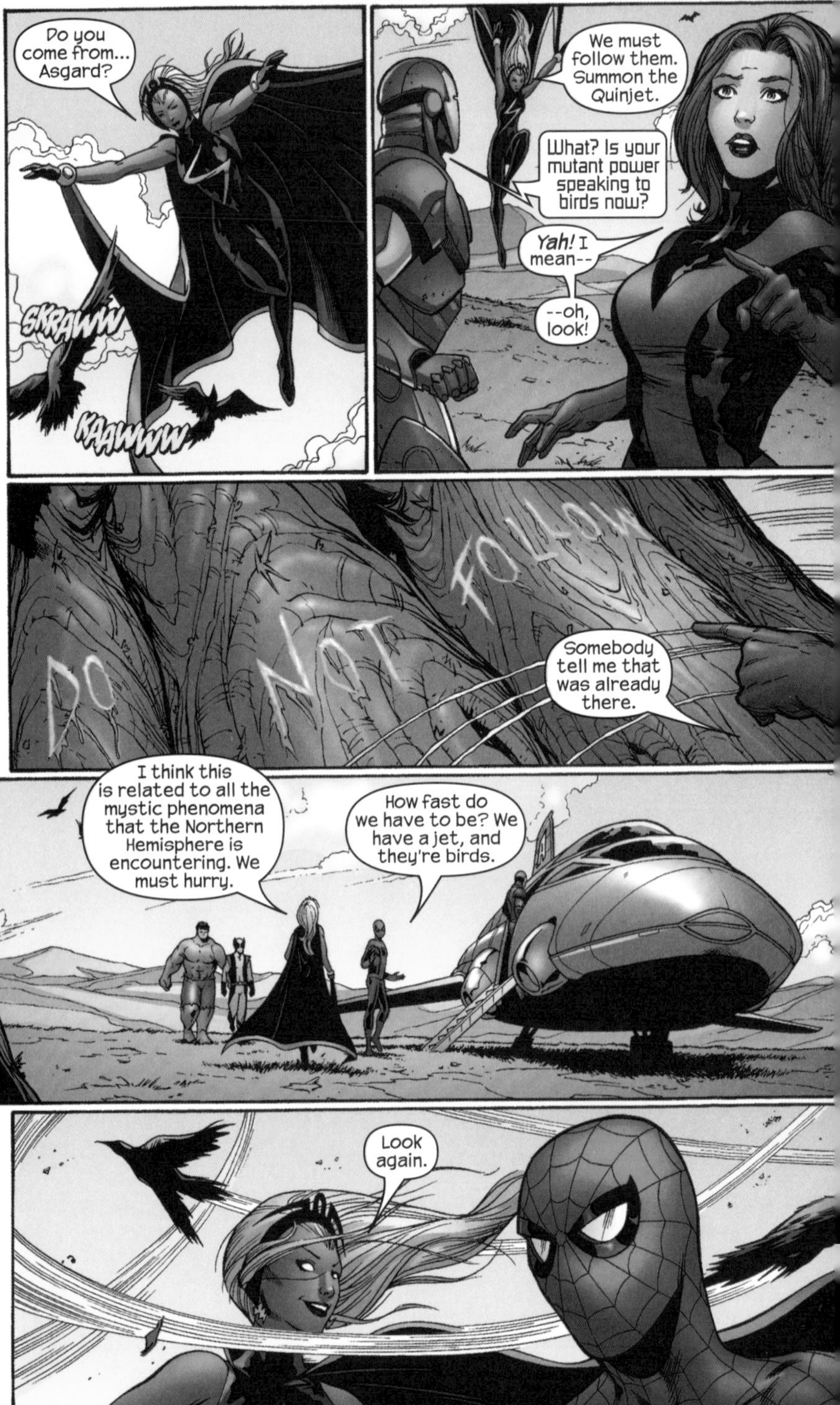

Do you come from... Asgard?
SKRAWW
KAAWWW
We must follow them. Summon the Quinjet.
What? Is your mutant power speaking to birds now?
Yah! I mean--
--oh, look!
DO NOT FOLLOW
Somebody tell me that was already there.
I think this is related to all the mystic phenomena that the Northern Hemisphere is encountering. We must hurry.
How fast do we have to be? We have a jet, and they're birds.
Look again.

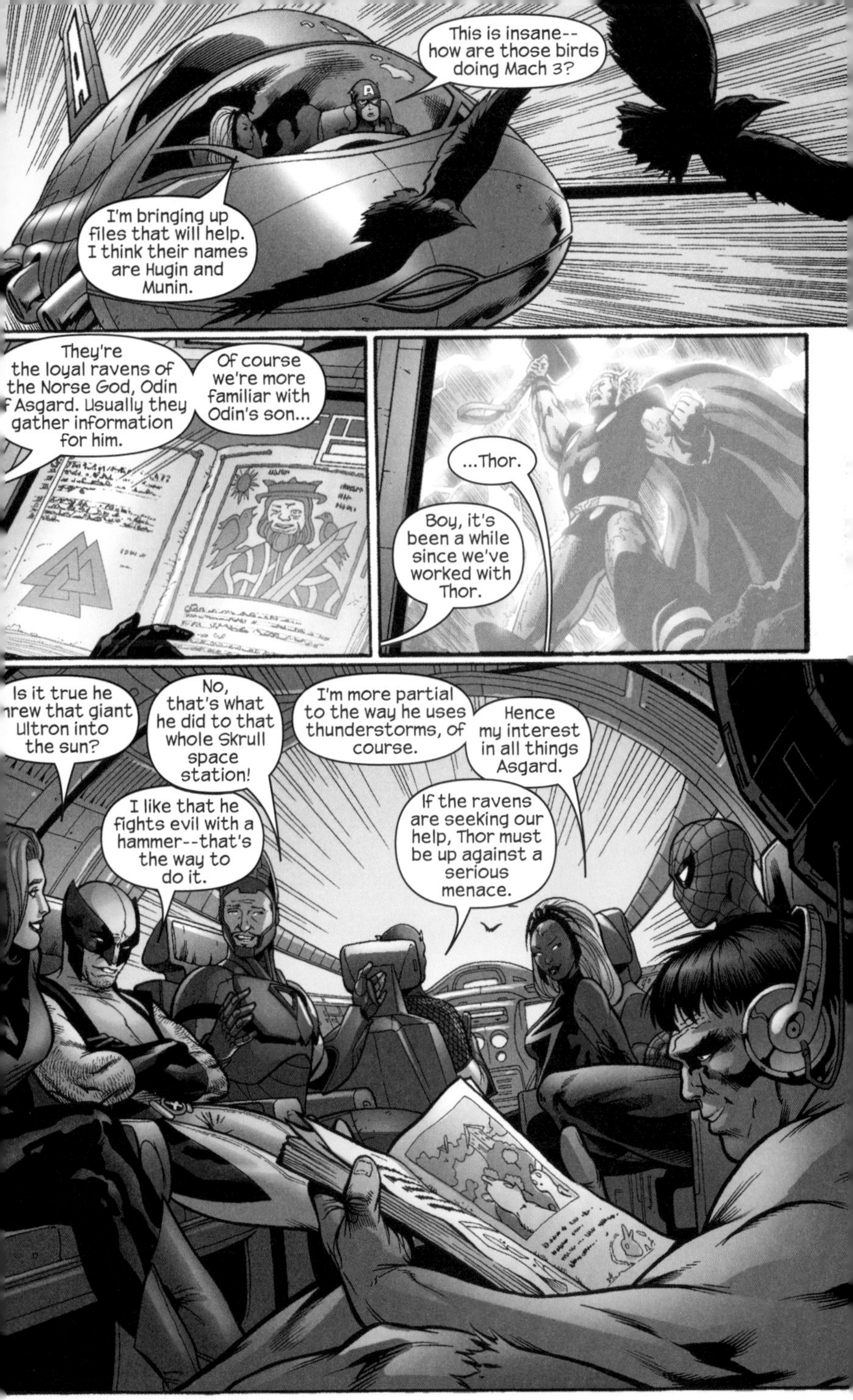

This is insane-- how are those birds doing Mach 3?
I'm bringing up files that will help. I think their names are Hugin and Munin.
They're the loyal ravens of the Norse God, Odin f Asgard. Usually they gather information for him.
Of course we're more familiar with Odin's son...
...Thor.
Boy, it's been a while since we've worked with Thor.
Is it true he hrew that giant Ultron into the sun?
No, that's what he did to that whole Skrull space station!
I like that he fights evil with a hammer--that's the way to do it.
I'm more partial to the way he uses thunderstorms, of course.
Hence my interest in all things Asgard.
If the ravens are seeking our help, Thor must be up against a serious menace.

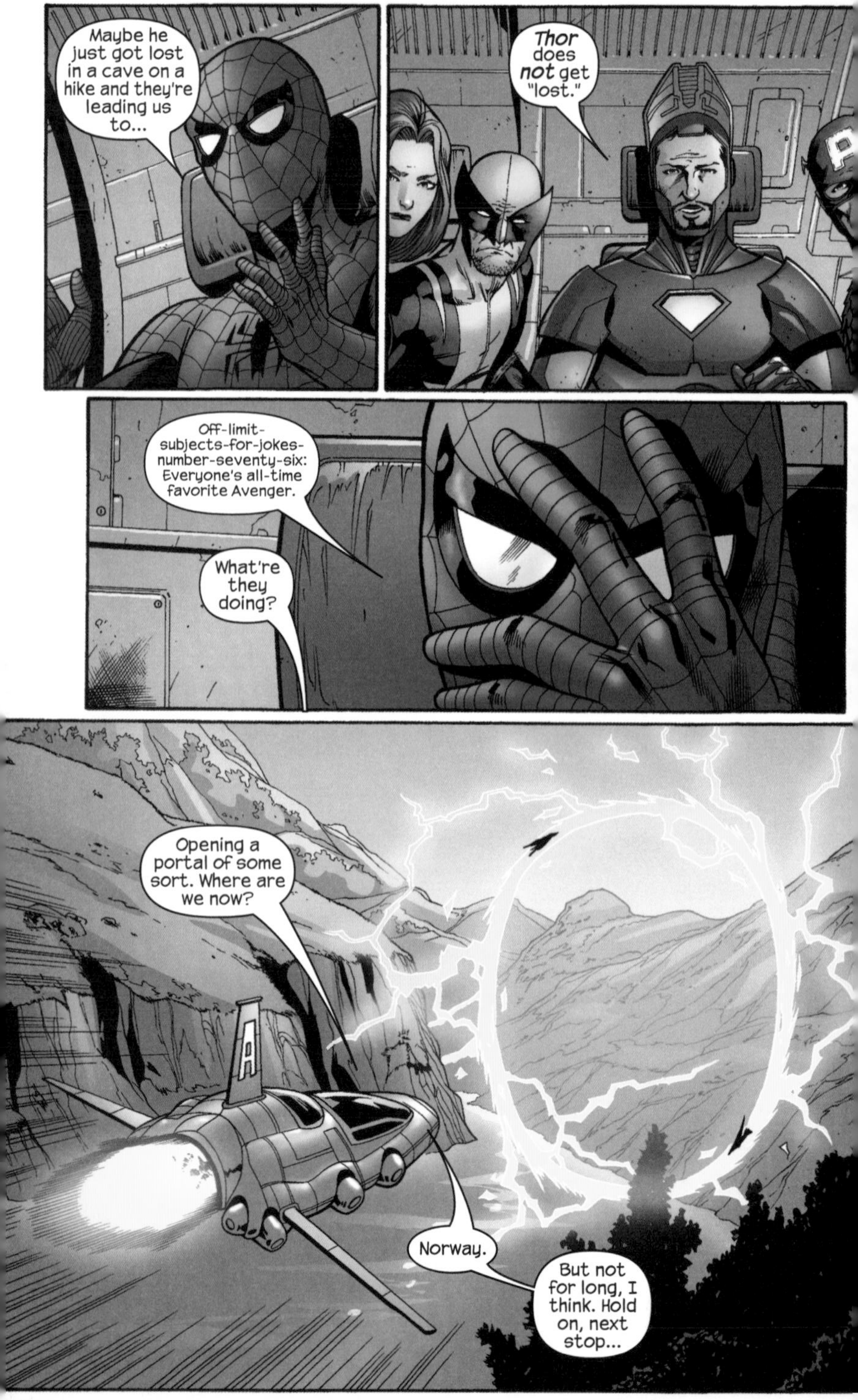
Maybe he just got lost in a cave on a hike and they're leading us to...
Thor does not get "lost."
Off-limit-subjects-for-jokes-number-seventy-six: Everyone's all-time favorite Avenger.
What're they doing?
Opening a portal of some sort. Where are we now?
Norway.
But not for long, I think. Hold on, next stop...

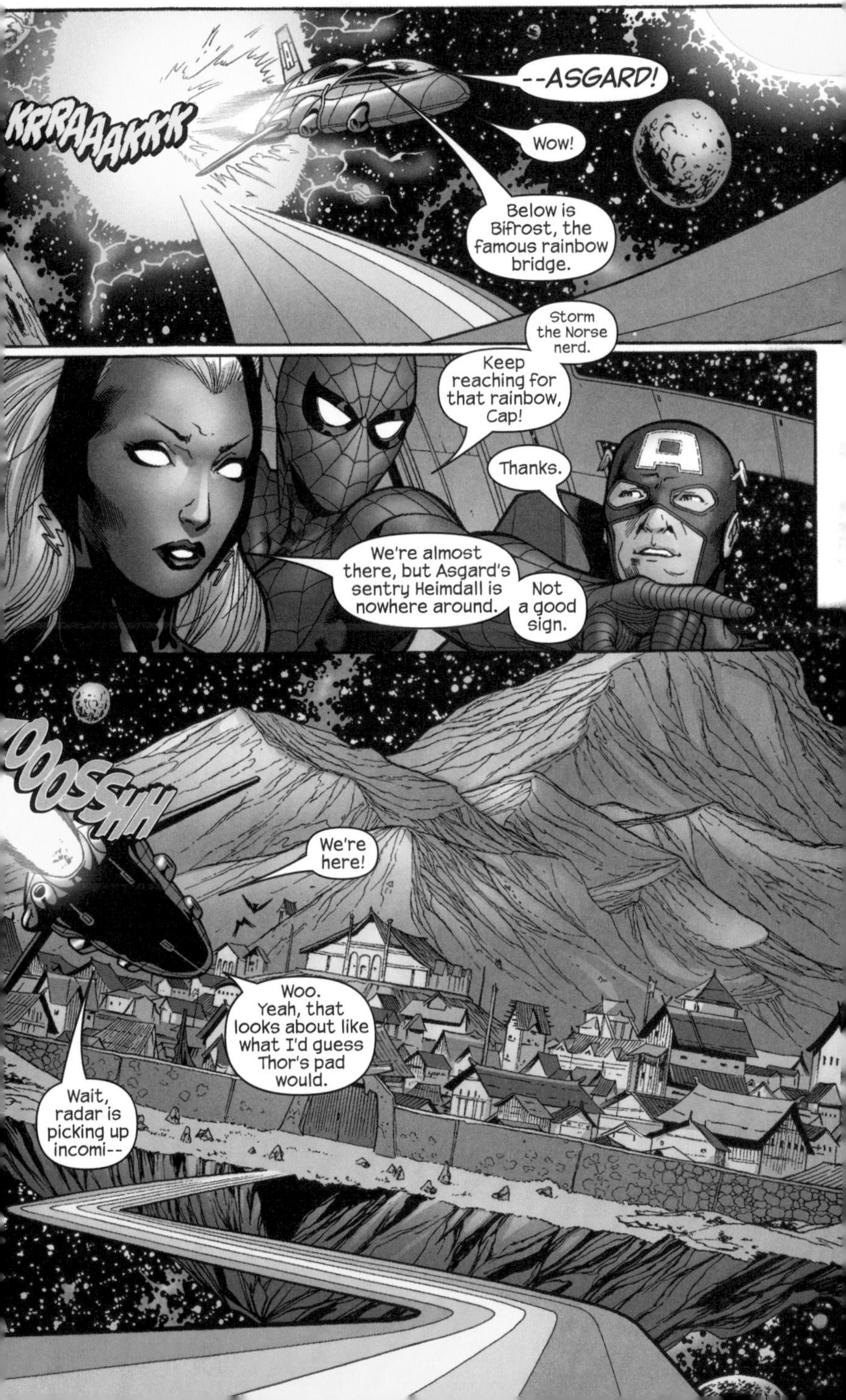
KRRAAAKKK
--ASGARD!
Wow!
Below is Bifrost, the famous rainbow bridge.
Storm the Norse nerd.
Keep reaching for that rainbow, Cap!
Thanks.
We're almost there, but Asgard's sentry Heimdall is nowhere around.
Not a good sign.
OOOSSHH
We're here!
Woo. Yeah, that looks about like what I'd guess Thor's pad would.
Wait, radar is picking up incomi--

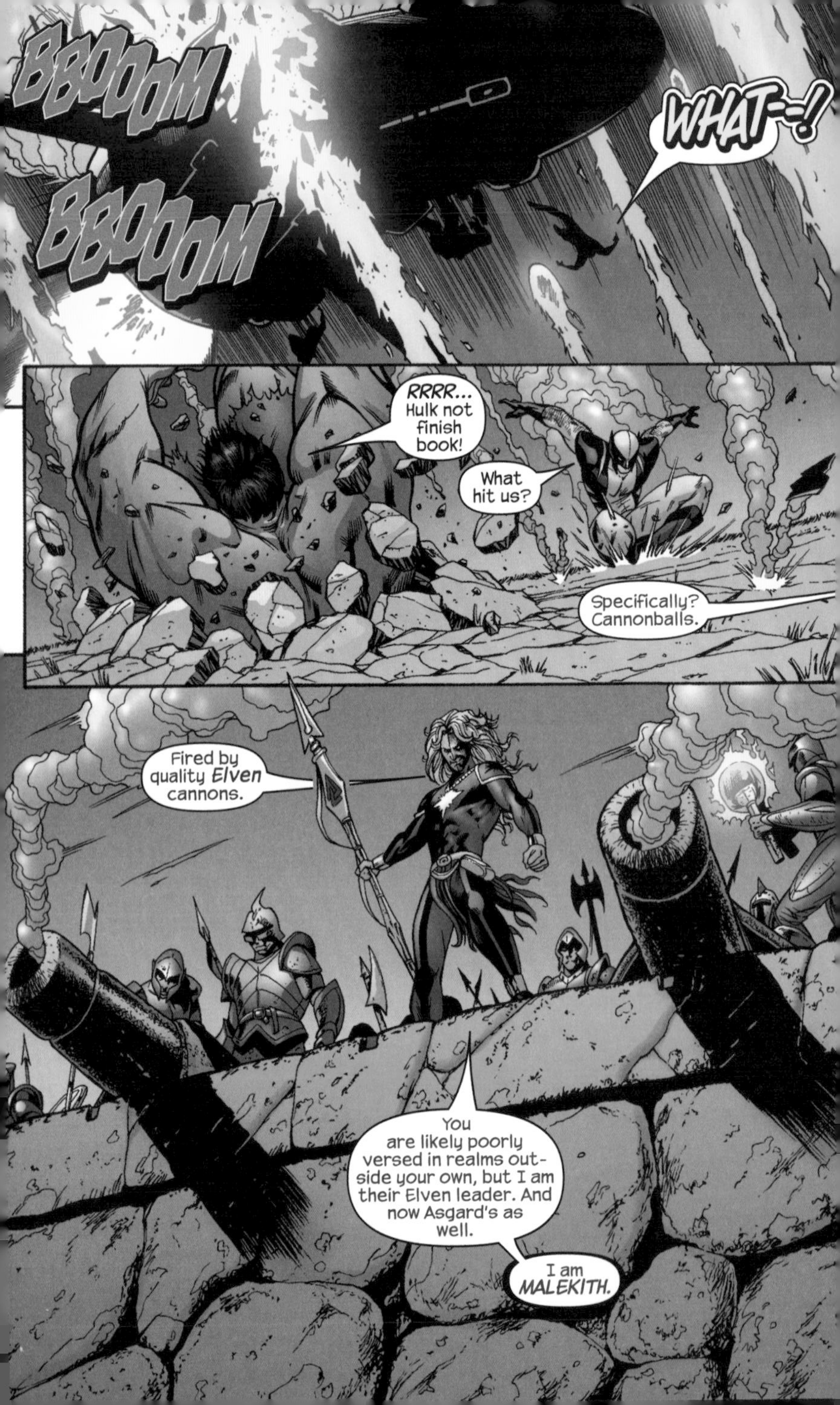
BBOOOOM
BBOOOOM
WHAT--!
RRRR... Hulk not finish book!
What hit us?
Specifically? Cannonballs.
Fired by quality *Elven* cannons.
You are likely poorly versed in realms out-side your own, but I am their Elven leader. And now Asgard's as well.
I am *MALEKITH.*

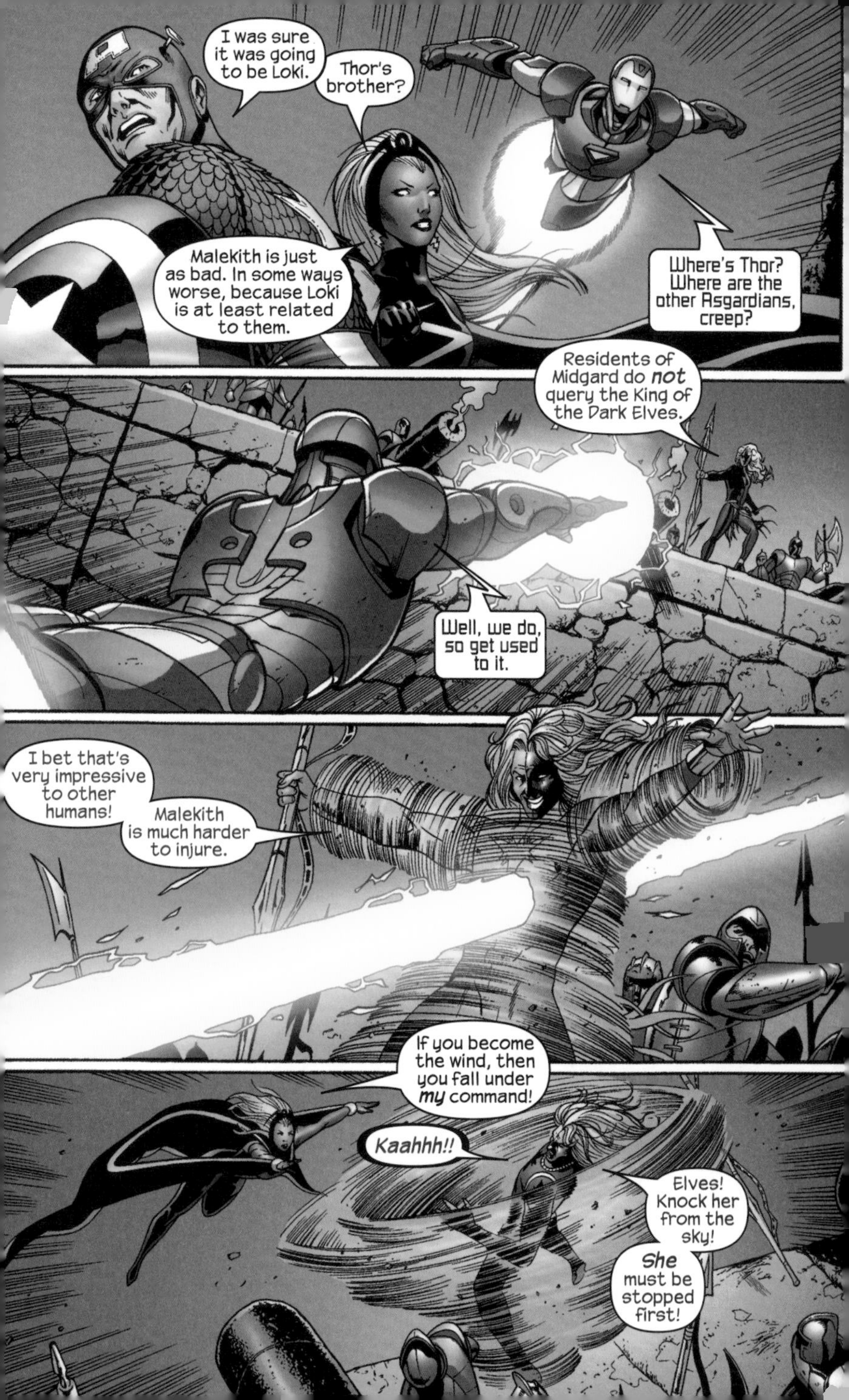
I was sure it was going to be Loki.
Thor's brother?
Malekith is just as bad. In some ways worse, because Loki is at least related to them.
Where's Thor? Where are the other Asgardians, creep?
Residents of Midgard do *not* query the King of the Dark Elves.
Well, we do, so get used to it.
I bet that's very impressive to other humans!
Malekith is much harder to injure.
If you become the wind, then you fall under *my* command!
Kaahhh!!
Elves! Knock her from the sky!
She must be stopped first!

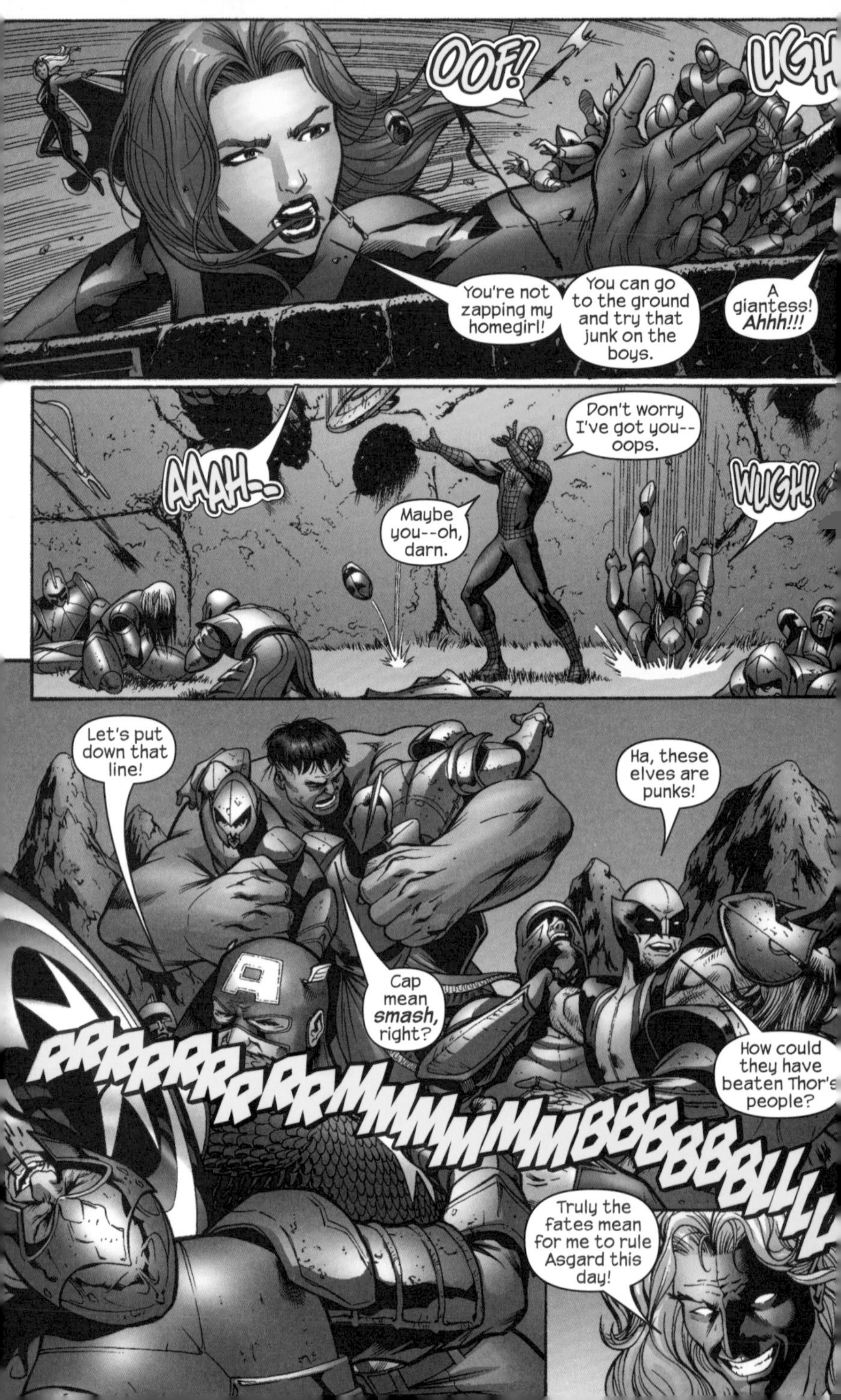

OOF!
UGH
You're not zapping my homegirl!
You can go to the ground and try that junk on the boys.
A giantess! *Ahhh!!!*
AAAH--
Don't worry I've got you-- oops.
Maybe you--oh, darn.
WUGH!
Let's put down that line!
Ha, these elves are punks!
Cap mean *smash,* right?
How could they have beaten Thor's people?
RRRRRRRRRMMMMMMMMMBBBBBBLLL
Truly the fates mean for me to rule Asgard this day!

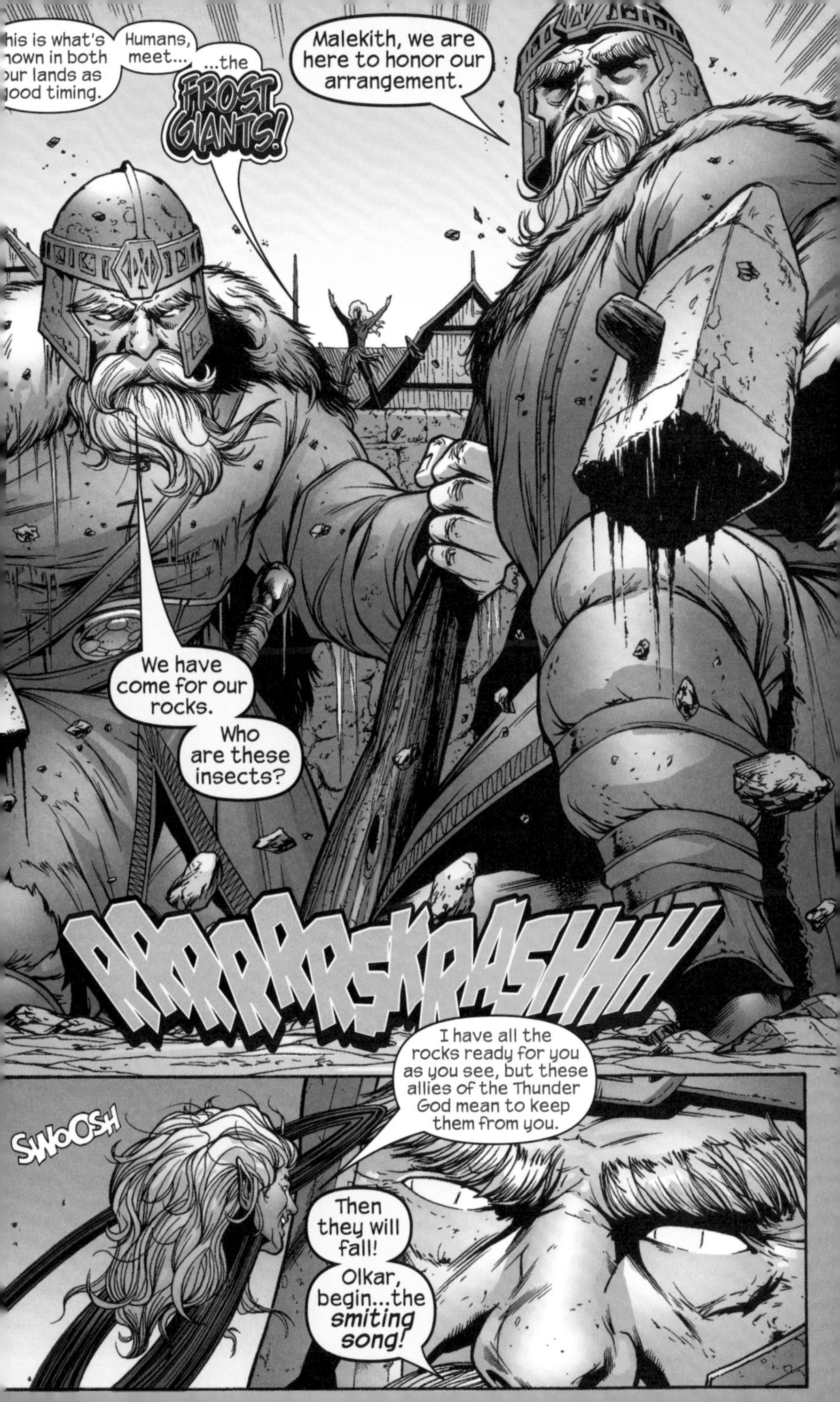

his is what's
nown in both
our lands as
good timing.
Humans, meet...
...the FROST GIANTS!
Malekith, we are here to honor our arrangement.
We have come for our rocks.
Who are these insects?
RRRRRRSKRASHHH
I have all the rocks ready for you as you see, but these allies of the Thunder God mean to keep them from you.
SWOOSH
Then they will fall!
Olkar, begin...the *smiting song!*

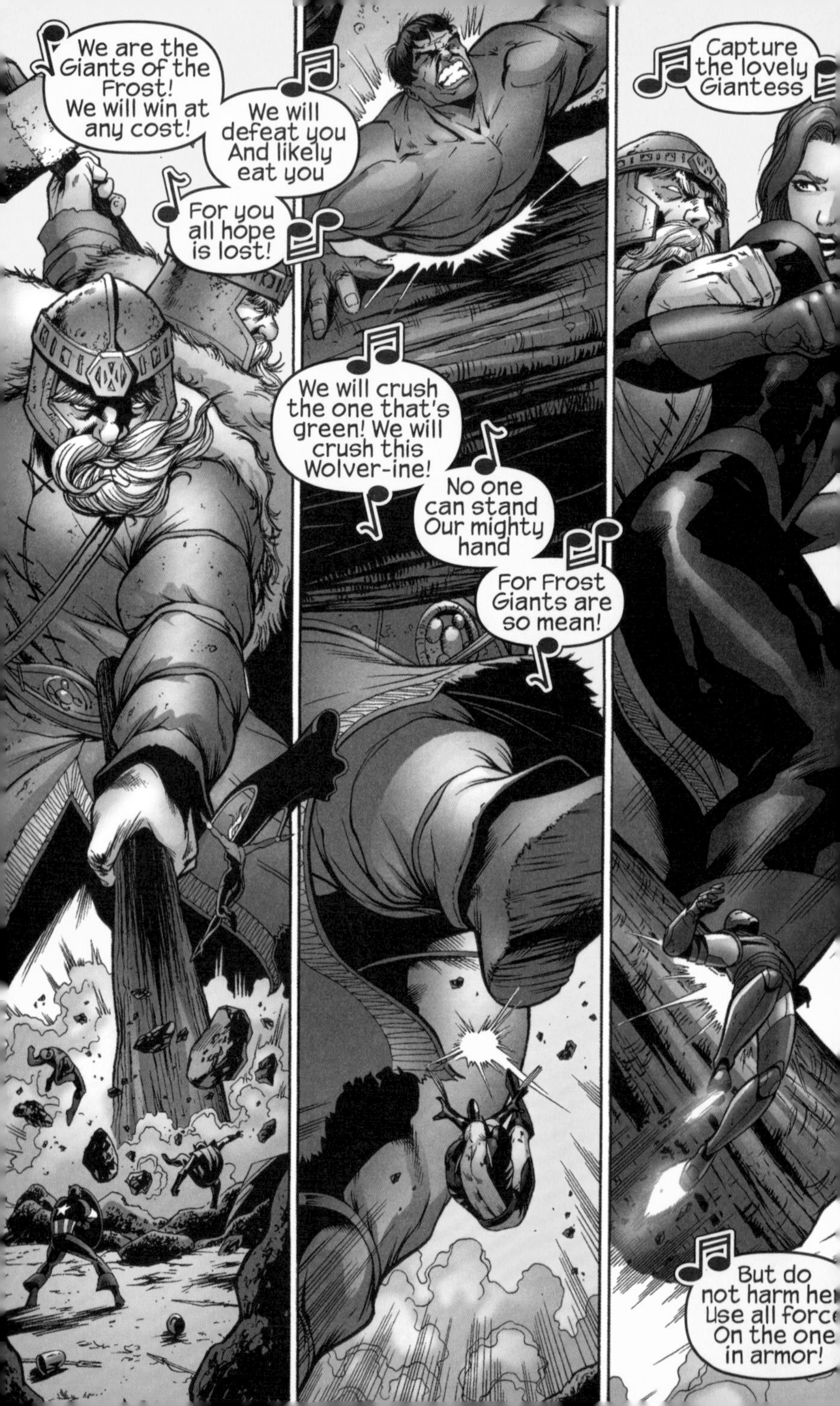

We are the Giants of the Frost! We will win at any cost!
We will defeat you And likely eat you
For you all hope is lost!
We will crush the one that's green! We will crush this Wolver-ine!
No one can stand Our mighty hand
For Frost Giants are so mean!
Capture the lovely Giantess
But do not harm her Use all force On the one in armor!

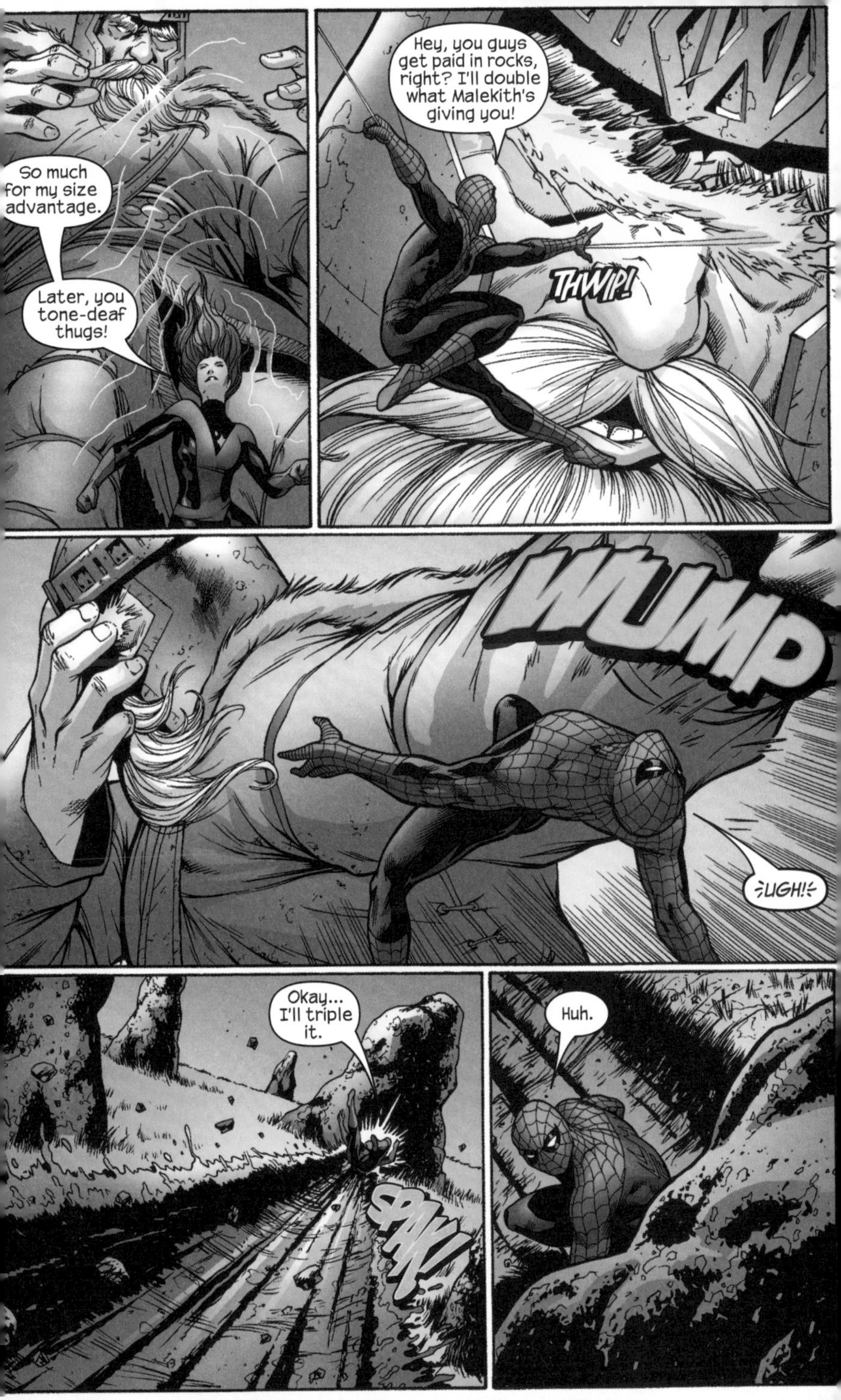
So much for my size advantage.
Later, you tone-deaf thugs!
Hey, you guys get paid in rocks, right? I'll double what Malekith's giving you!
THWIP!
WUMP
UGH!
Okay... I'll triple it.
SPAK!
Huh.

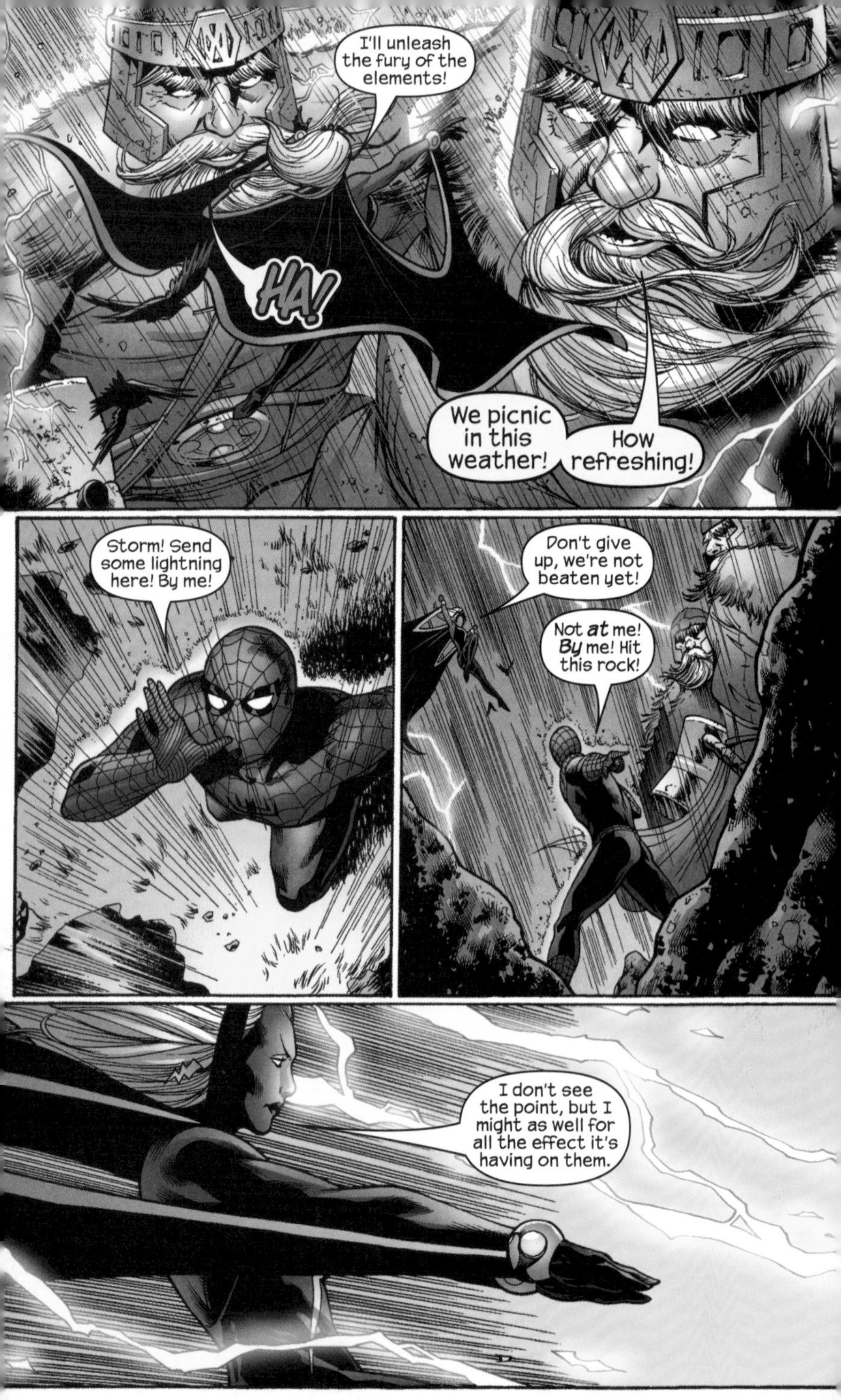

I'll unleash the fury of the elements!
HA!
We picnic in this weather!
How refreshing!
Storm! Send some lightning here! By me!
Don't give up, we're not beaten yet!
Not *at* me! *By* me! Hit this rock!
I don't see the point, but I might as well for all the effect it's having on them.

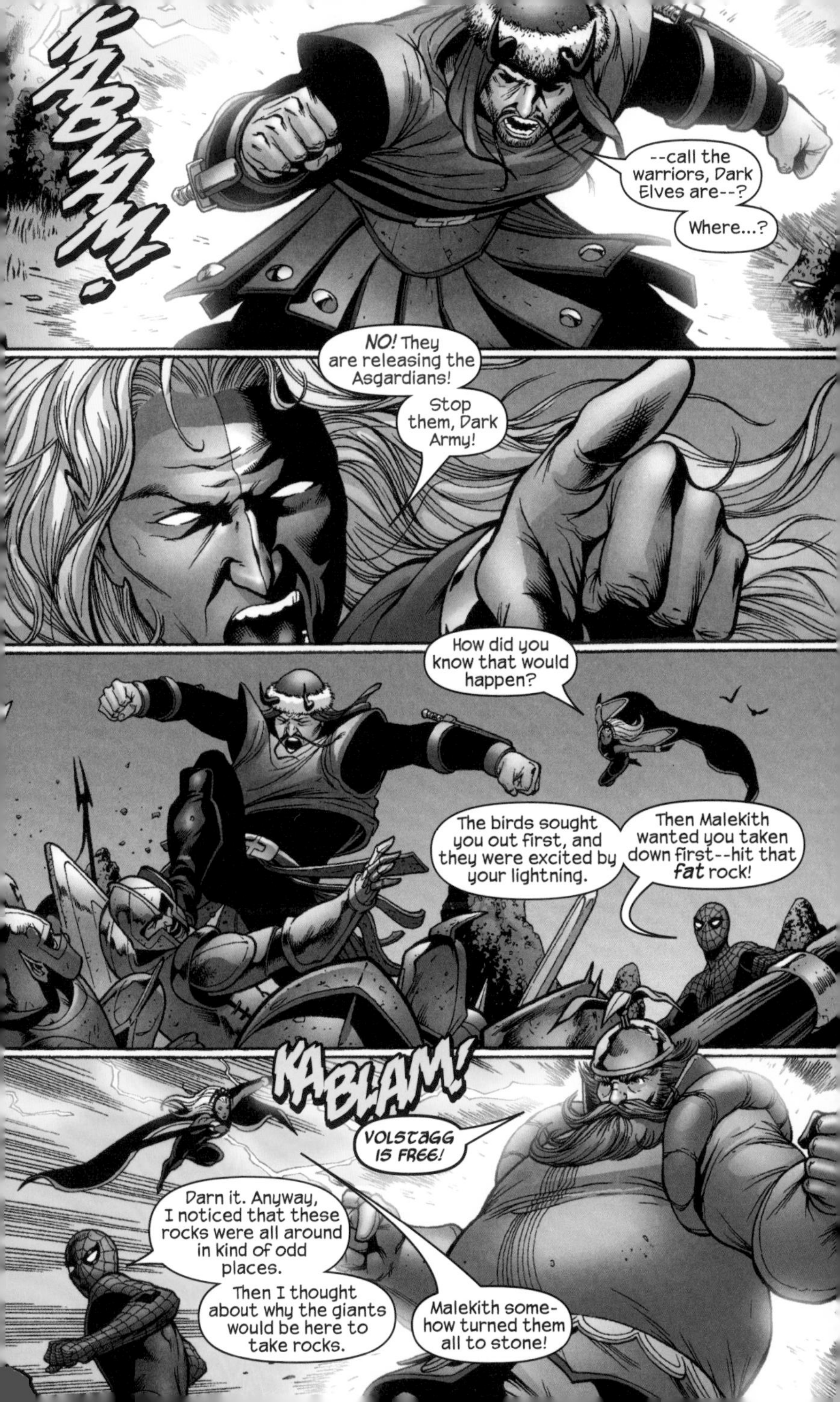
KABLAM!
--call the warriors, Dark Elves are--?
Where...?
NO! They are releasing the Asgardians!
Stop them, Dark Army!
How did you know that would happen?
The birds sought you out first, and they were excited by your lightning.
Then Malekith wanted you taken down first--hit that fat rock!
KABLAM!
VOLSTAGG IS FREE!
Darn it. Anyway, I noticed that these rocks were all around in kind of odd places.
Then I thought about why the giants would be here to take rocks.
Malekith some-how turned them all to stone!

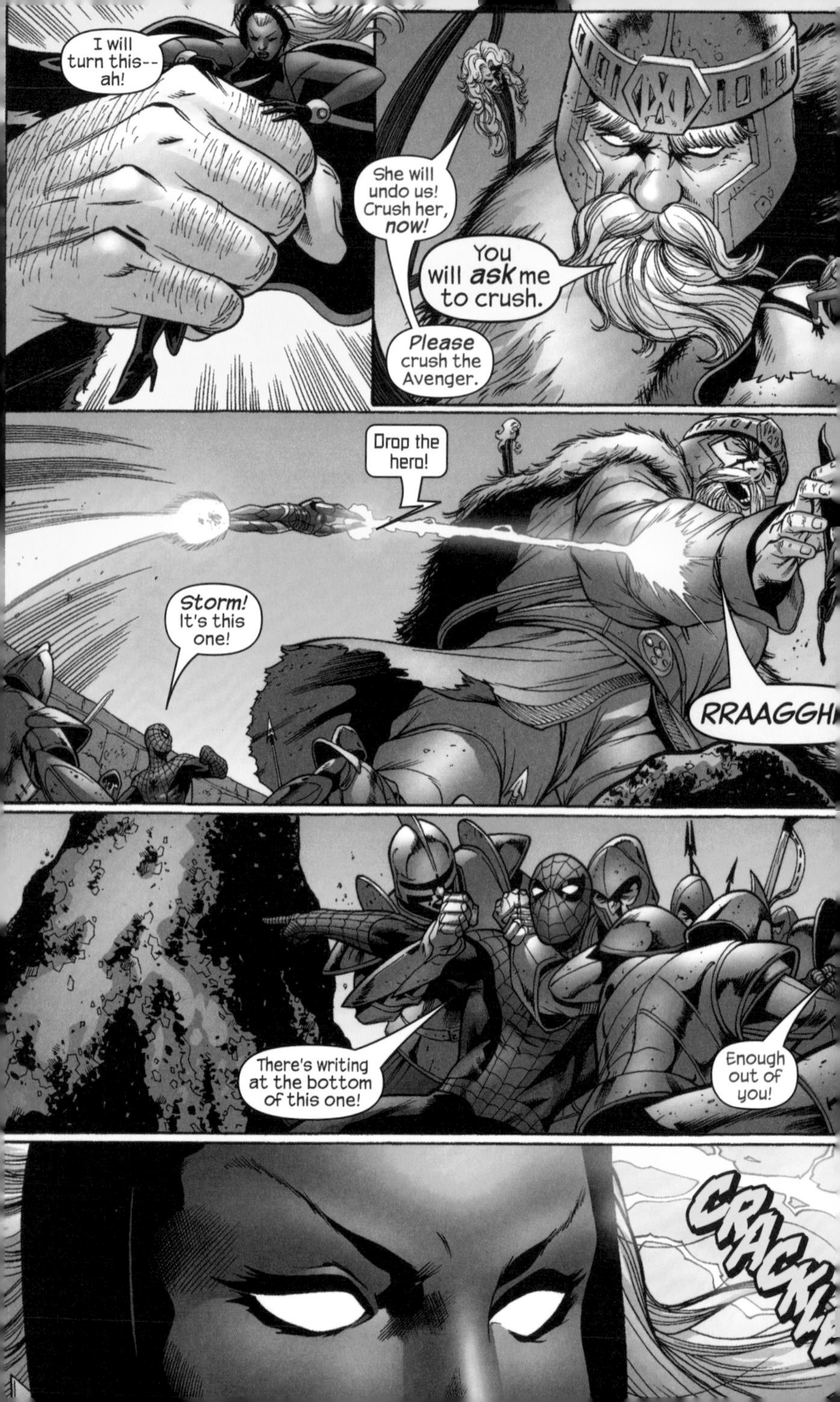

I will turn this-- ah!
She will undo us! Crush her, *now!*
You will ***ask*** me to crush.
Please crush the Avenger.
Drop the hero!
Storm! It's this one!
RRAAGGH
There's writing at the bottom of this one!
Enough out of you!
CRACKLE

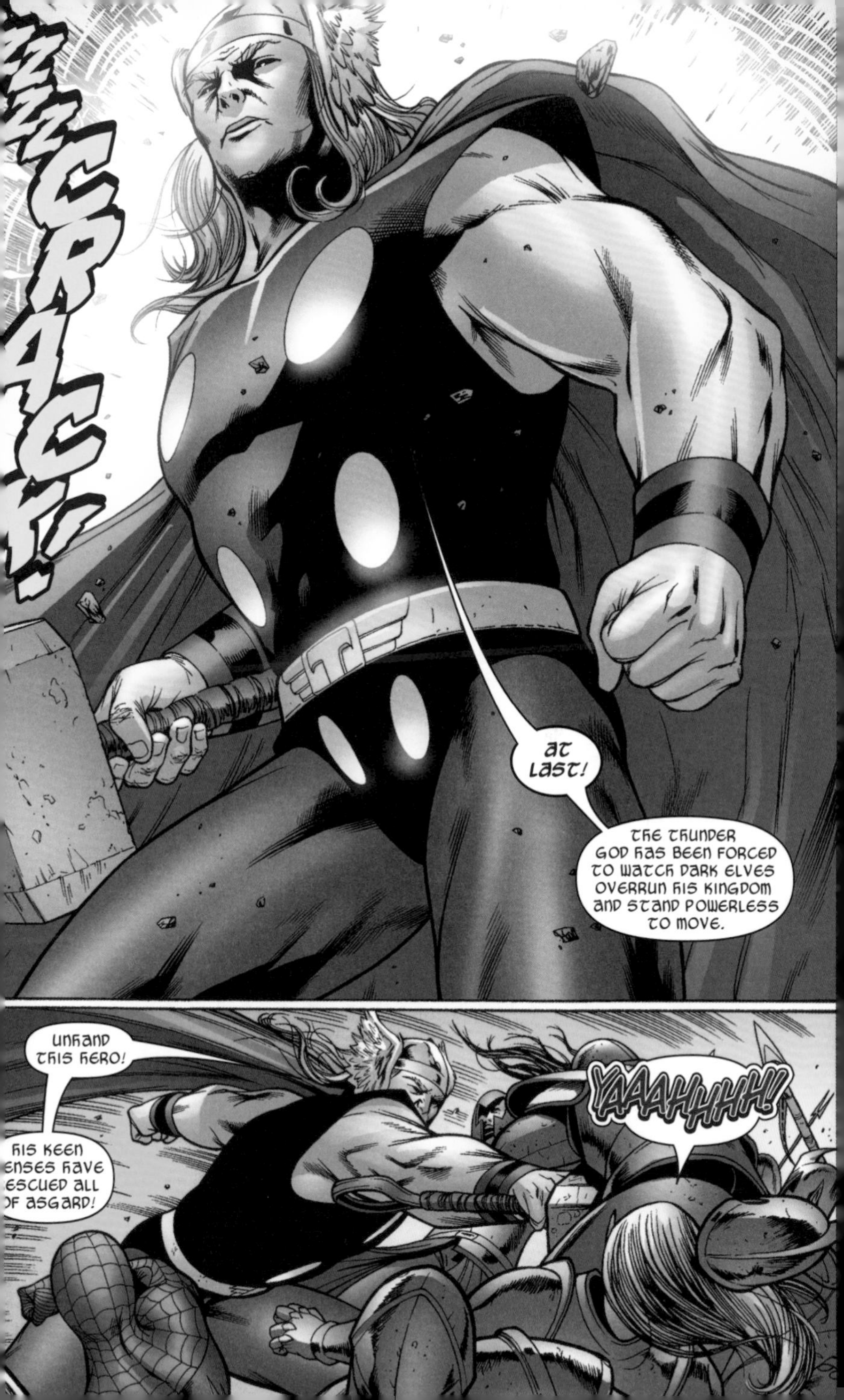
ZZZZCRACK!
AT LAST!
THE THUNDER GOD HAS BEEN FORCED TO WATCH DARK ELVES OVERRUN HIS KINGDOM AND STAND POWERLESS TO MOVE.
UNHAND THIS HERO!
HIS KEEN ENSES HAVE ESCUED ALL OF ASGARD!
YAAAHHHH!

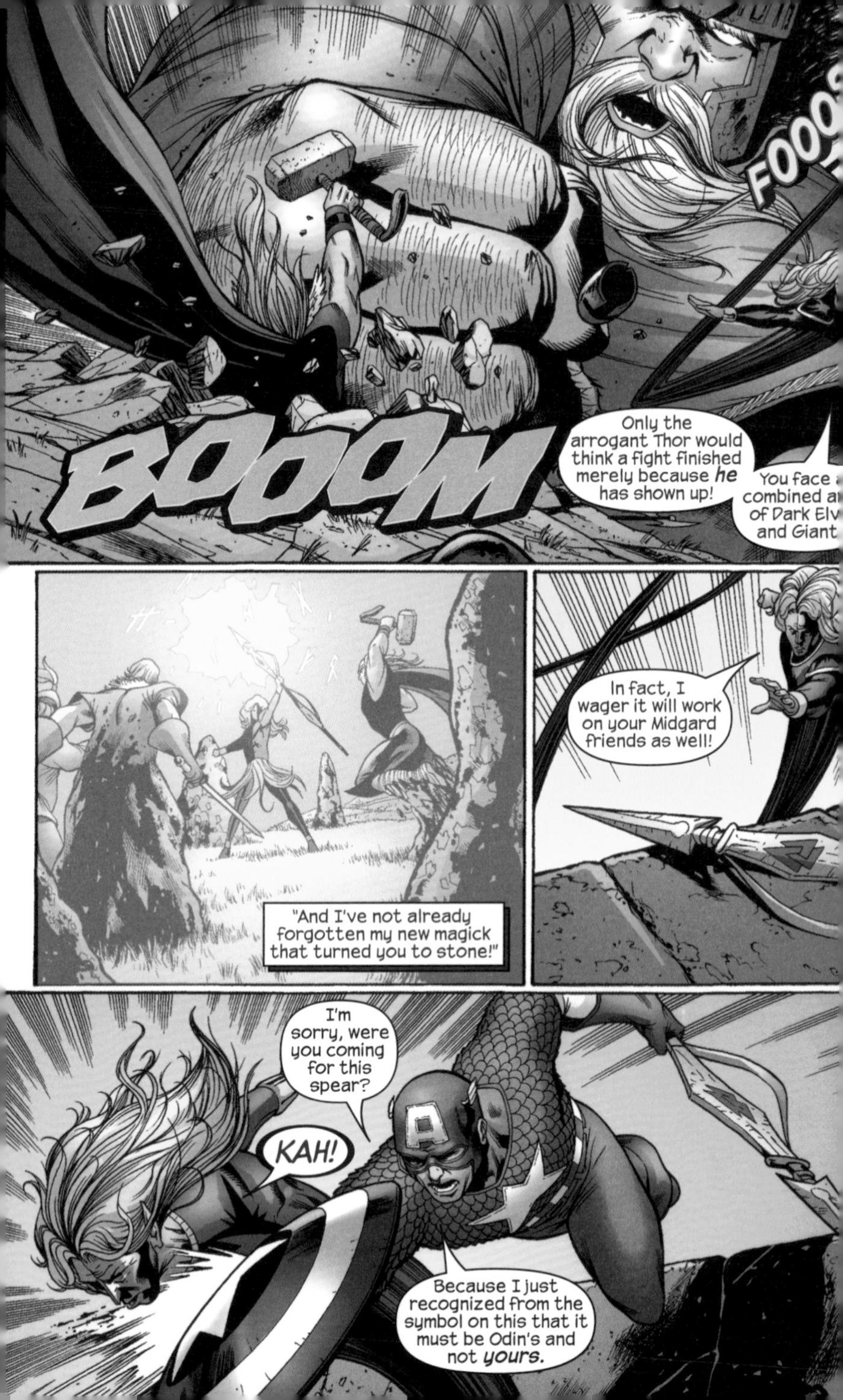
FOOO
BOOOM
Only the arrogant Thor would think a fight finished merely because *he* has shown up!
You face
combined a
of Dark Elv
and Giant
"And I've not already forgotten my new magick that turned you to stone!"
In fact, I wager it will work on your Midgard friends as well!
I'm sorry, were you coming for this spear?
KAH!
Because I just recognized from the symbol on this that it must be Odin's and not *yours.*

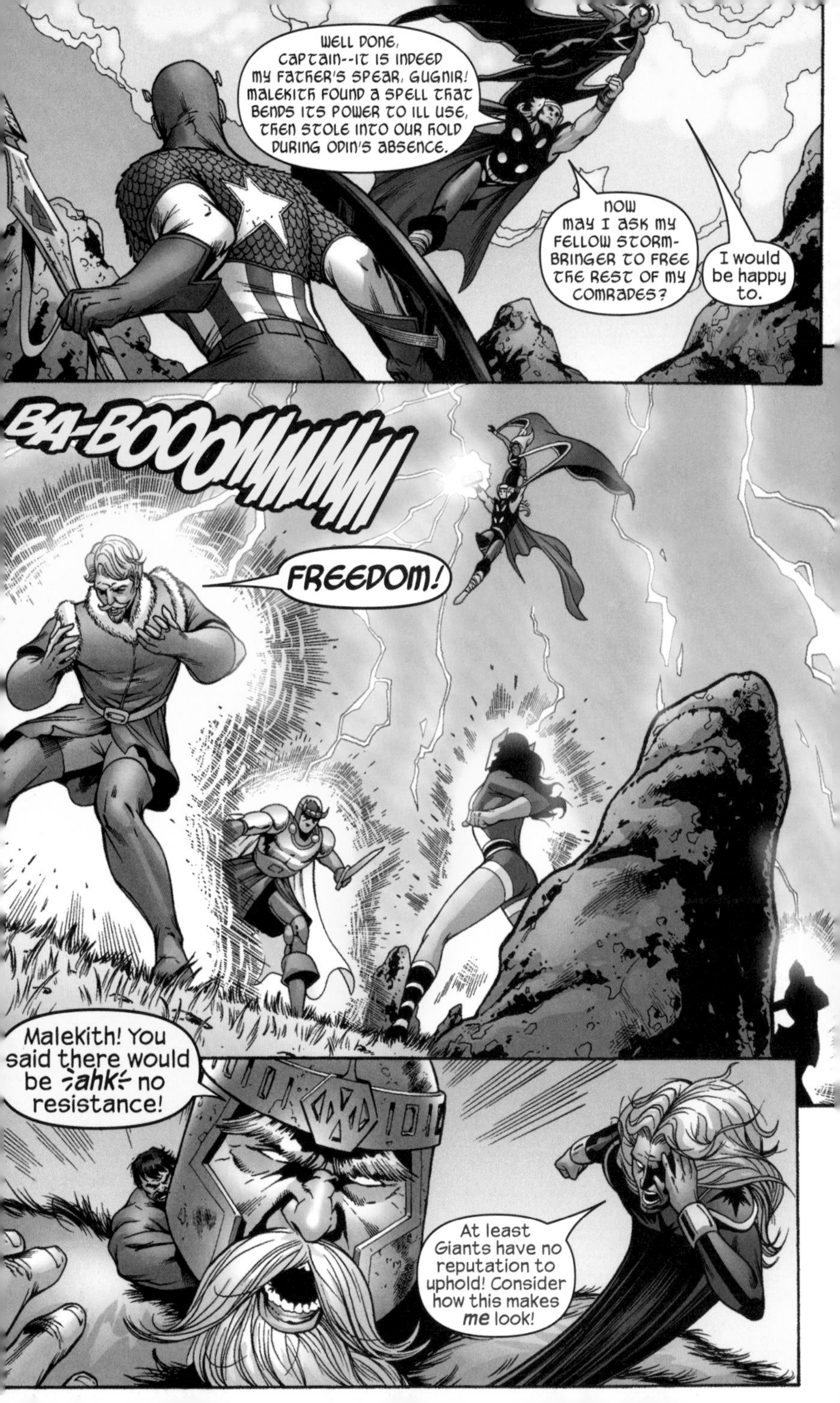

WELL DONE, CAPTAIN--IT IS INDEED MY FATHER'S SPEAR, GUGNIR! MALEKITH FOUND A SPELL THAT BENDS ITS POWER TO ILL USE, THEN STOLE INTO OUR HOLD DURING ODIN'S ABSENCE.
NOW MAY I ASK MY FELLOW STORM-BRINGER TO FREE THE REST OF MY COMRADES?
I would be happy to.
BA-BOOOMMMMM
FREEDOM!
Malekith! You said there would be *ahk* no resistance!
At least Giants have no reputation to uphold! Consider how this makes *me* look!

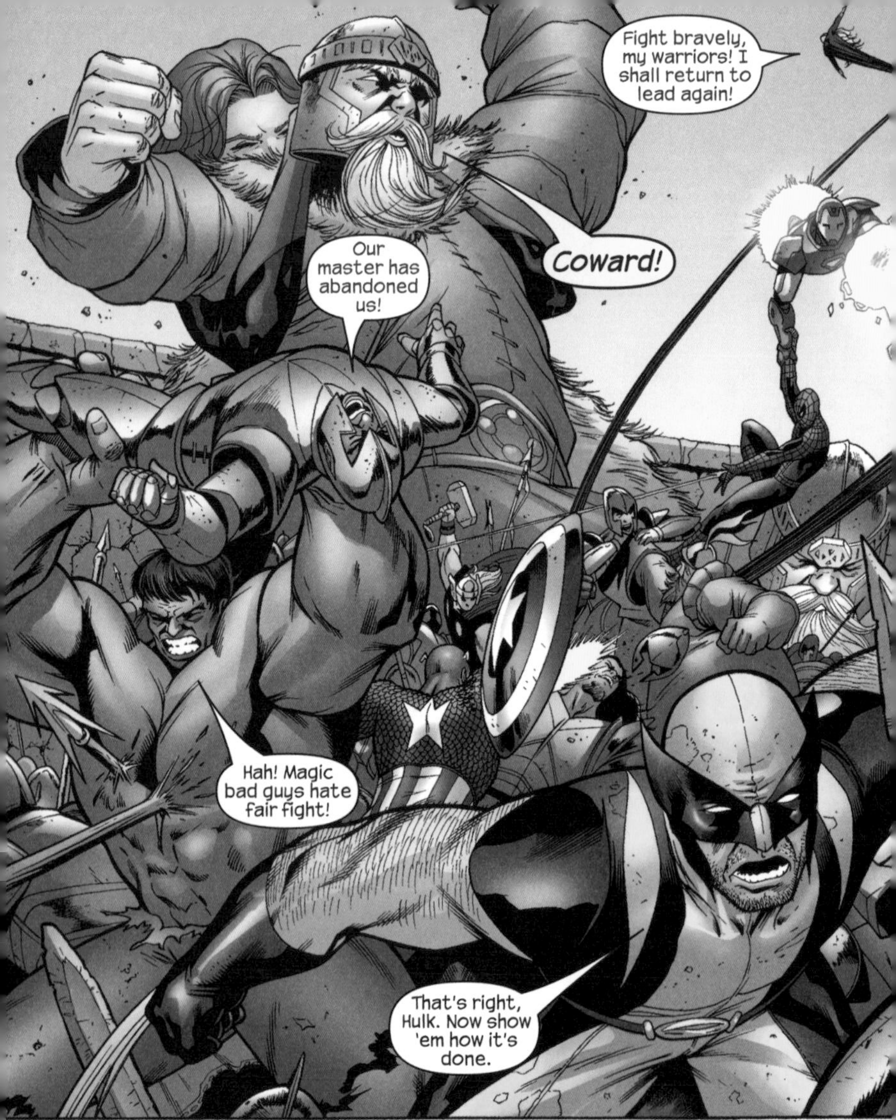
Fight bravely, my warriors! I shall return to lead again!
Coward!
Our master has abandoned us!
Hah! Magic bad guys hate fair fight!
That's right, Hulk. Now show 'em how it's done.

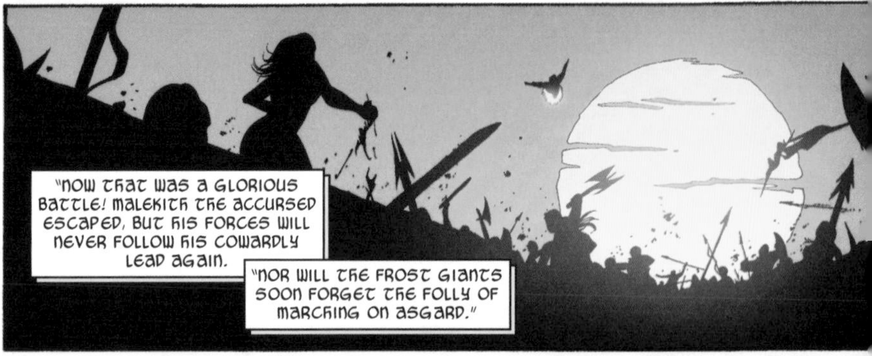
"NOW THAT WAS A GLORIOUS BATTLE! MALEKITH THE ACCURSED ESCAPED, BUT HIS FORCES WILL NEVER FOLLOW HIS COWARDLY LEAD AGAIN.
"NOR WILL THE FROST GIANTS SOON FORGET THE FOLLY OF MARCHING ON ASGARD."

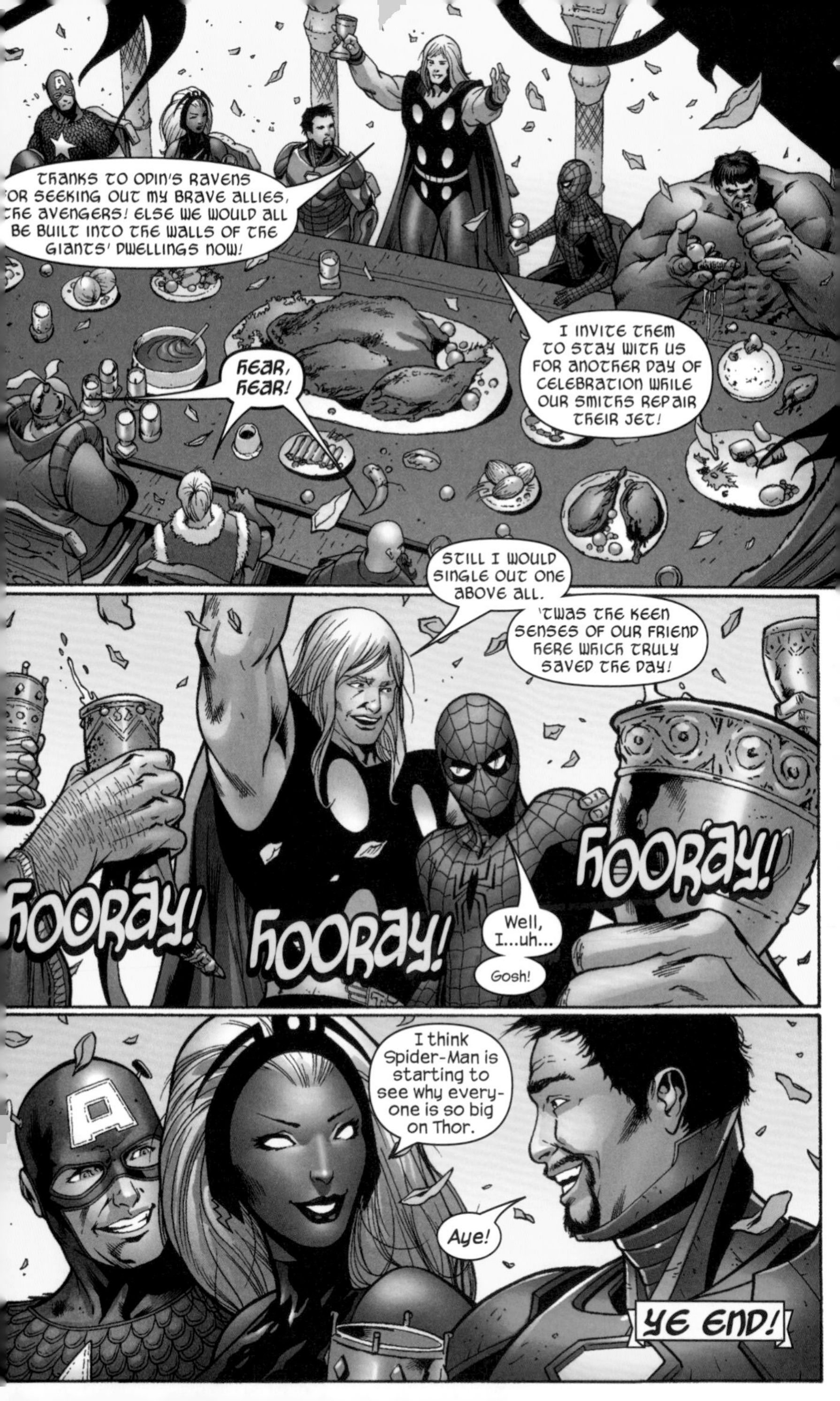

THANKS TO ODIN'S RAVENS FOR SEEKING OUT MY BRAVE ALLIES, THE AVENGERS! ELSE WE WOULD ALL BE BUILT INTO THE WALLS OF THE GIANTS' DWELLINGS NOW!
I INVITE THEM TO STAY WITH US FOR ANOTHER DAY OF CELEBRATION WHILE OUR SMITHS REPAIR THEIR JET!
HEAR, HEAR!
STILL I WOULD SINGLE OUT ONE ABOVE ALL.
'TWAS THE KEEN SENSES OF OUR FRIEND HERE WHICH TRULY SAVED THE DAY!
HOORAY!
HOORAY!
HOORAY!
Well, I...uh...
Gosh!
I think Spider-Man is starting to see why every-one is so big on Thor.
Aye!
YE END!

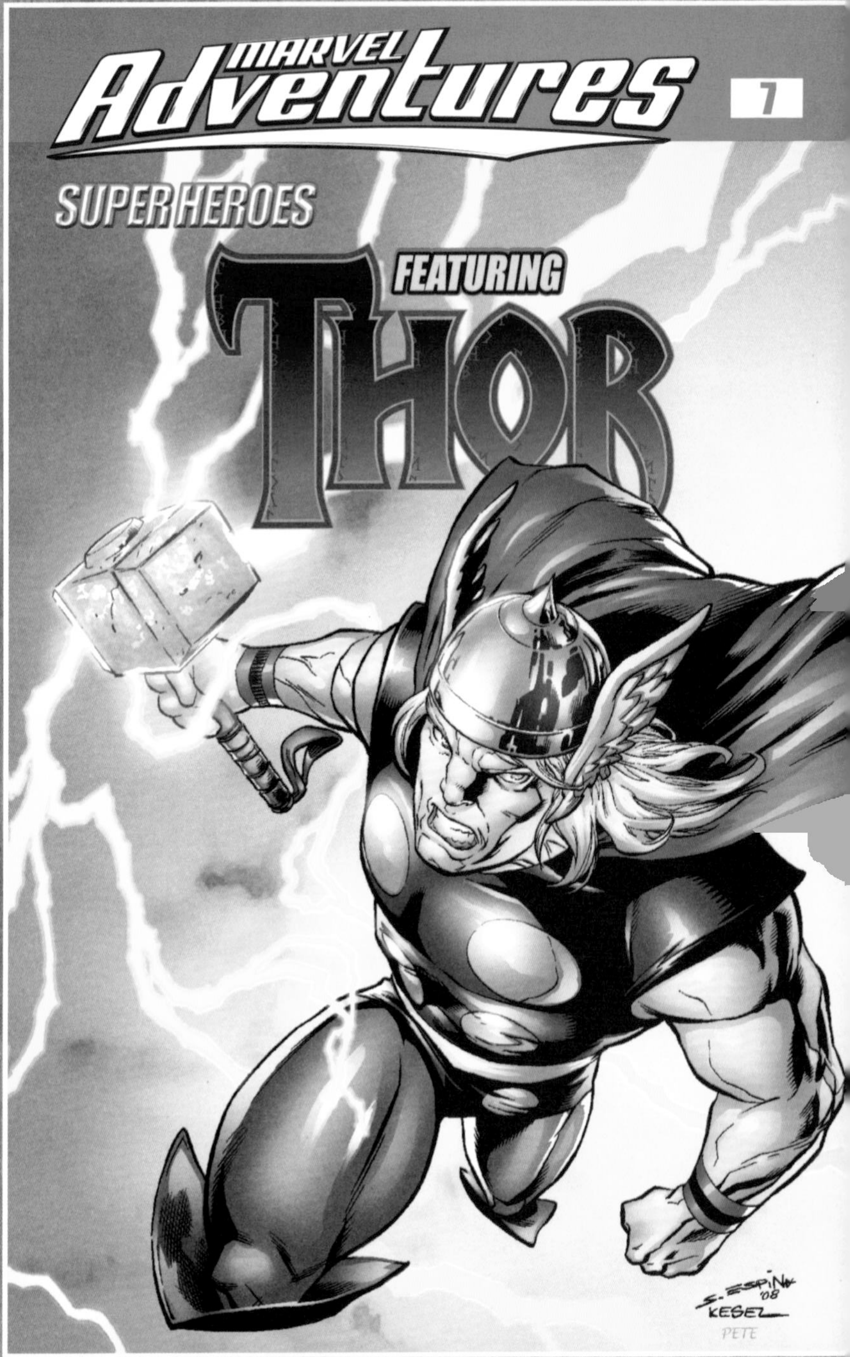
MARVEL
Adventures
7
SUPER HEROES
FEATURING
THOR
S. ESPIN '08
KESEL
PETE

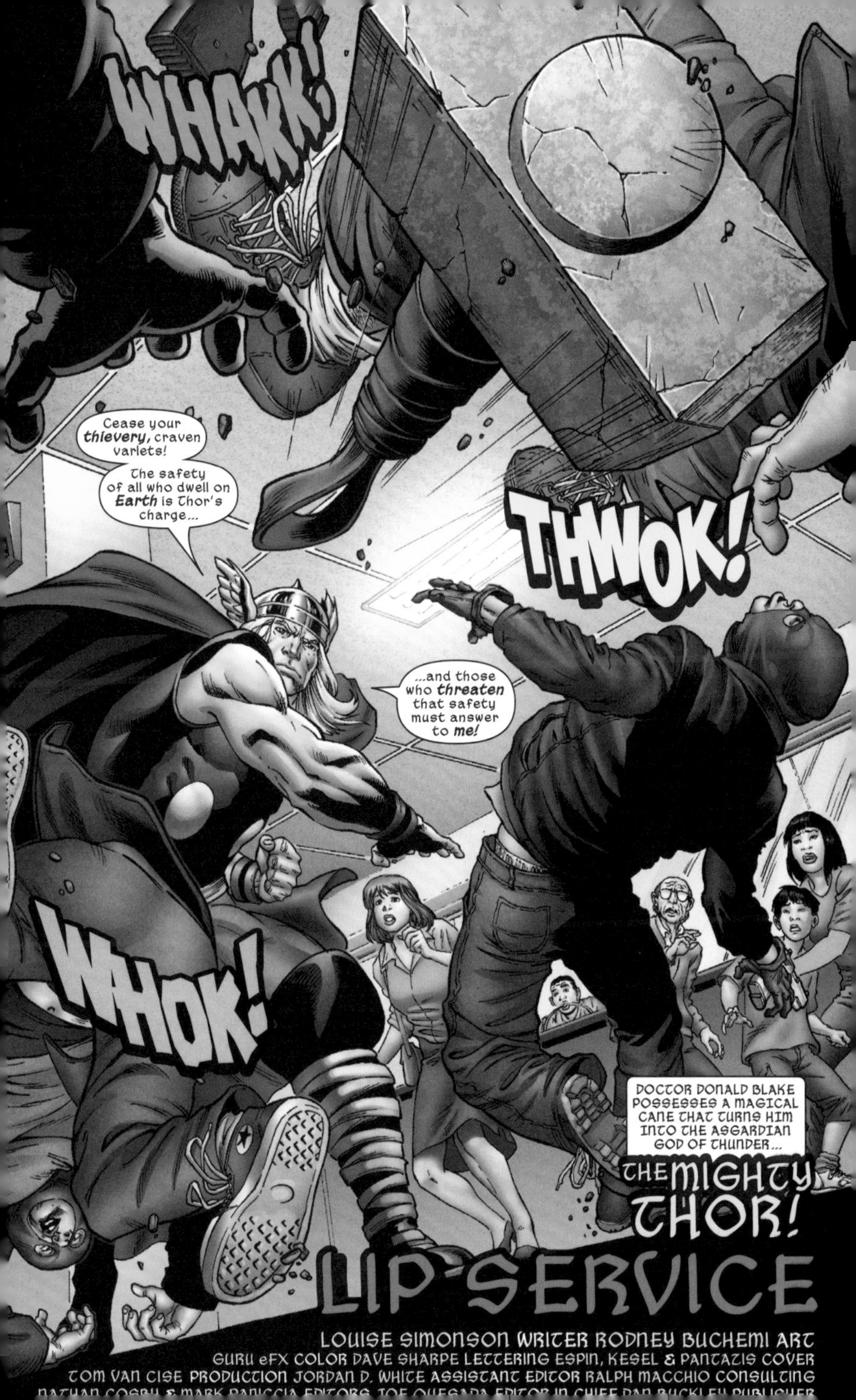
WHAKK!
Cease your thievery, craven varlets!
The safety of all who dwell on Earth is Thor's charge...
THWOK!
...and those who threaten that safety must answer to me!
WHOK!
DOCTOR DONALD BLAKE POSSESSES A MAGICAL CANE THAT TURNS HIM INTO THE ASGARDIAN GOD OF THUNDER...
THE MIGHTY THOR!
LIP SERVICE
LOUISE SIMONSON WRITER RODNEY BUCHEMI ART
GURU eFX COLOR DAVE SHARPE LETTERING ESPIN, KESEL & PANTAZIS COVER
TOM VAN CISE PRODUCTION JORDAN D. WHITE ASSISTANT EDITOR RALPH MACCHIO CONSULTING

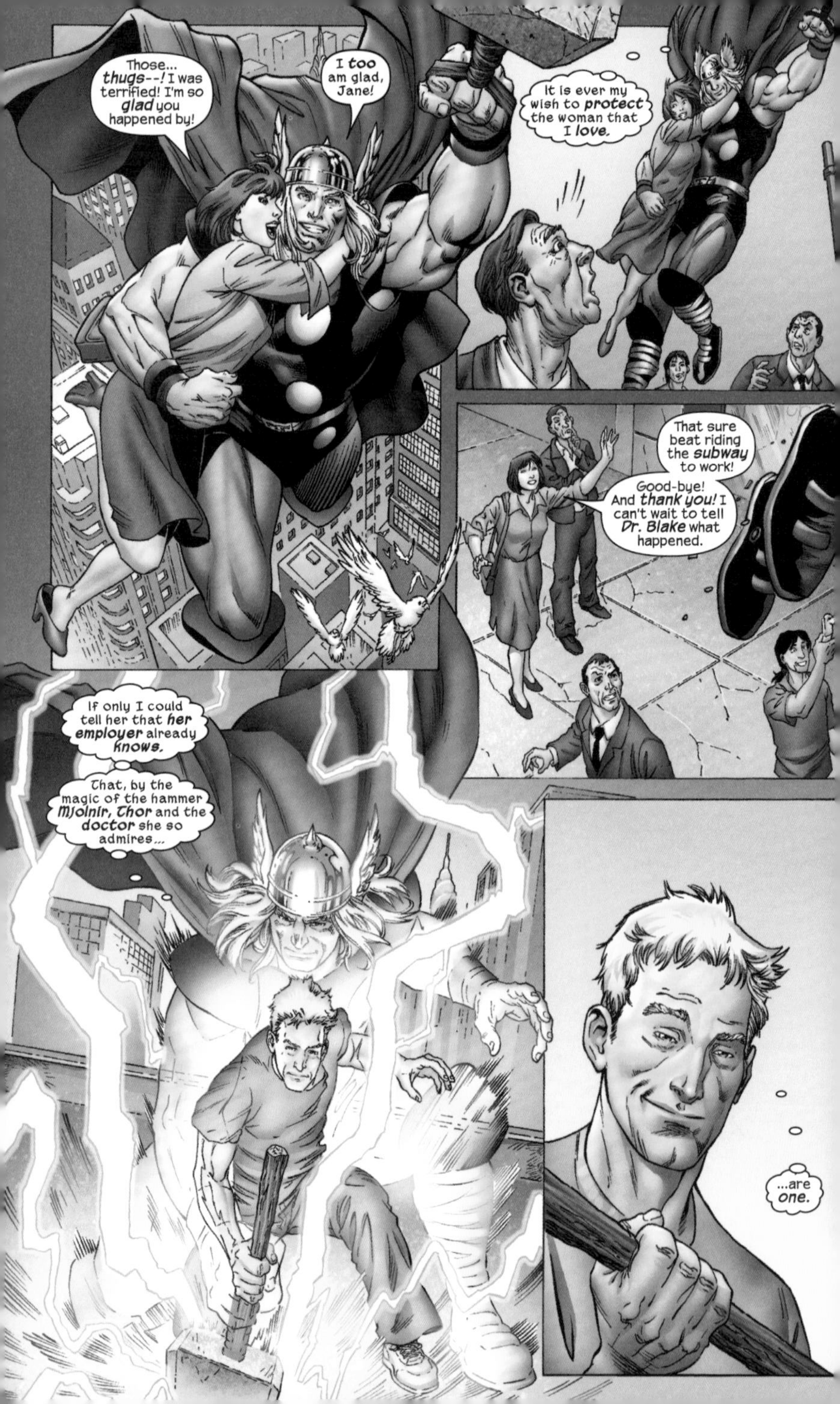

Those... thugs--! I was terrified! I'm so glad you happened by!
I too am glad, Jane!
It is ever my wish to protect the woman that I love.
That sure beat riding the subway to work!
Good-bye! And thank you! I can't wait to tell Dr. Blake what happened.
If only I could tell her that her employer already knows.
That, by the magic of the hammer Mjolnir, Thor and the doctor she so admires...
...are one.

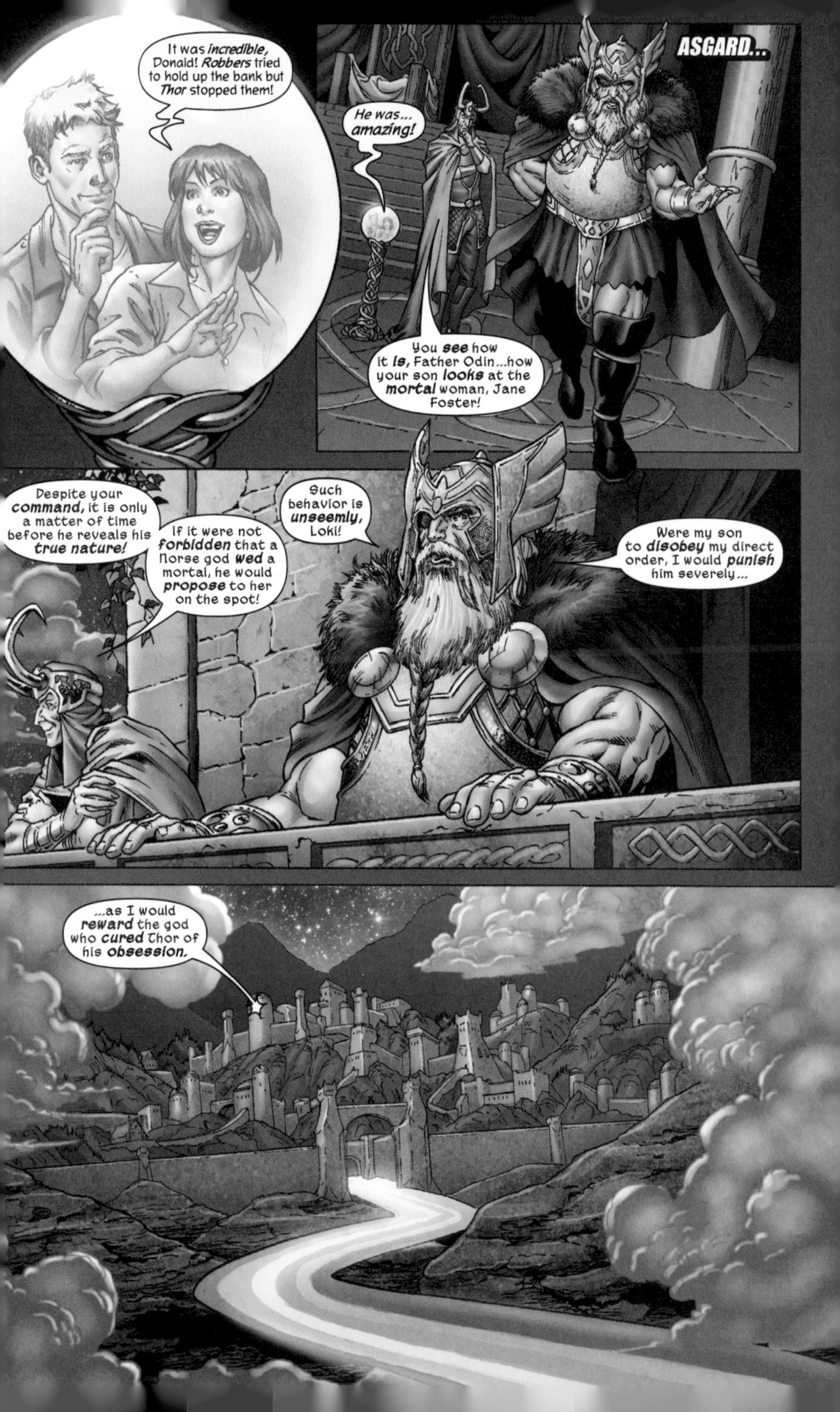

It was *incredible,* Donald! *Robbers* tried to hold up the bank but *Thor* stopped them!
ASGARD...
He was... *amazing!*
You **see** how it **is,** Father Odin...how your son **looks** at the **mortal** woman, Jane Foster!
Such behavior is **unseemly,** Loki!
Despite your **command,** it is only a matter of time before he reveals his **true nature!**
If it were not **forbidden** that a Norse god **wed** a mortal, he would **propose** to her on the spot!
Were my son to **disobey** my direct order, I would **punish** him severely...
...as I would **reward** the god who **cured** Thor of his **obsession.**

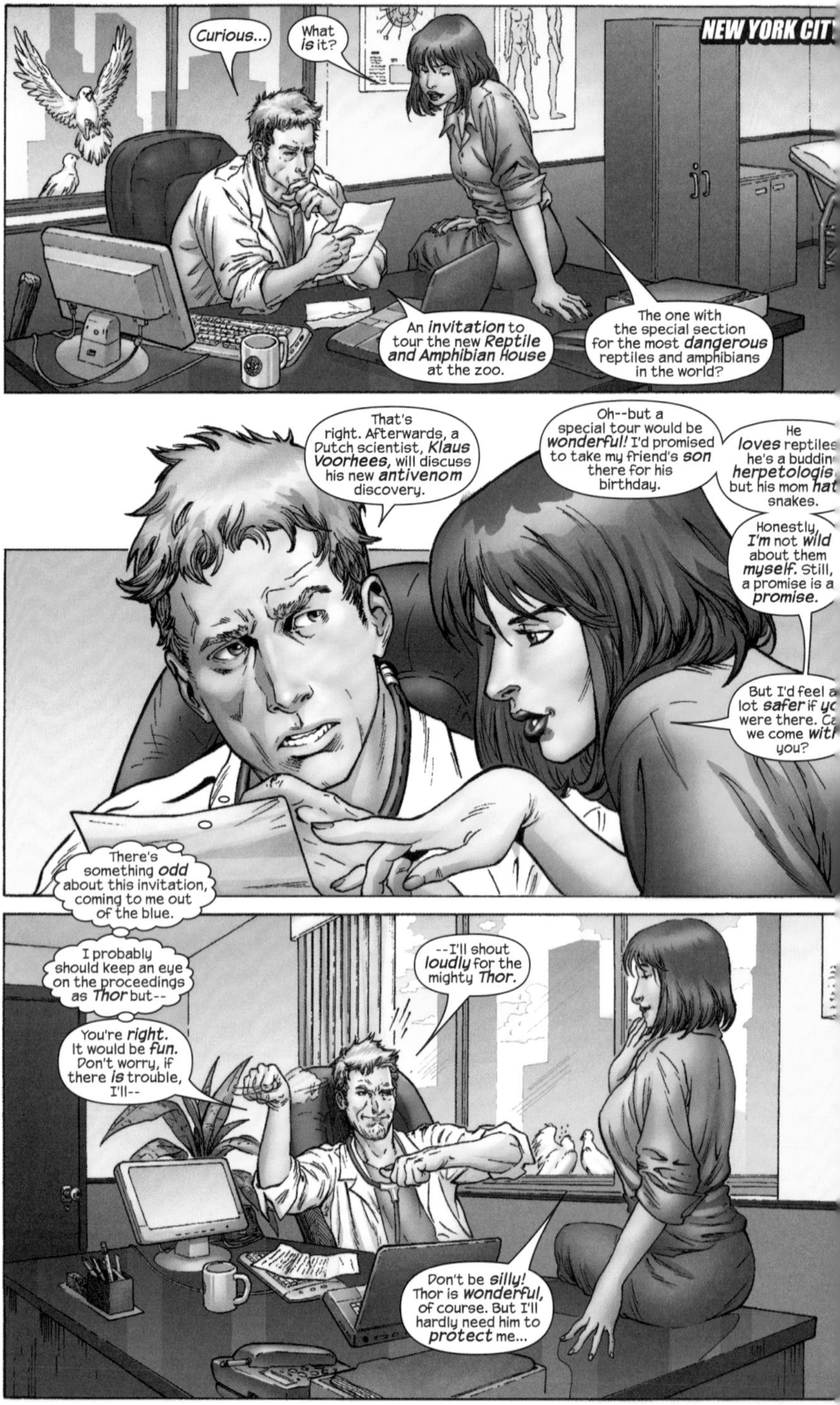
NEW YORK CIT
Curious...
What is it?
An invitation to tour the new Reptile and Amphibian House at the zoo.
The one with the special section for the most dangerous reptiles and amphibians in the world?
That's right. Afterwards, a Dutch scientist, Klaus Voorhees, will discuss his new antivenom discovery.
Oh--but a special tour would be wonderful! I'd promised to take my friend's son there for his birthday.
He loves reptile he's a buddin herpetologis but his mom hat snakes.
Honestly, I'm not wild about them myself. Still, a promise is a promise.
But I'd feel a lot safer if y were there. C we come wit you?
There's something odd about this invitation, coming to me out of the blue.
I probably should keep an eye on the proceedings as Thor but--
You're right. It would be fun. Don't worry, if there is trouble, I'll--
--I'll shout loudly for the mighty Thor.
Don't be silly! Thor is wonderful, of course. But I'll hardly need him to protect me...

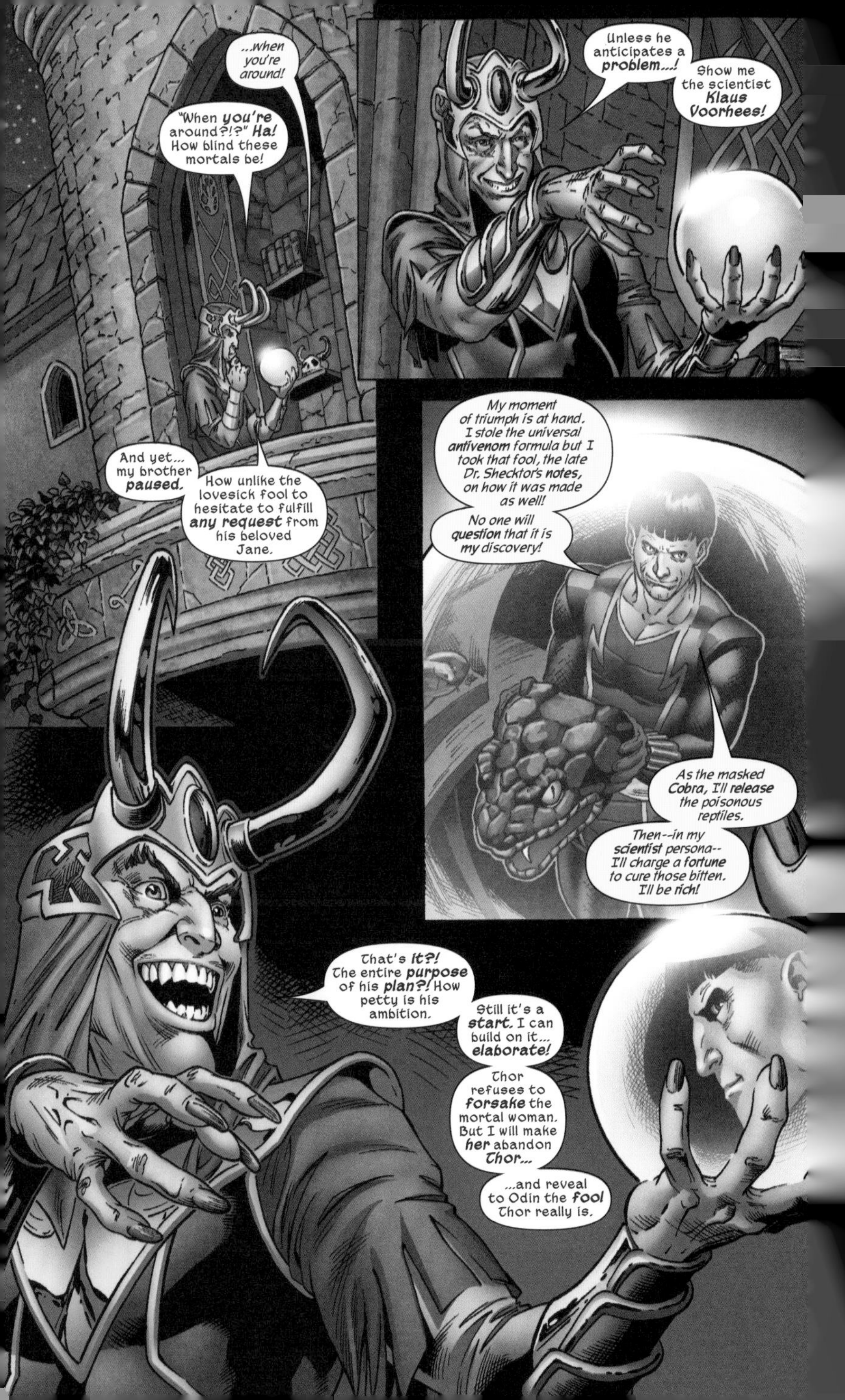
...when you're around!
"When you're around?!?" Ha! How blind these mortals be!
Unless he anticipates a problem...!
Show me the scientist Klaus Voorhees!
And yet... my brother paused.
How unlike the lovesick fool to hesitate to fulfill any request from his beloved Jane.
My moment of triumph is at hand. I stole the universal antivenom formula but I took that fool, the late Dr. Shecktor's notes, on how it was made as well!
No one will question that it is my discovery!
As the masked Cobra, I'll release the poisonous reptiles.
Then--in my scientist persona--I'll charge a fortune to cure those bitten. I'll be rich!
That's it?! The entire purpose of his plan?! How petty is his ambition.
Still it's a start. I can build on it... elaborate!
Thor refuses to forsake the mortal woman. But I will make her abandon Thor...
...and reveal to Odin the fool Thor really is.

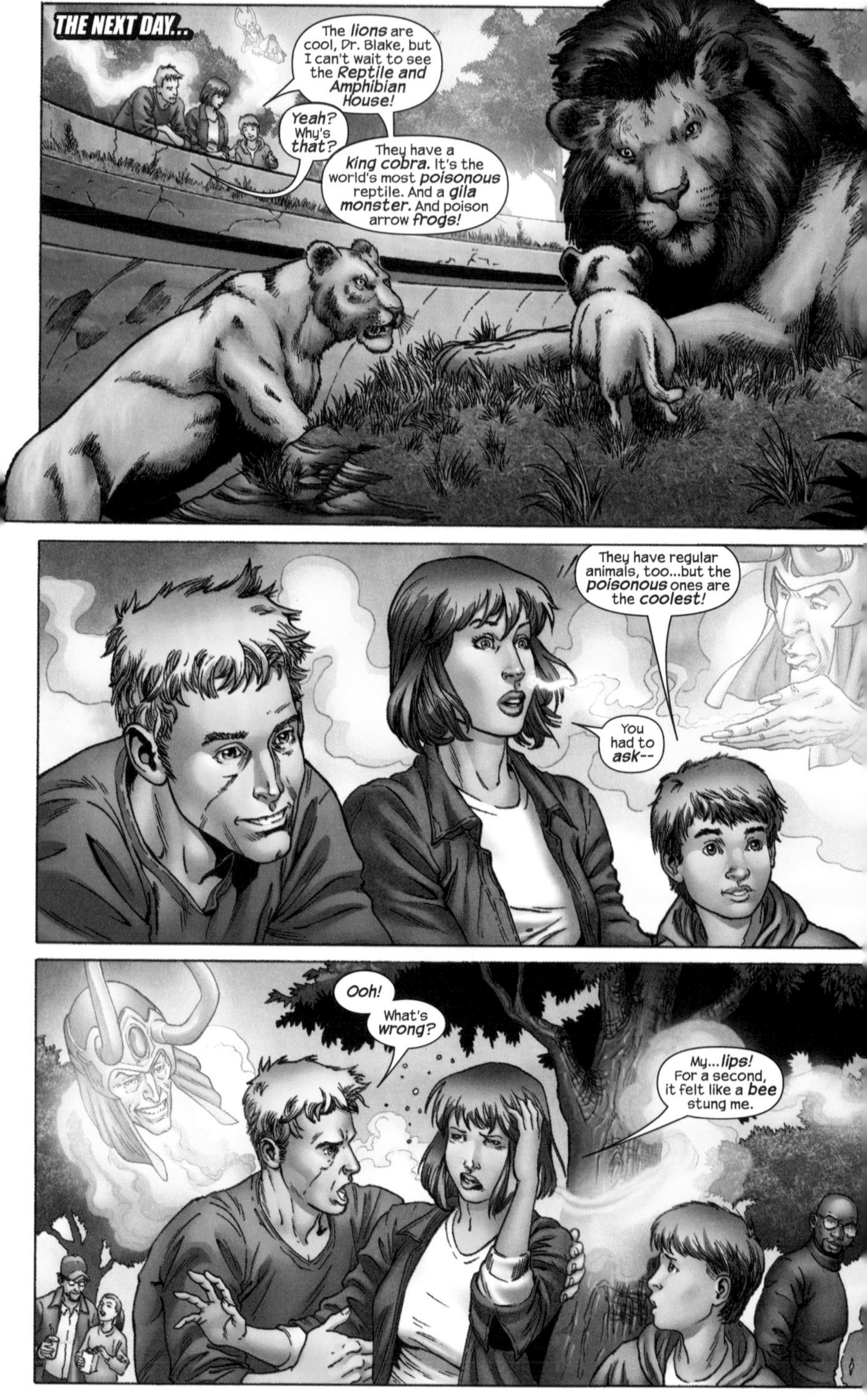
THE NEXT DAY...
The lions are cool, Dr. Blake, but I can't wait to see the Reptile and Amphibian House!
Yeah? Why's that?
They have a king cobra. It's the world's most poisonous reptile. And a gila monster. And poison arrow frogs!
They have regular animals, too...but the poisonous ones are the coolest!
You had to ask--
Ooh!
What's wrong?
My...lips! For a second, it felt like a bee stung me.

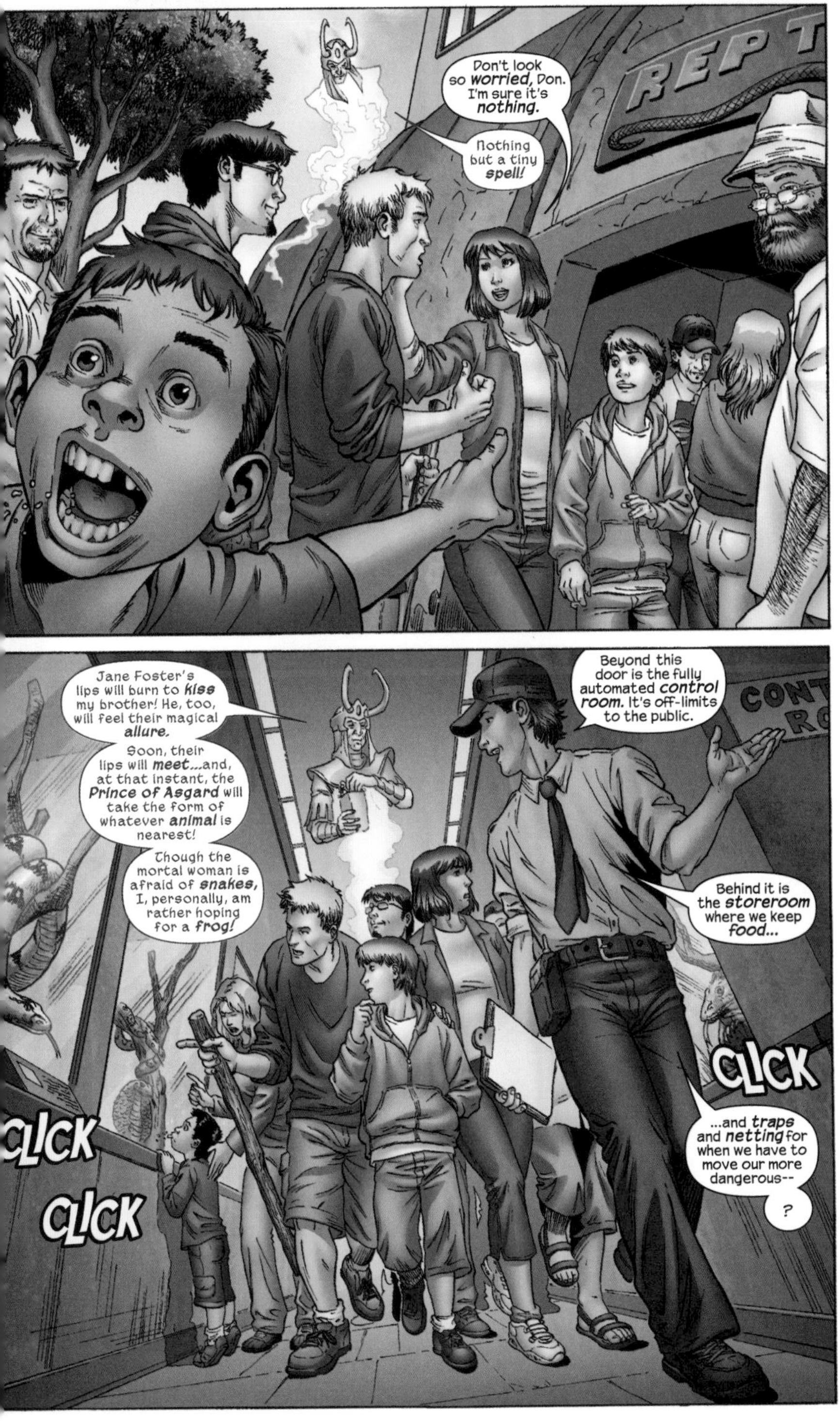
REPT
Don't look so worried, Don. I'm sure it's nothing.
Nothing but a tiny spell!
CONT RO
Jane Foster's lips will burn to kiss my brother! He, too, will feel their magical allure.
Soon, their lips will meet...and, at that instant, the Prince of Asgard will take the form of whatever animal is nearest!
Though the mortal woman is afraid of snakes, I, personally, am rather hoping for a frog!
Beyond this door is the fully automated control room. It's off-limits to the public.
Behind it is the storeroom where we keep food...
CLICK
CLICK
CLICK
...and traps and netting for when we have to move our more dangerous--
?

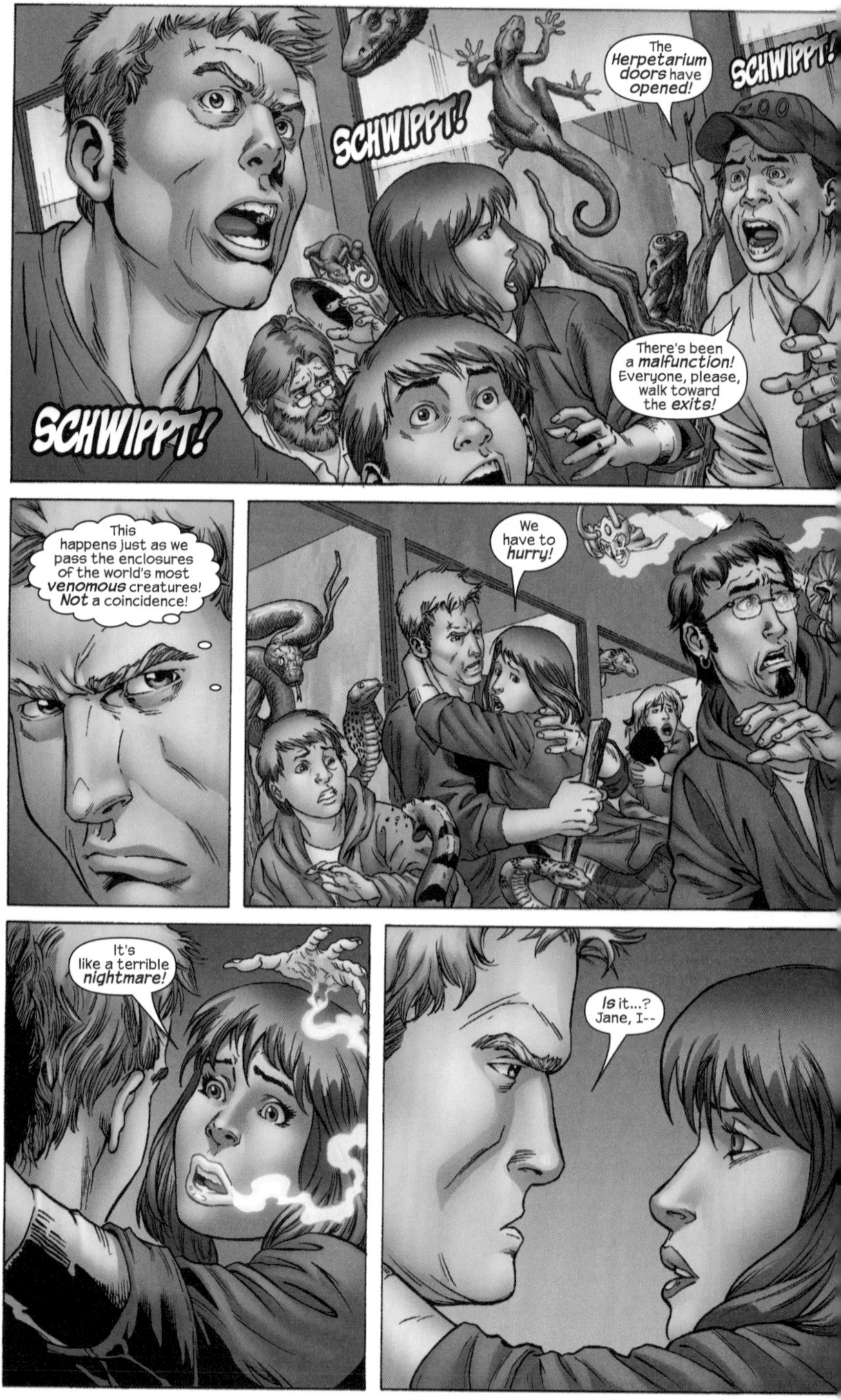
The Herpetarium doors have opened!
SCHWIPPT!
SCHWIPPT!
There's been a malfunction! Everyone, please, walk toward the exits!
SCHWIPPT!
This happens just as we pass the enclosures of the world's most venomous creatures! Not a coincidence!
We have to hurry!
It's like a terrible nightmare!
Is it...? Jane, I--

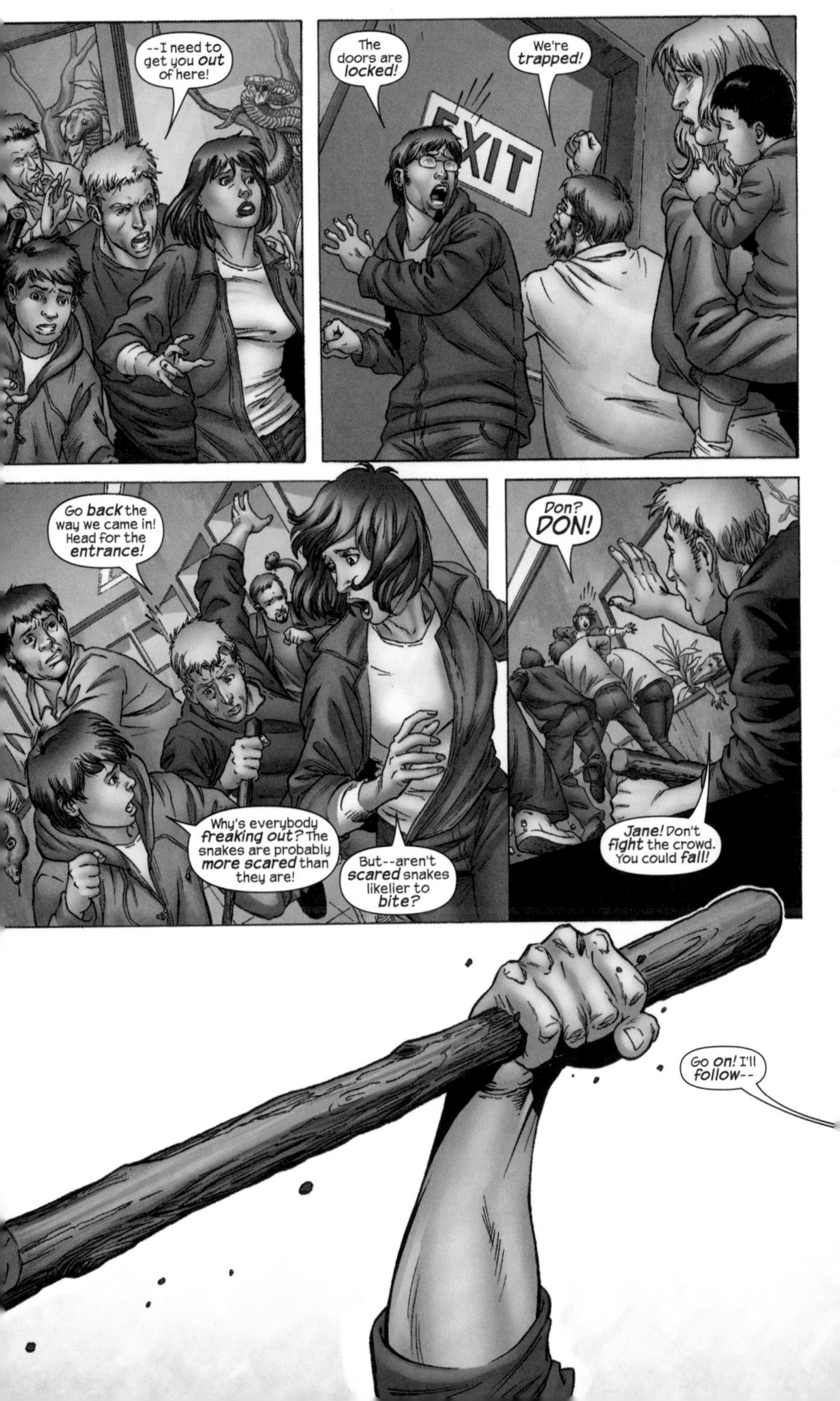

--I need to get you out of here!
The doors are locked!
We're trapped!
EXIT
Go back the way we came in! Head for the entrance!
Don? DON!
Why's everybody freaking out? The snakes are probably more scared than they are!
But--aren't scared snakes likelier to bite?
Jane! Don't fight the crowd. You could fall!
Go on! I'll follow--

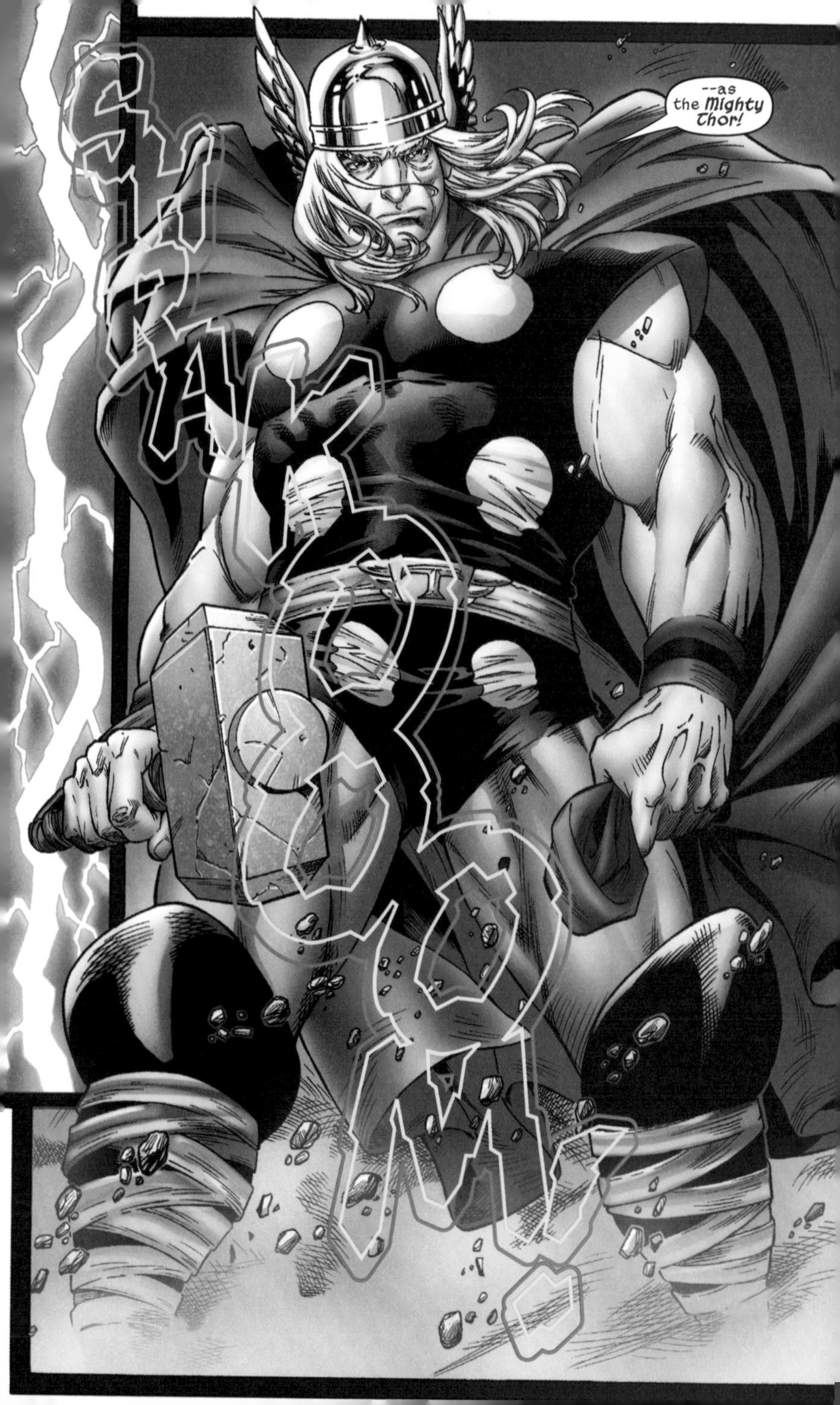
--as the Mighty Thor!

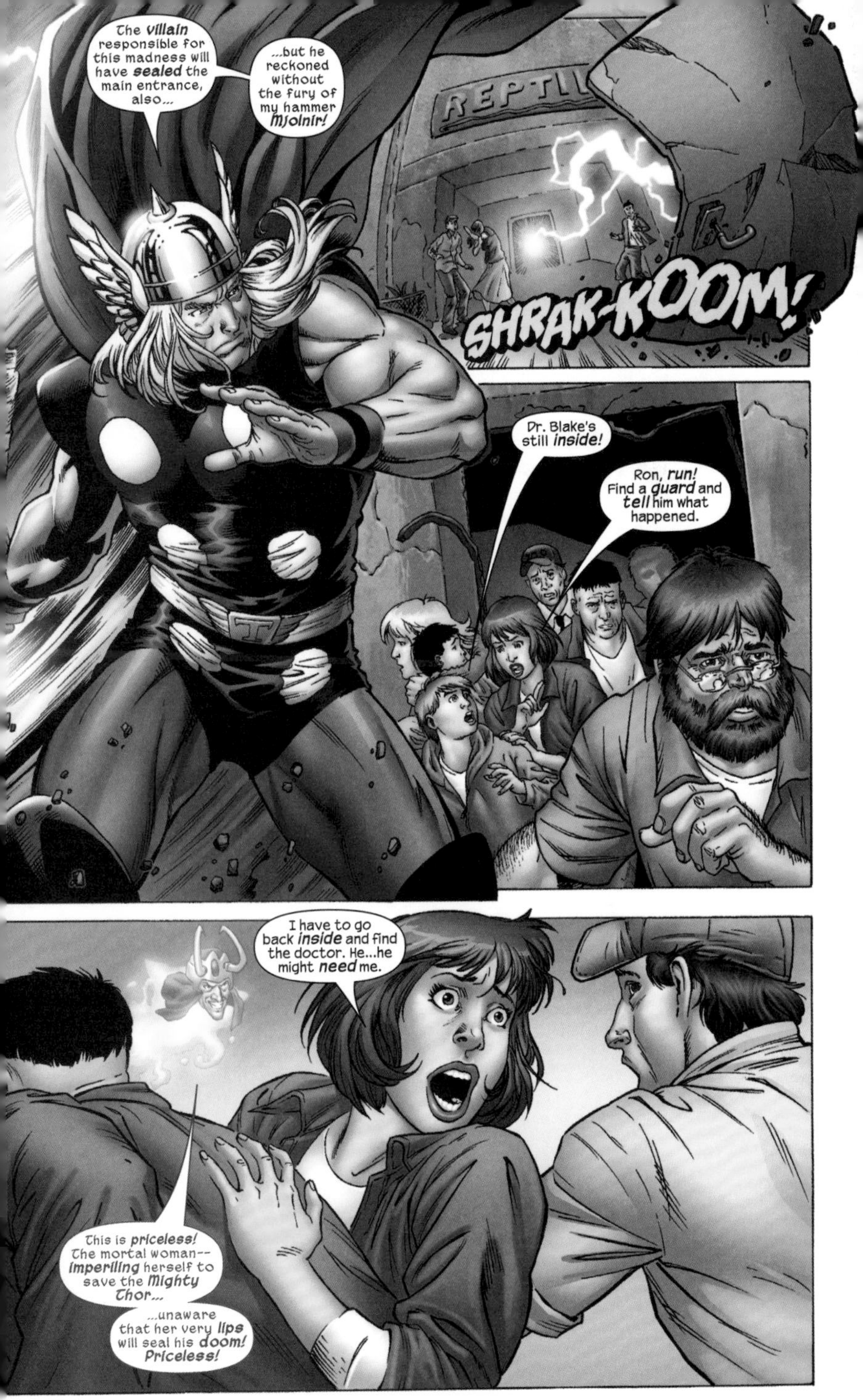
The villain responsible for this madness will have sealed the main entrance, also...
...but he reckoned without the fury of my hammer Mjolnir!
REPTIL
SHRAK-KOOM!
Dr. Blake's still inside!
Ron, run! Find a guard and tell him what happened.
I have to go back inside and find the doctor. He...he might need me.
This is priceless! The mortal woman--imperiling herself to save the Mighty Thor...
...unaware that her very lips will seal his doom! Priceless!

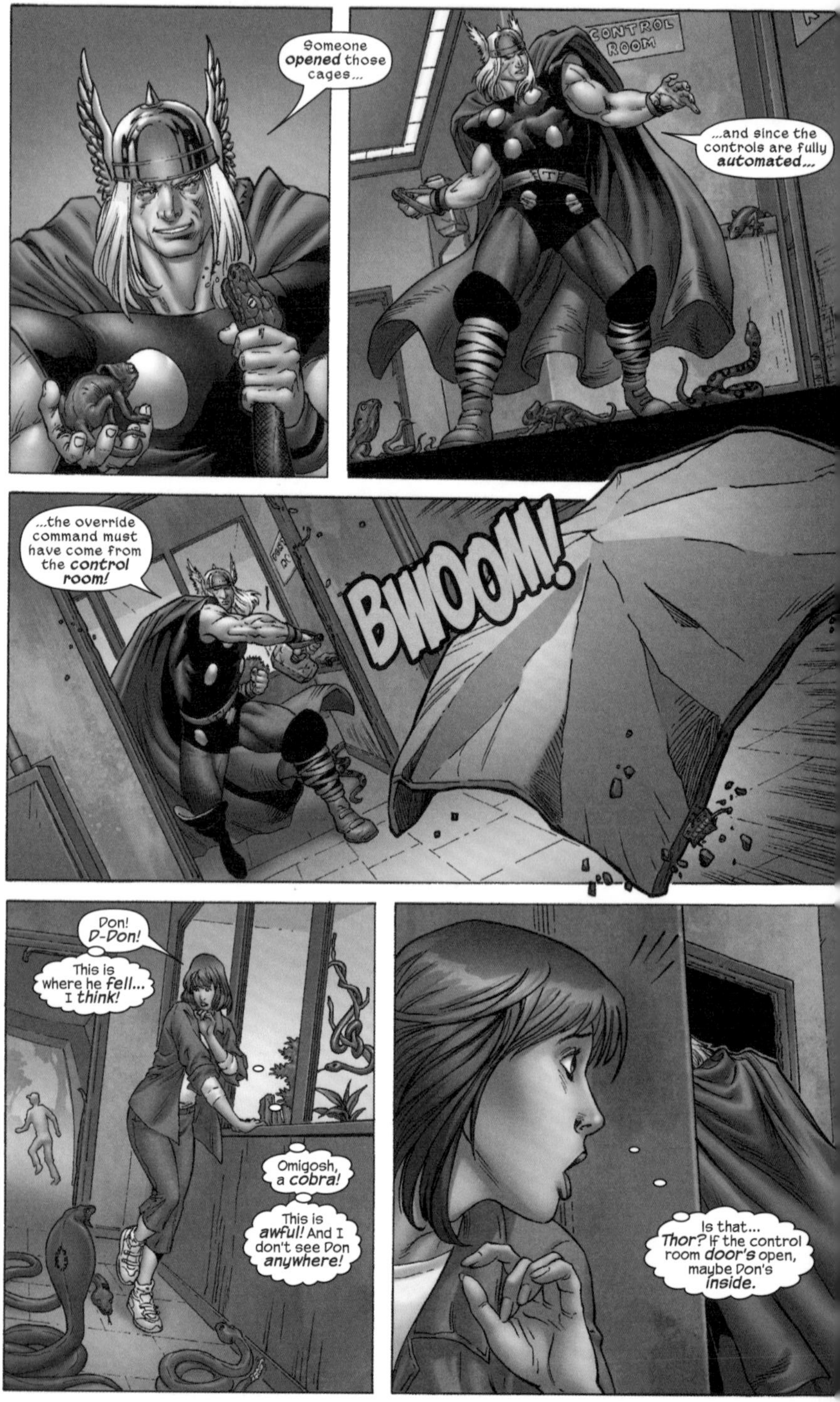

Someone opened those cages...
...and since the controls are fully automated...
CONTROL ROOM
...the override command must have come from the control room!
BWOOM!
Don! D-Don!
This is where he fell... I think!
Omigosh, a cobra!
This is awful! And I don't see Don anywhere!
Is that... Thor? If the control room door's open, maybe Don's inside.

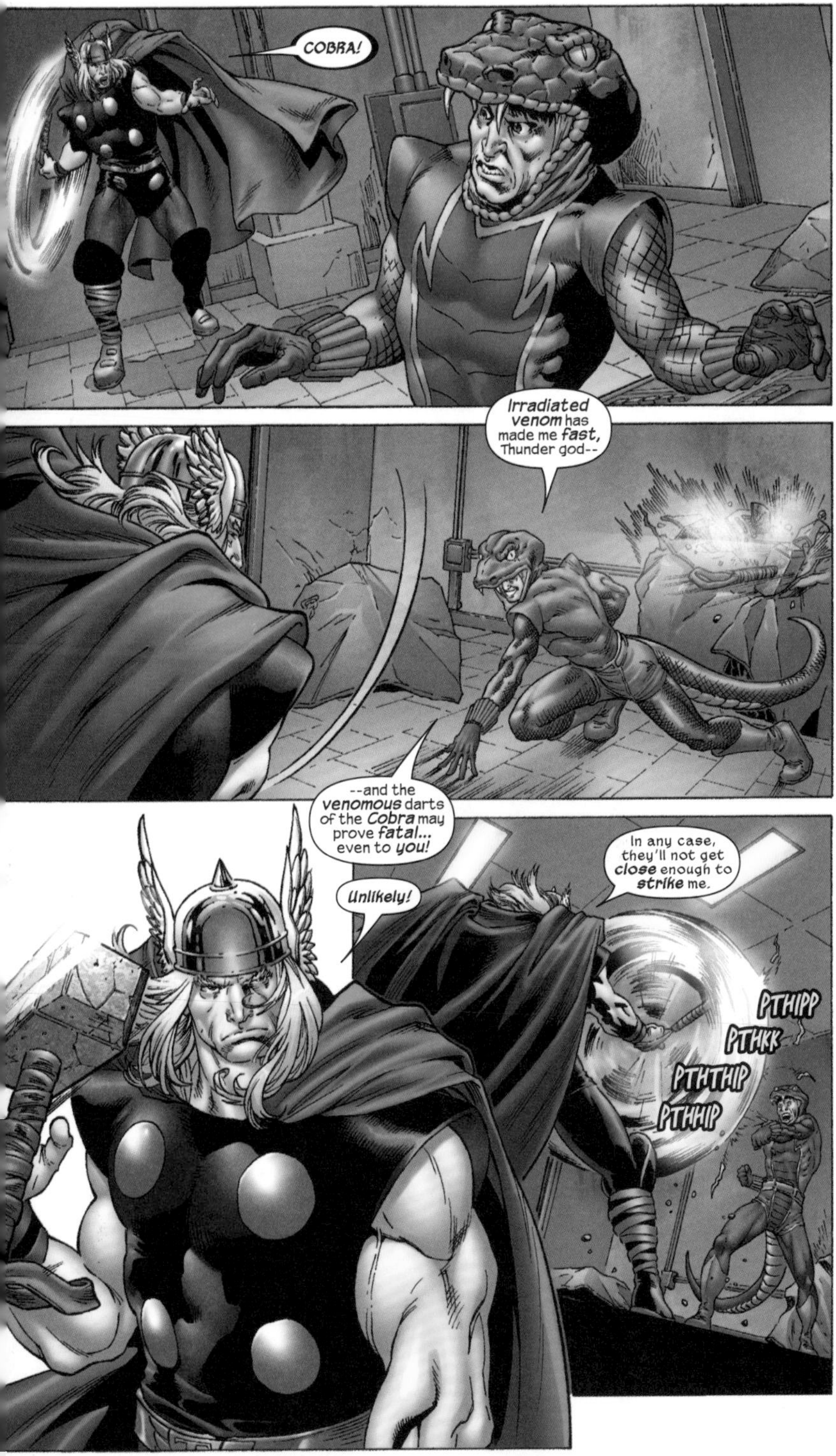
COBRA!
Irradiated venom has made me fast, Thunder god--
--and the venomous darts of the Cobra may prove fatal... even to you!
Unlikely!
In any case, they'll not get close enough to strike me.
PTHIPP
PTHKK
PTHTHIP
PTHHIP

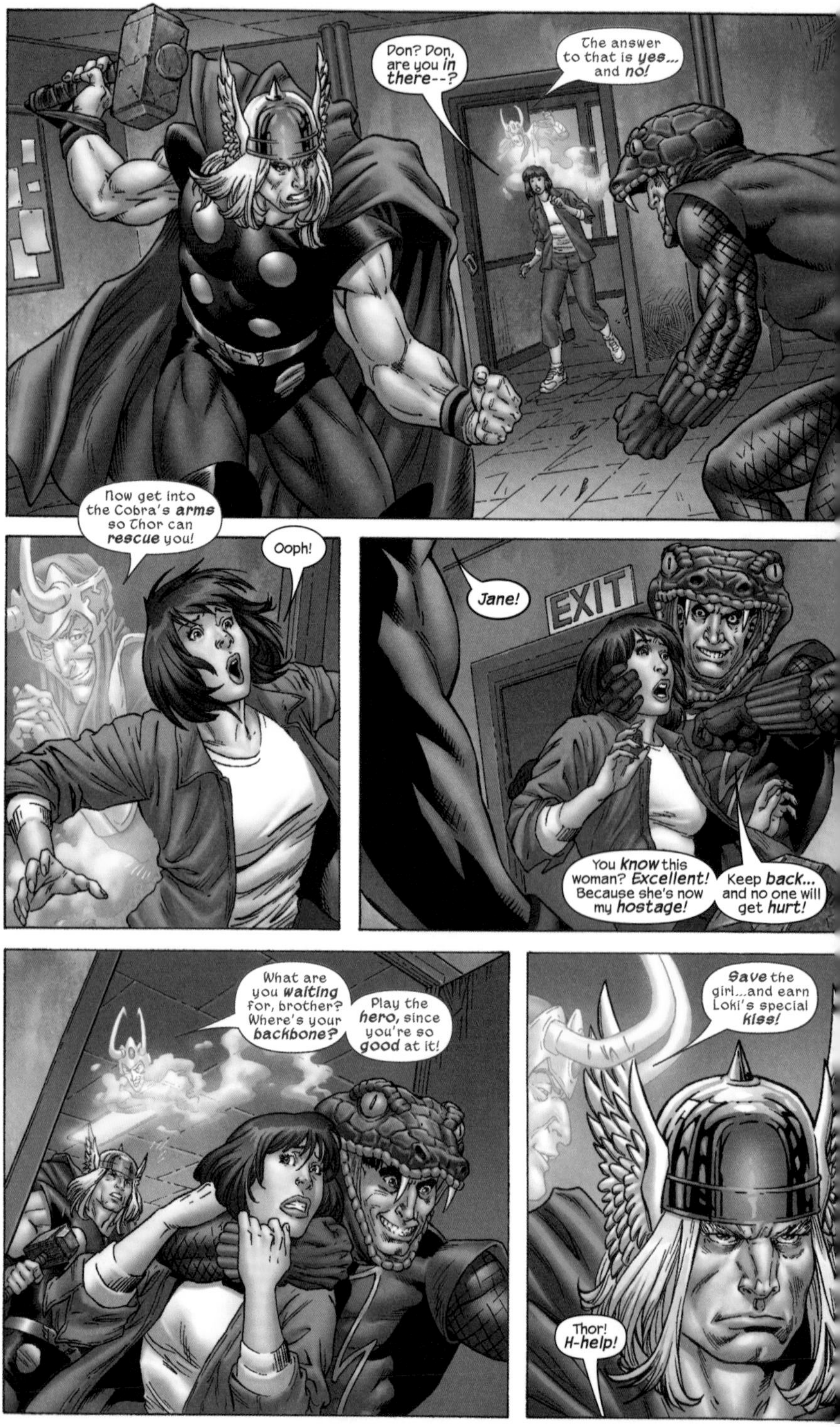
Don? Don, are you in there--?
The answer to that is yes... and no!
Now get into the Cobra's arms so Thor can rescue you!
Ooph!
Jane!
EXIT
You know this woman? Excellent! Because she's now my hostage!
Keep back... and no one will get hurt!
What are you waiting for, brother? Where's your backbone?
Play the hero, since you're so good at it!
Save the girl...and earn Loki's special kiss!
Thor! H-help!

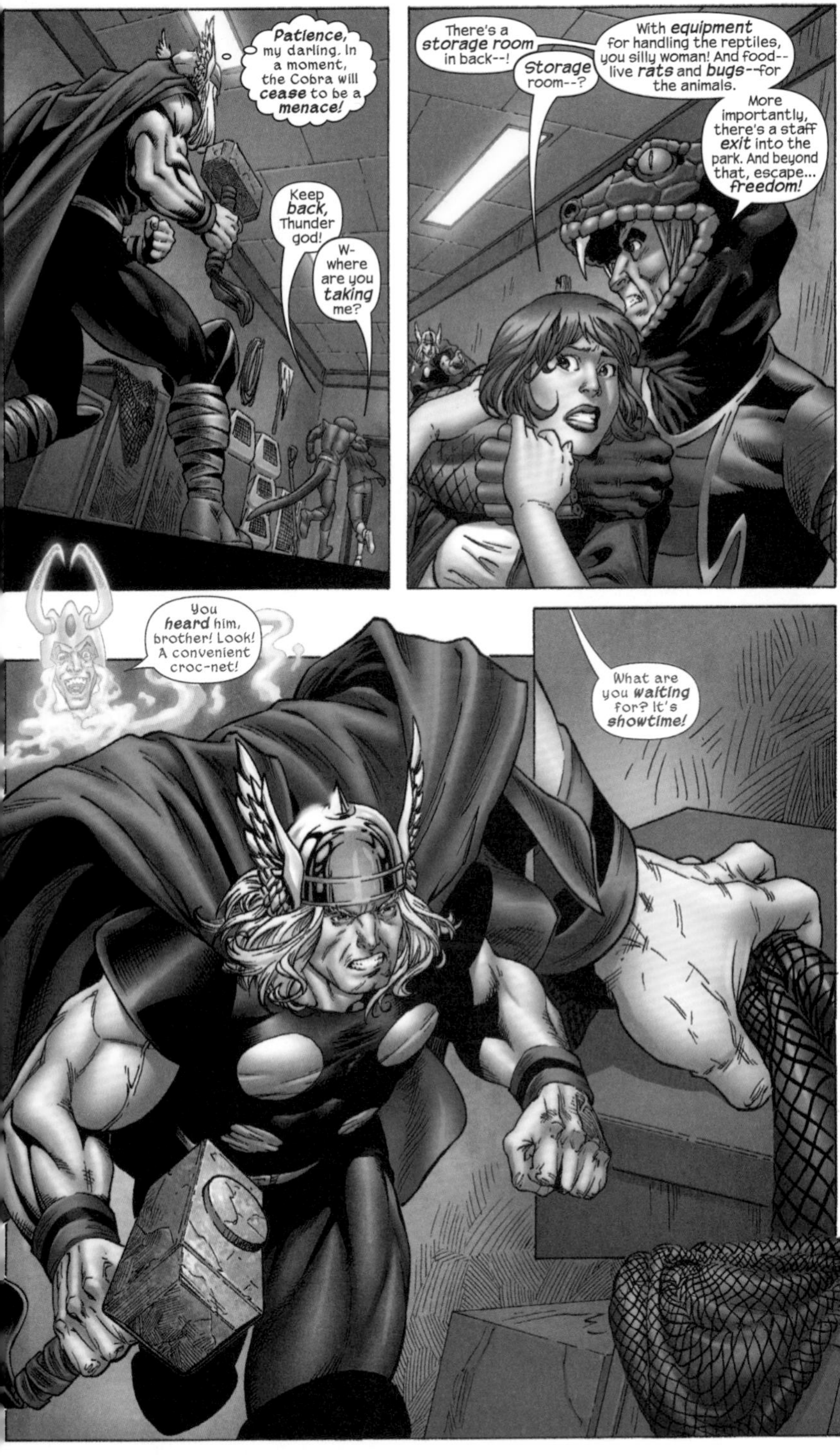

Patience, my darling. In a moment, the Cobra will cease to be a menace!
Keep back, Thunder god!
W-where are you taking me?
There's a storage room in back--!
Storage room--?
With equipment for handling the reptiles, you silly woman! And food--live rats and bugs--for the animals.
More importantly, there's a staff exit into the park. And beyond that, escape... freedom!
You heard him, brother! Look! A convenient croc-net!
What are you waiting for? It's showtime!

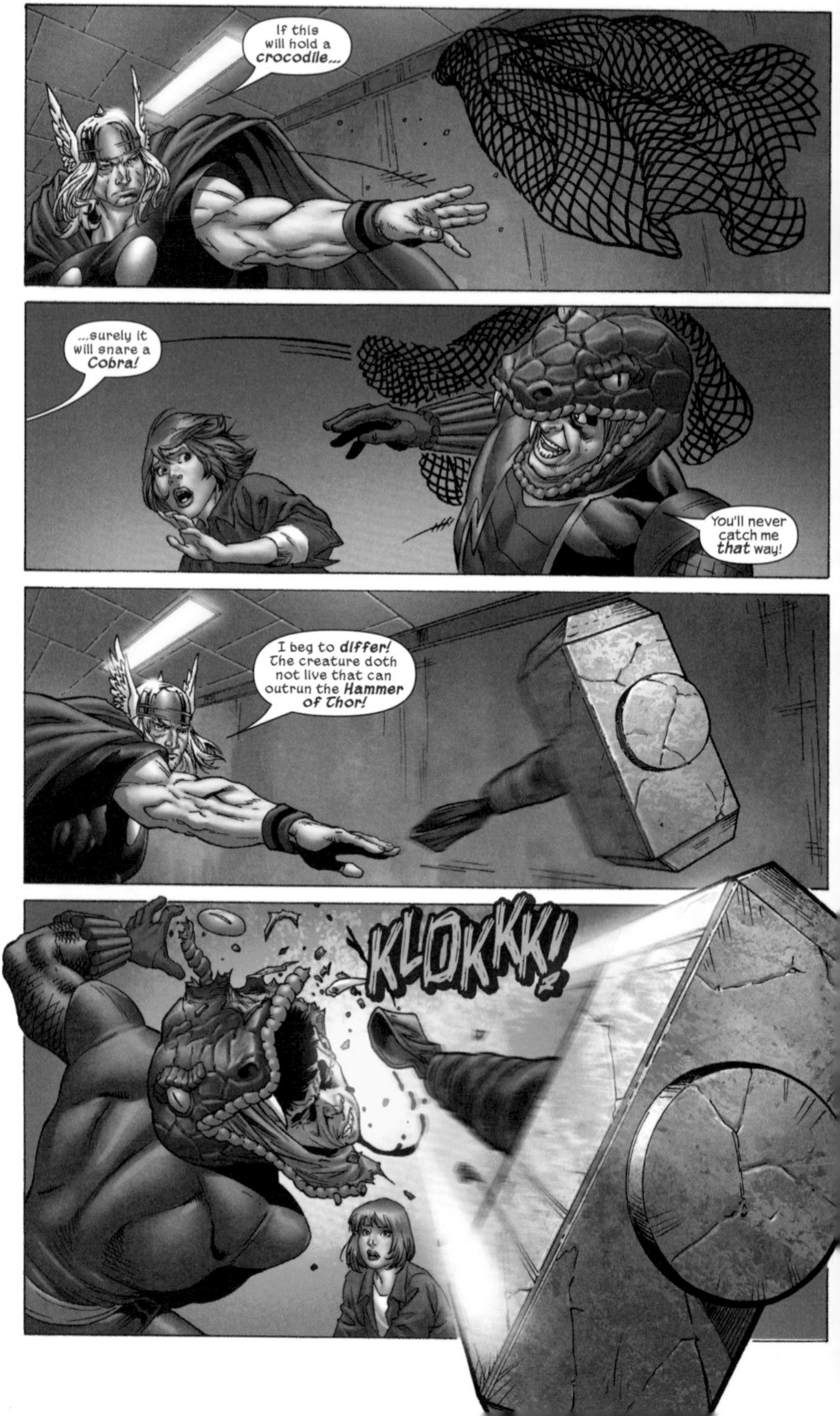
If this will hold a crocodile...
...surely it will snare a Cobra!
You'll never catch me that way!
I beg to differ! The creature doth not live that can outrun the Hammer of Thor!
KLOKKK!

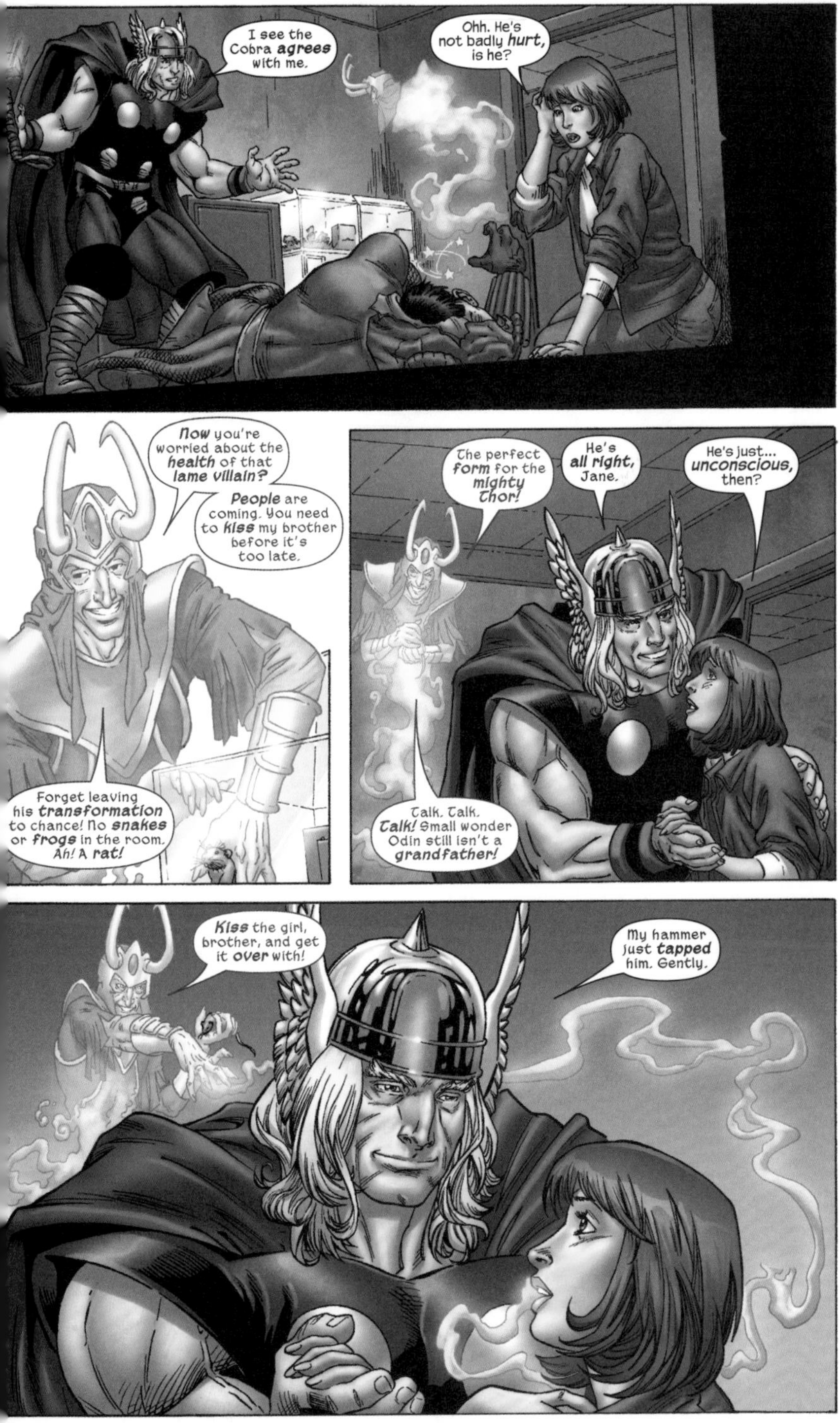
I see the Cobra agrees with me.
Ohh. He's not badly hurt, is he?
Now you're worried about the health of that lame villain?
People are coming. You need to kiss my brother before it's too late.
Forget leaving his transformation to chance! No snakes or frogs in the room. Ah! A rat!
The perfect form for the mighty Thor!
He's all right, Jane.
He's just... unconscious, then?
Talk. Talk. Talk! Small wonder Odin still isn't a grandfather!
Kiss the girl, brother, and get it over with!
My hammer just tapped him. Gently.

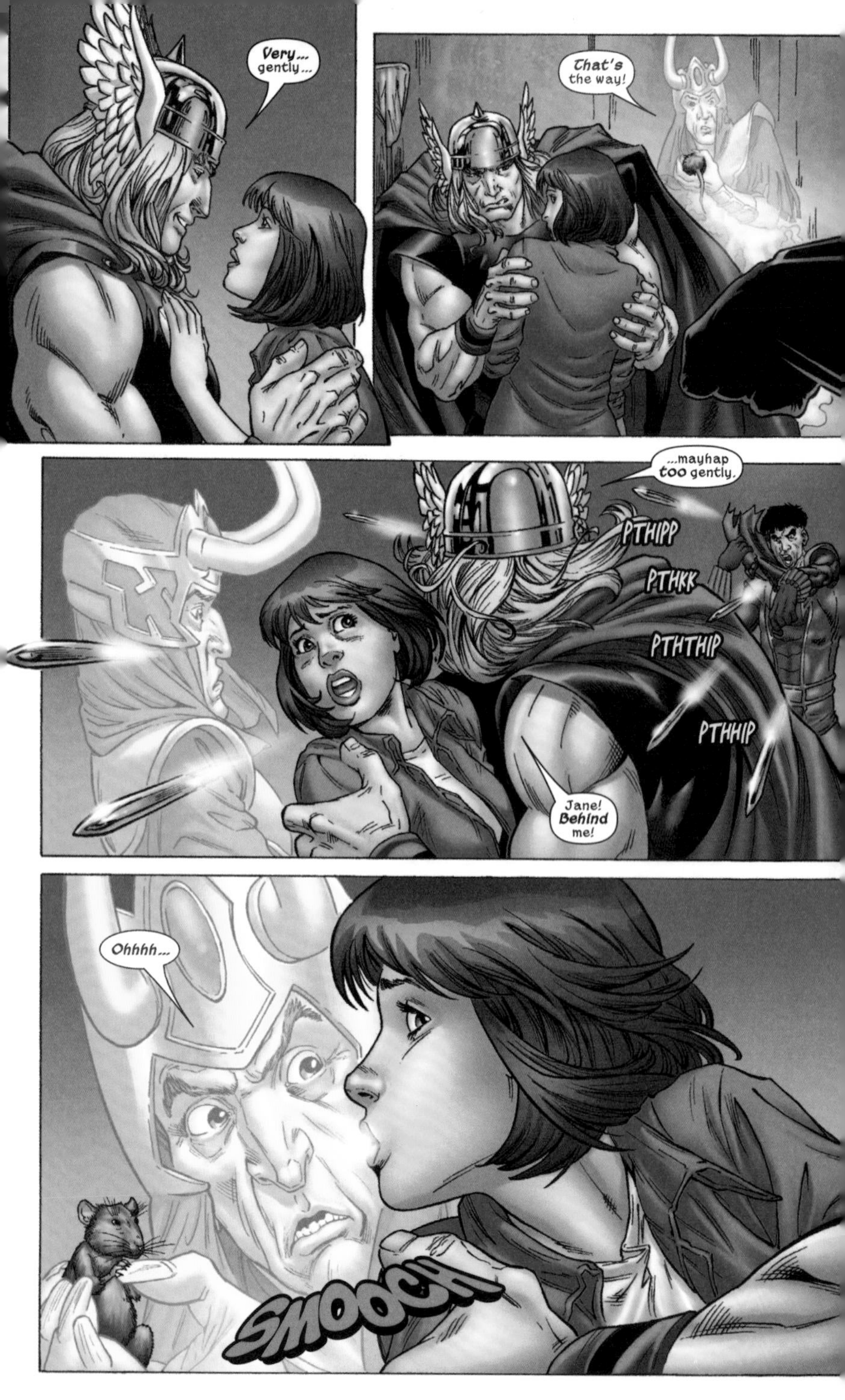
Very... gently...
That's the way!
...mayhap too gently.
PTHIPP
PTHKK
PTHTHIP
PTHHIP
Jane! Behind me!
Ohhhh...
SMOOCH

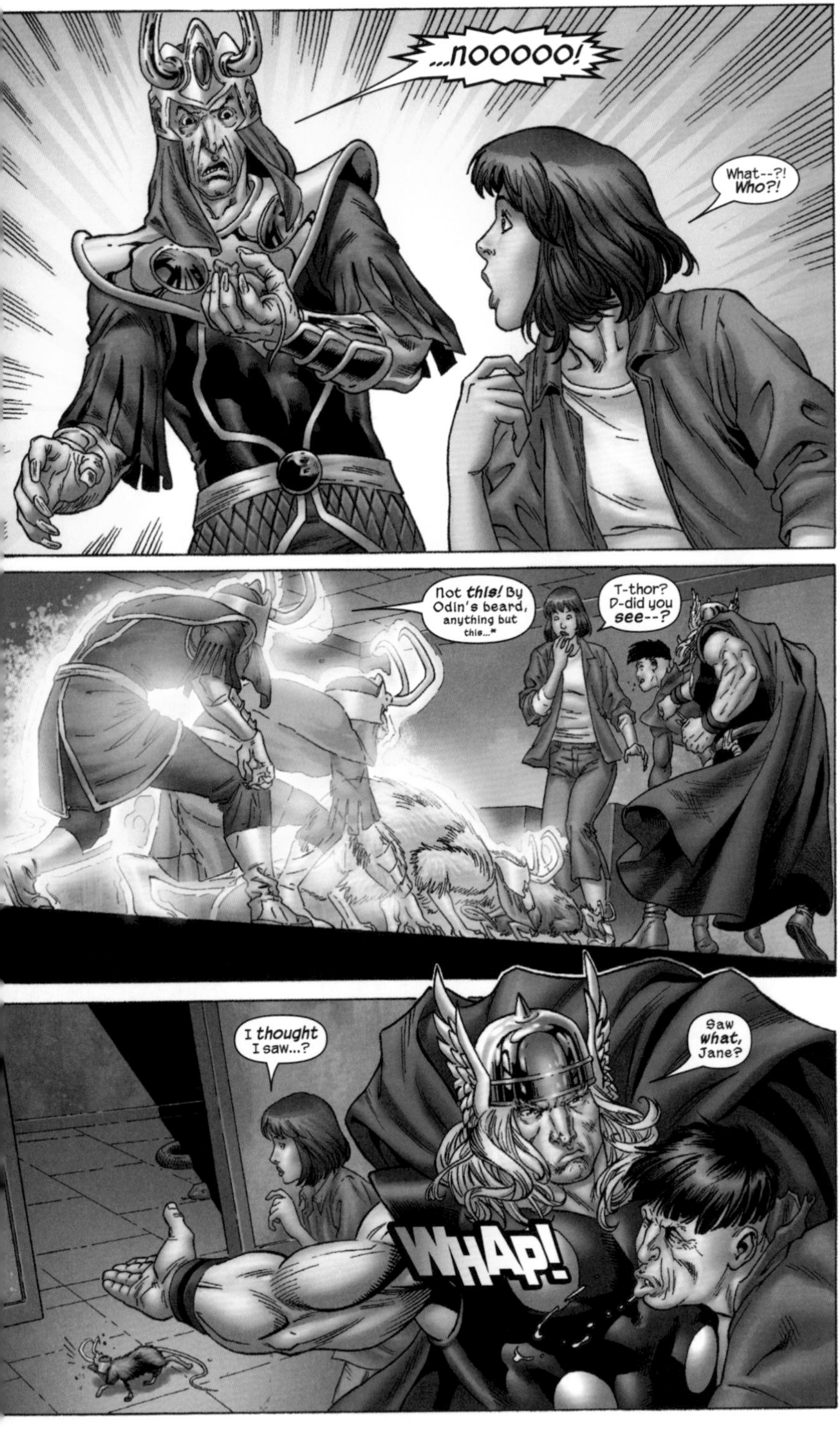
...nOOOOO!
What--?! Who?!
Not this! By Odin's beard, anything but this...*
T-thor? D-did you see--?
I thought I saw...?
Saw what, Jane?
WHAP!

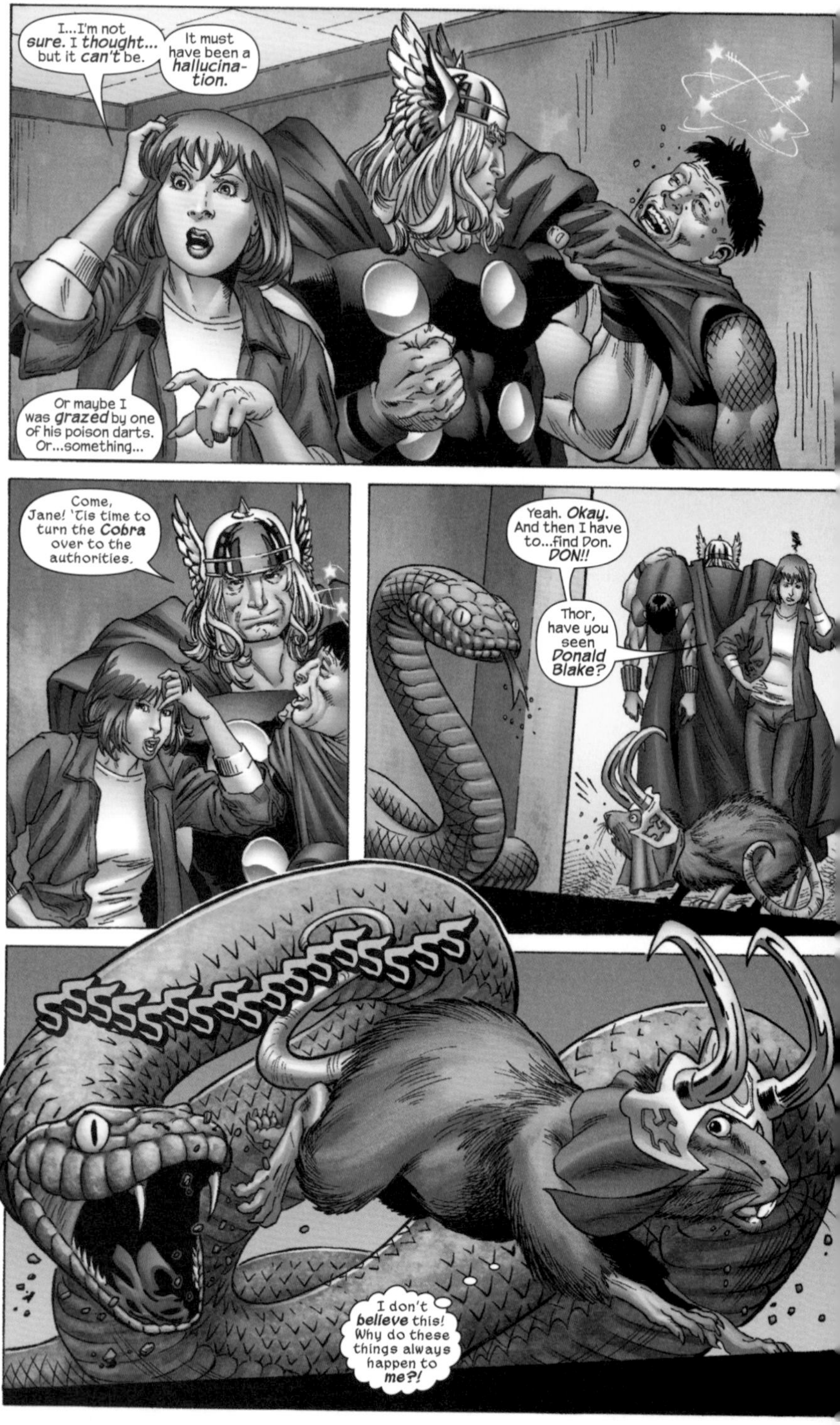
I...I'm not sure. I thought... but it can't be.
It must have been a hallucination.
Or maybe I was grazed by one of his poison darts. Or...something...
Come, Jane! 'Tis time to turn the Cobra over to the authorities.
Yeah. Okay. And then I have to...find Don. DON!!
Thor, have you seen Donald Blake?
SSSSSSSSSSSSSSSS
I don't believe this! Why do these things always happen to me?!

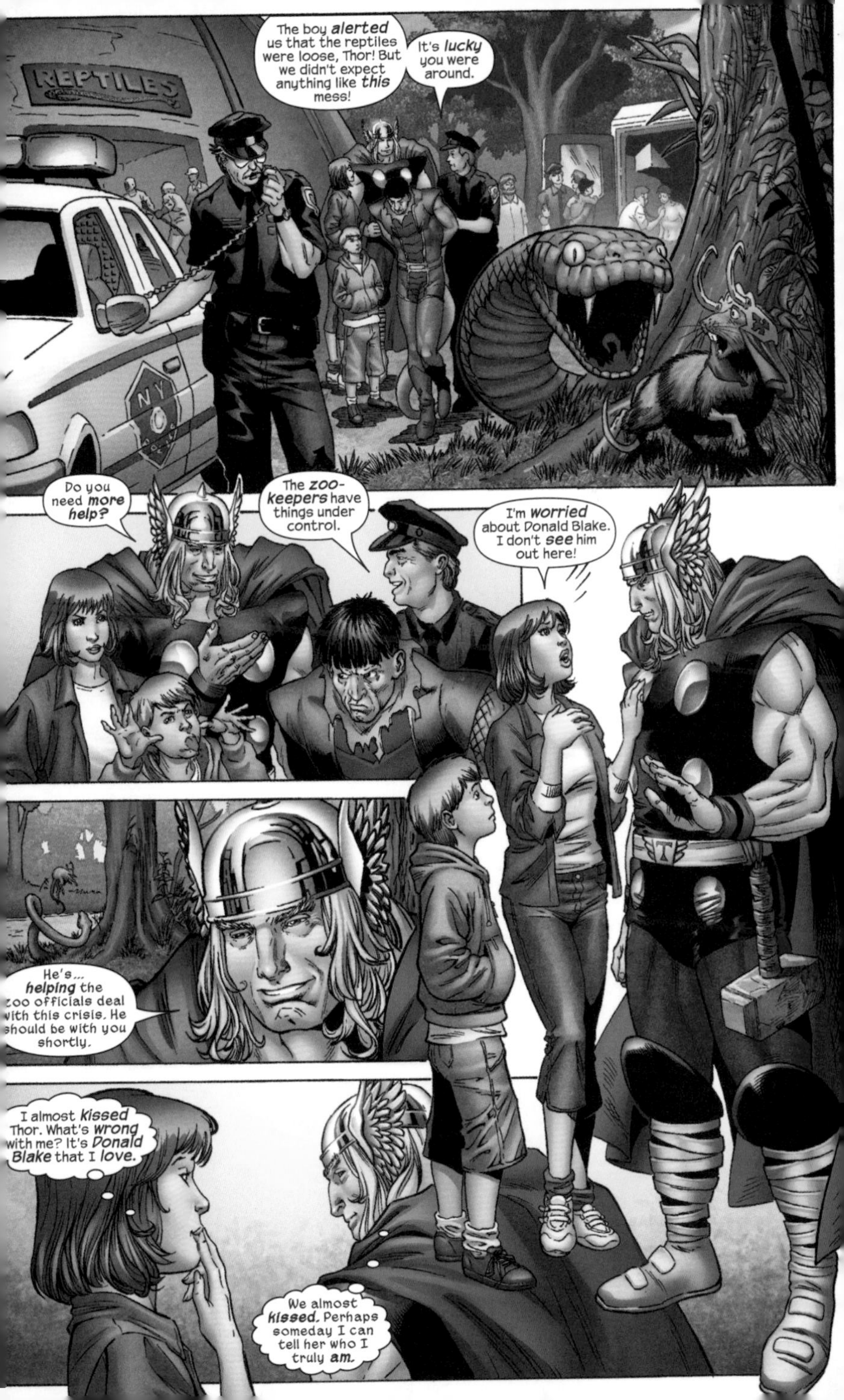
REPTILES
The boy alerted us that the reptiles were loose, Thor! But we didn't expect anything like this mess!
It's lucky you were around.
NY
Do you need more help?
The zoo-keepers have things under control.
I'm worried about Donald Blake. I don't see him out here!
He's... helping the zoo officials deal with this crisis. He should be with you shortly.
I almost kissed Thor. What's wrong with me? It's Donald Blake that I love.
We almost kissed. Perhaps someday I can tell her who I truly am.

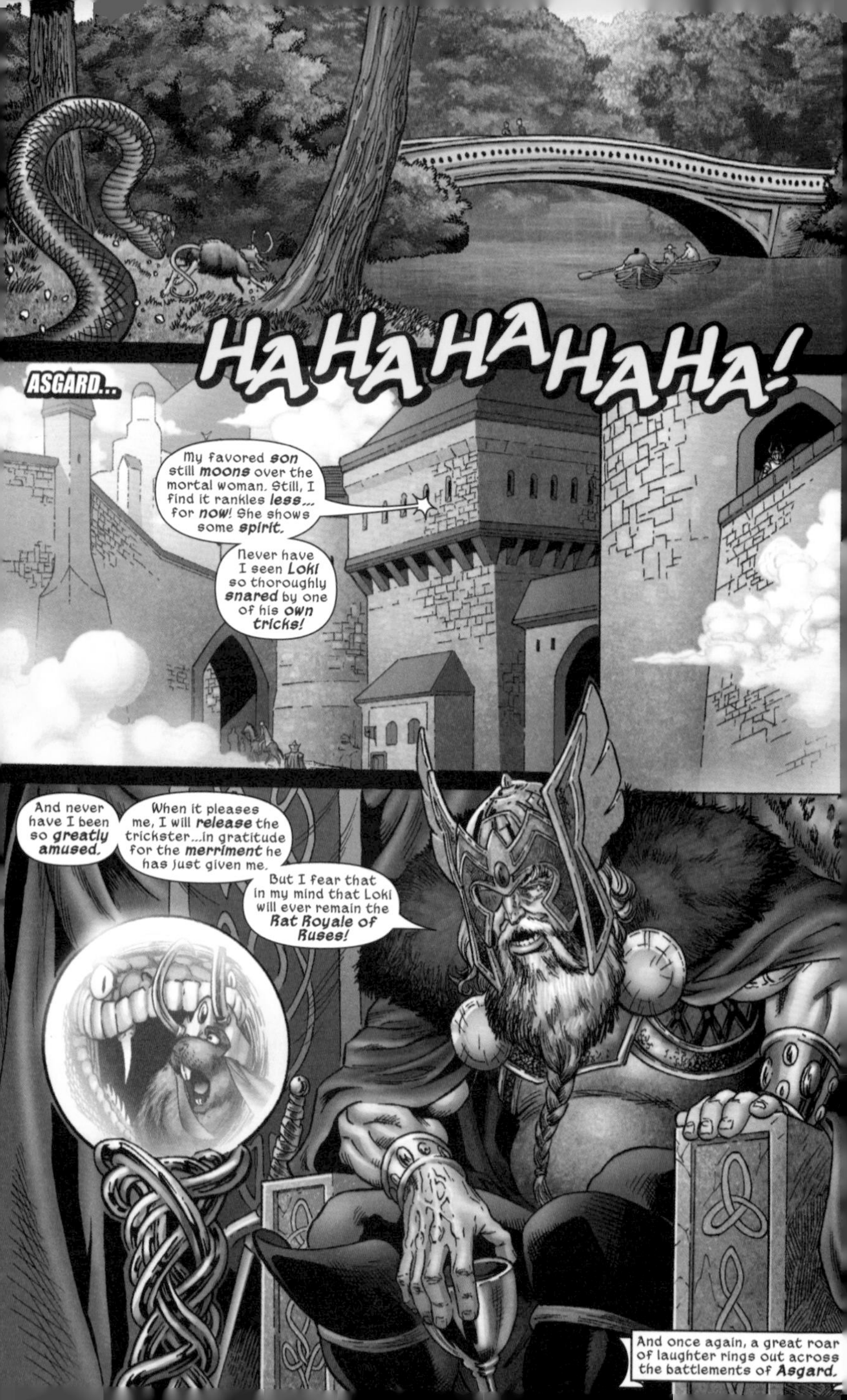
HAHAHAHAHAHA!
ASGARD...
My favored son still moons over the mortal woman. Still, I find it rankles less... for now! She shows some spirit.
Never have I seen Loki so thoroughly snared by one of his own tricks!
And never have I been so greatly amused.
When it pleases me, I will release the trickster...in gratitude for the merriment he has just given me.
But I fear that in my mind that Loki will ever remain the Rat Royale of Ruses!
And once again, a great roar of laughter rings out across the battlements of Asgard.

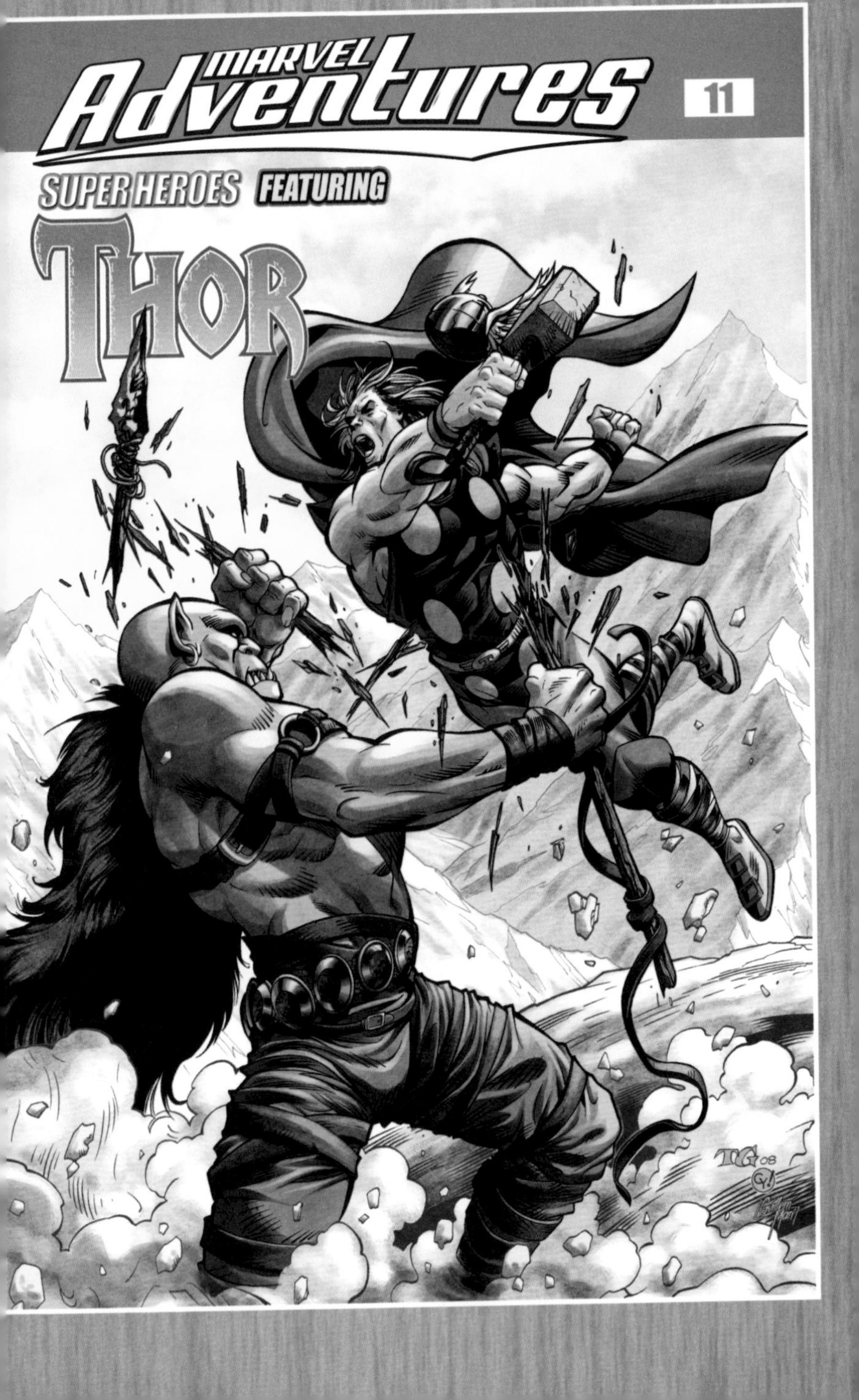
MARVEL
Adventures
11
SUPER HEROES FEATURING
THOR

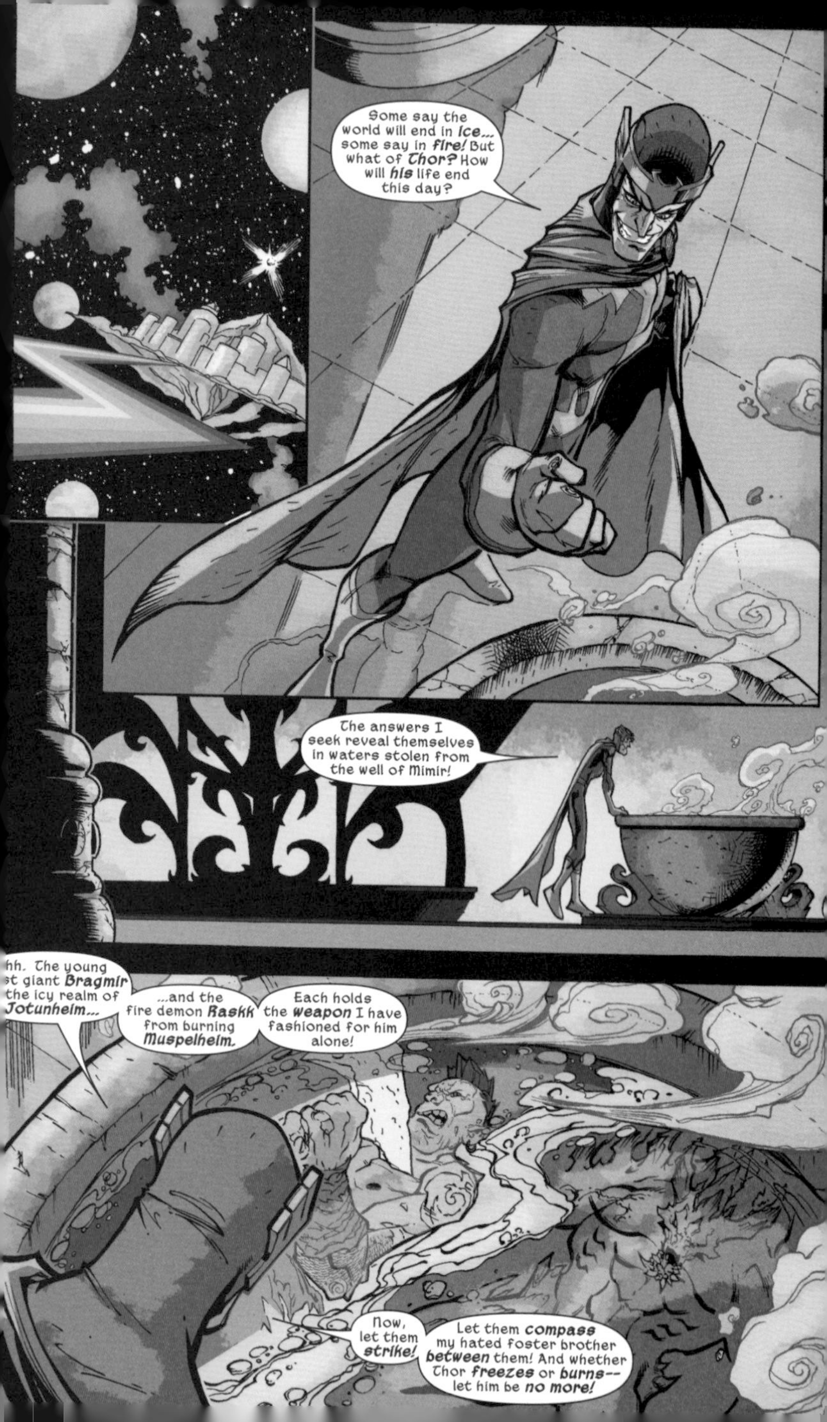

Some say the world will end in ice... some say in fire! But what of Thor? How will his life end this day?
The answers I seek reveal themselves in waters stolen from the well of Mimir!
hh. The young st giant Bragmir the icy realm of Jotunheim...
...and the fire demon Raskk from burning Muspelheim.
Each holds the weapon I have fashioned for him alone!
Now, let them strike!
Let them compass my hated foster brother between them! And whether Thor freezes or burns-- let him be no more!

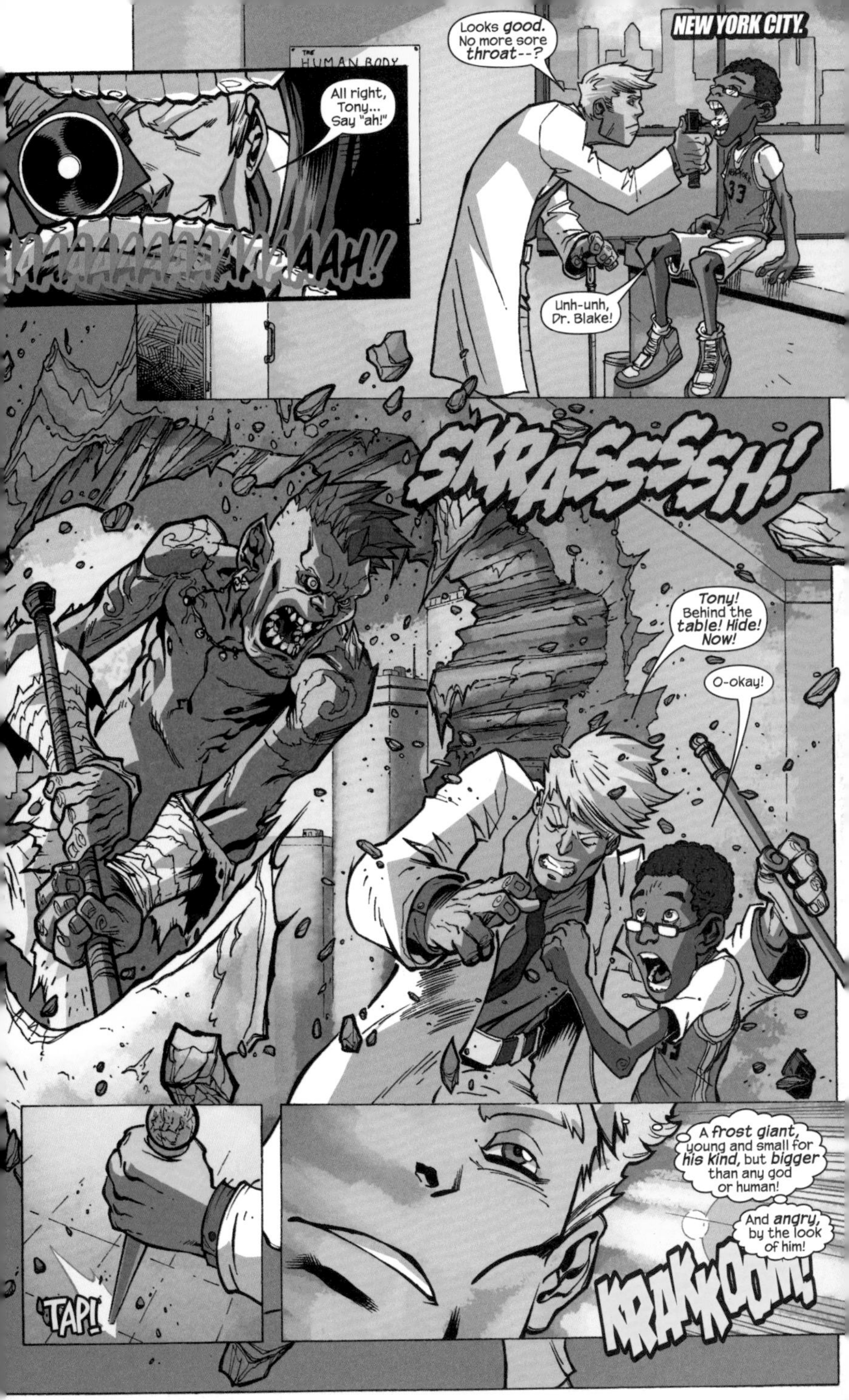
NEW YORK CITY.
THE HUMAN BODY
All right, Tony... Say "ah!"
AAAAAAAAAAAAAH!!
Looks good. No more sore throat--?
Unh-unh, Dr. Blake!
SKRASSSSH!
Tony! Behind the table! Hide! Now!
O-okay!
TAP!
A frost giant, young and small for his kind, but bigger than any god or human!
And angry, by the look of him!
KRAKOOM!

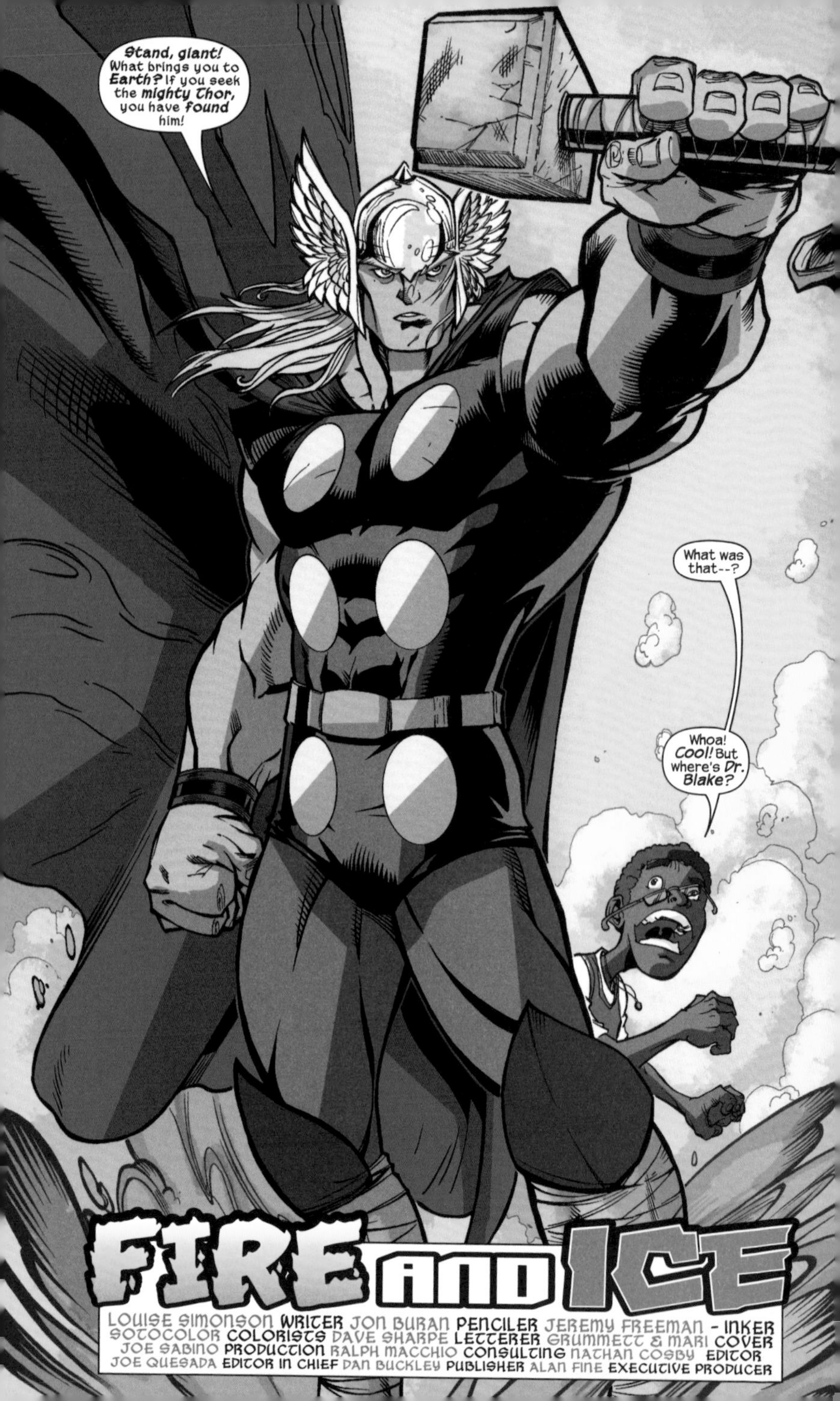
Stand, giant! What brings you to Earth? If you seek the mighty Thor, you have found him!
What was that--?
Whoa! Cool! But where's Dr. Blake?
FIRE AND ICE
LOUISE SIMONSON WRITER JON BURAN PENCILER JEREMY FREEMAN - INKER
SOTOCOLOR COLORISTS DAVE SHARPE LETTERER GRUMMETT & MARI COVER
JOE SABINO PRODUCTION RALPH MACCHIO CONSULTING NATHAN COSBY EDITOR
JOE QUESADA EDITOR IN CHIEF DAN BUCKLEY PUBLISHER ALAN FINE EXECUTIVE PRODUCER

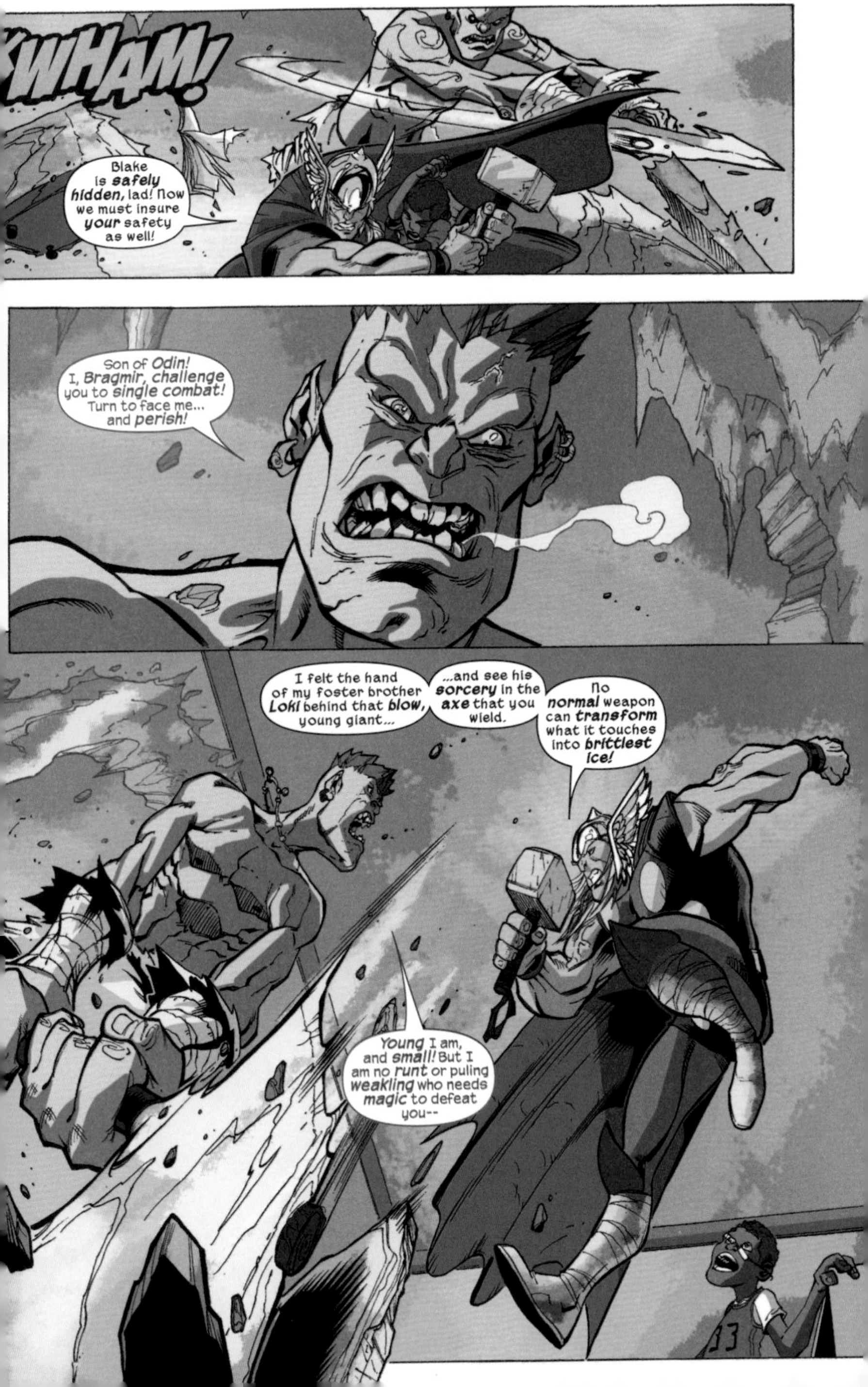

KWHAM!
Blake is safely hidden, lad! Now we must insure your safety as well!
Son of Odin! I, Bragmir, challenge you to single combat! Turn to face me... and perish!
I felt the hand of my foster brother Loki behind that blow, young giant...
...and see his sorcery in the axe that you wield.
No normal weapon can transform what it touches into brittlest ice!
Young I am, and small! But I am no runt or puling weakling who needs magic to defeat you--

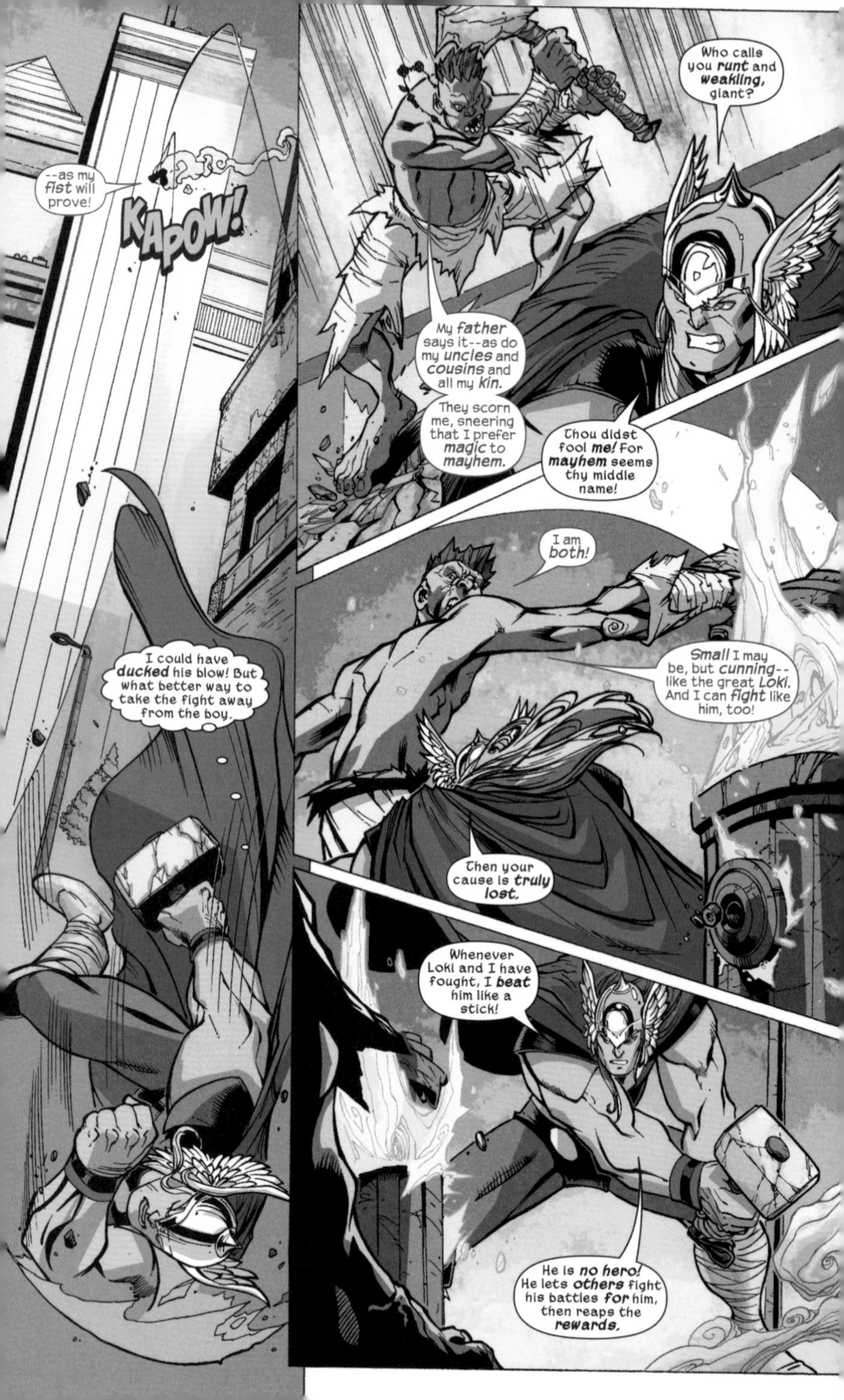

--as my fist will prove!
KAPOW!
I could have ducked his blow! But what better way to take the fight away from the boy.
Who calls you runt and weakling, giant?
My father says it--as do my uncles and cousins and all my kin.
They scorn me, sneering that I prefer magic to mayhem.
Thou didst fool me! For mayhem seems thy middle name!
I am both!
Small I may be, but cunning--like the great Loki. And I can fight like him, too!
Then your cause is truly lost.
Whenever Loki and I have fought, I beat him like a stick!
He is no hero! He lets others fight his battles for him, then reaps the rewards.

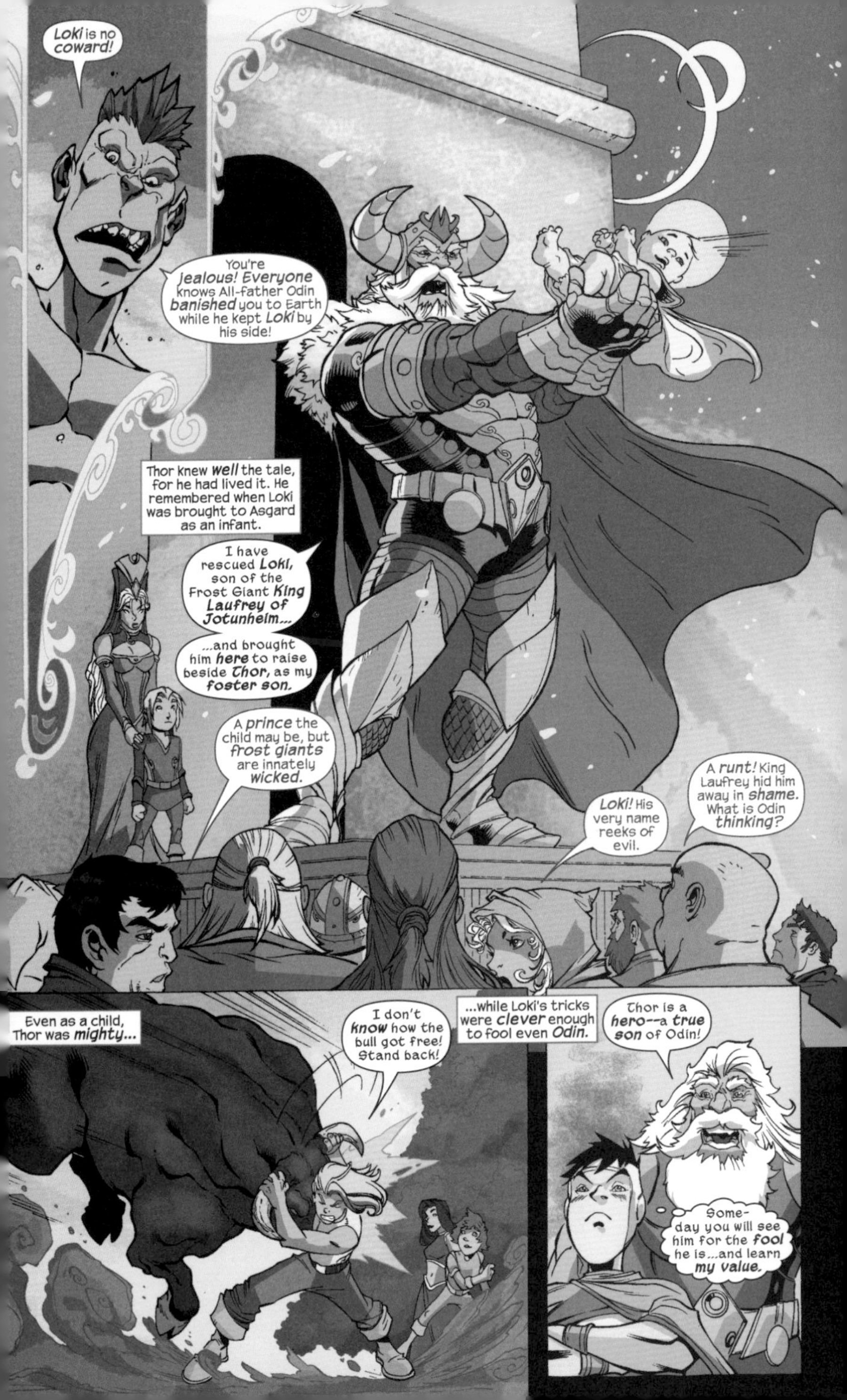
Loki is no coward!
You're jealous! Everyone knows All-father Odin banished you to Earth while he kept Loki by his side!
Thor knew well the tale, for he had lived it. He remembered when Loki was brought to Asgard as an infant.
I have rescued Loki, son of the Frost Giant King Laufrey of Jotunheim...
...and brought him here to raise beside Thor, as my foster son.
A prince the child may be, but frost giants are innately wicked.
Loki! His very name reeks of evil.
A runt! King Laufrey hid him away in shame. What is Odin thinking?
Even as a child, Thor was mighty...
I don't know how the bull got free! Stand back!
...while Loki's tricks were clever enough to fool even Odin.
Thor is a hero--a true son of Odin!
Someday you will see him for the fool he is...and learn my value.

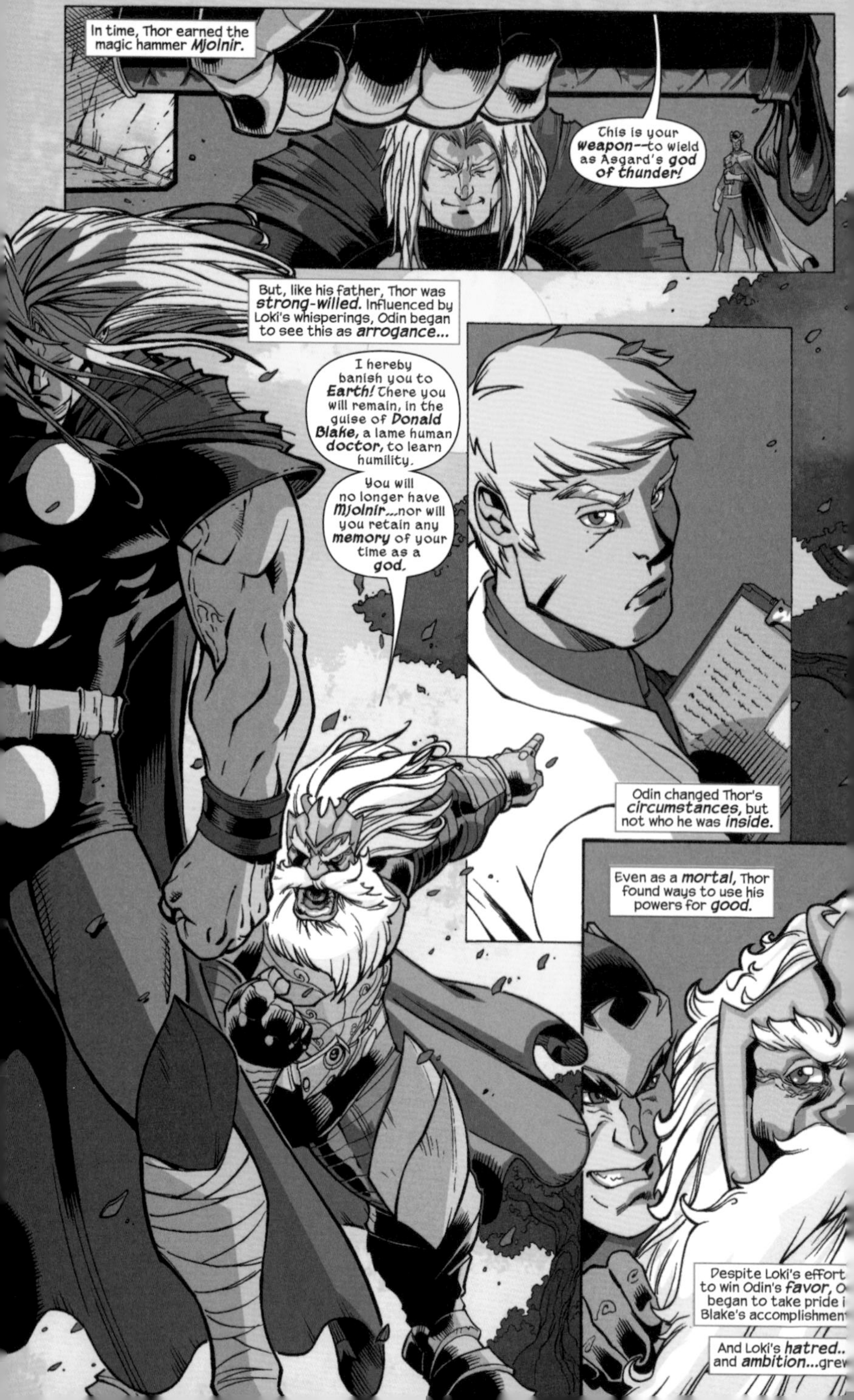
In time, Thor earned the magic hammer *Mjolnir*.
This is your *weapon*--to wield as Asgard's *god of thunder!*
But, like his father, Thor was *strong-willed.* Influenced by Loki's whisperings, Odin began to see this as *arrogance...*
I hereby banish you to *Earth!* There you will remain, in the guise of *Donald Blake*, a lame human *doctor*, to learn humility.
You will no longer have *Mjolnir*...nor will you retain any *memory* of your time as a *god*.
Odin changed Thor's *circumstances*, but not who he was *inside*.
Even as a *mortal*, Thor found ways to use his powers for *good*.
Despite Loki's effort to win Odin's *favor*, O began to take pride i Blake's accomplishmen
And Loki's *hatred*.. and *ambition*...grew

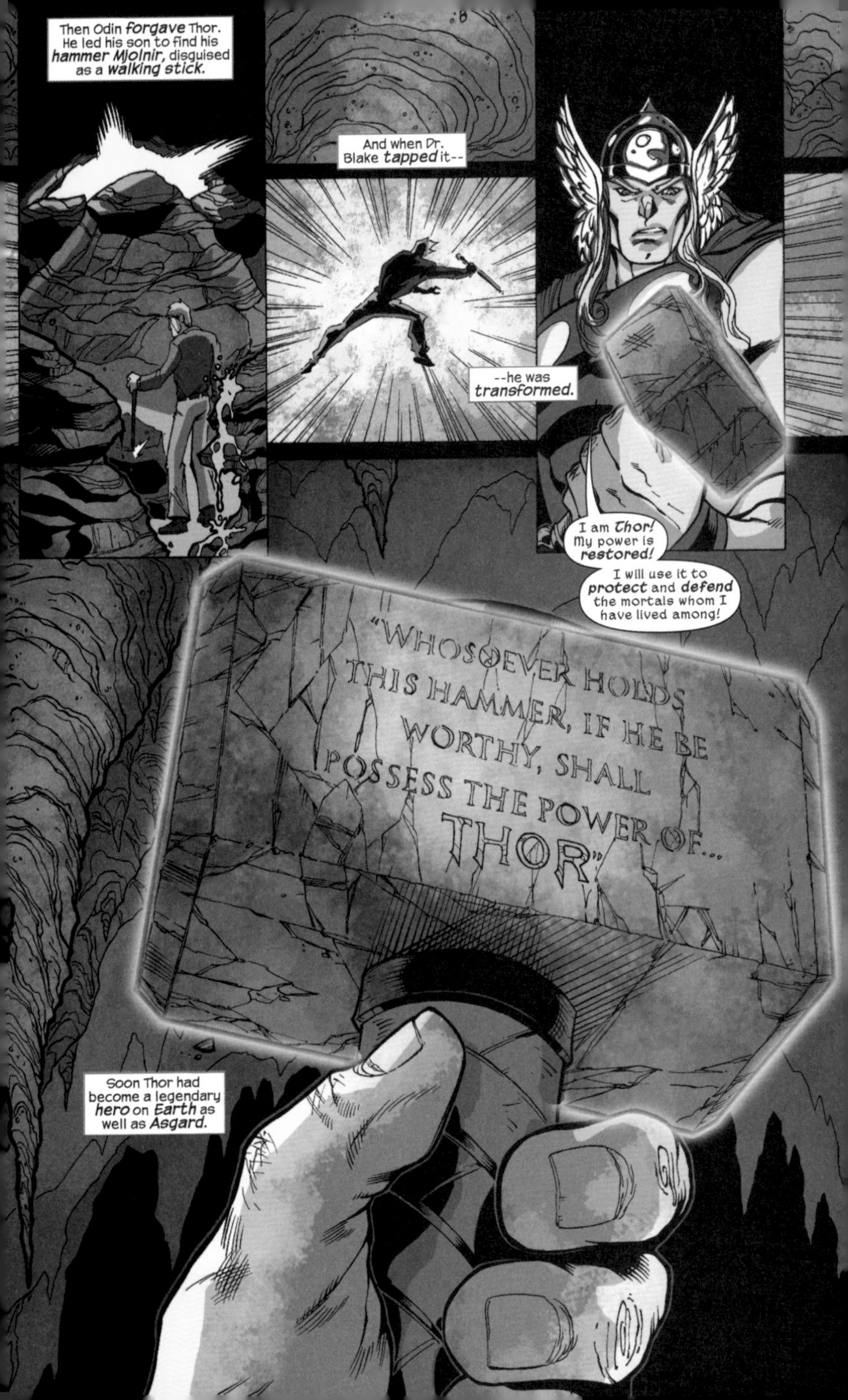
Then Odin forgave Thor. He led his son to find his hammer Mjolnir, disguised as a walking stick.
And when Dr. Blake tapped it--
--he was transformed.
I am Thor! My power is restored!
I will use it to protect and defend the mortals whom I have lived among!
"WHOSOEVER HOLDS THIS HAMMER, IF HE BE WORTHY, SHALL POSSESS THE POWER OF... THOR"
Soon Thor had become a legendary hero on Earth as well as Asgard.

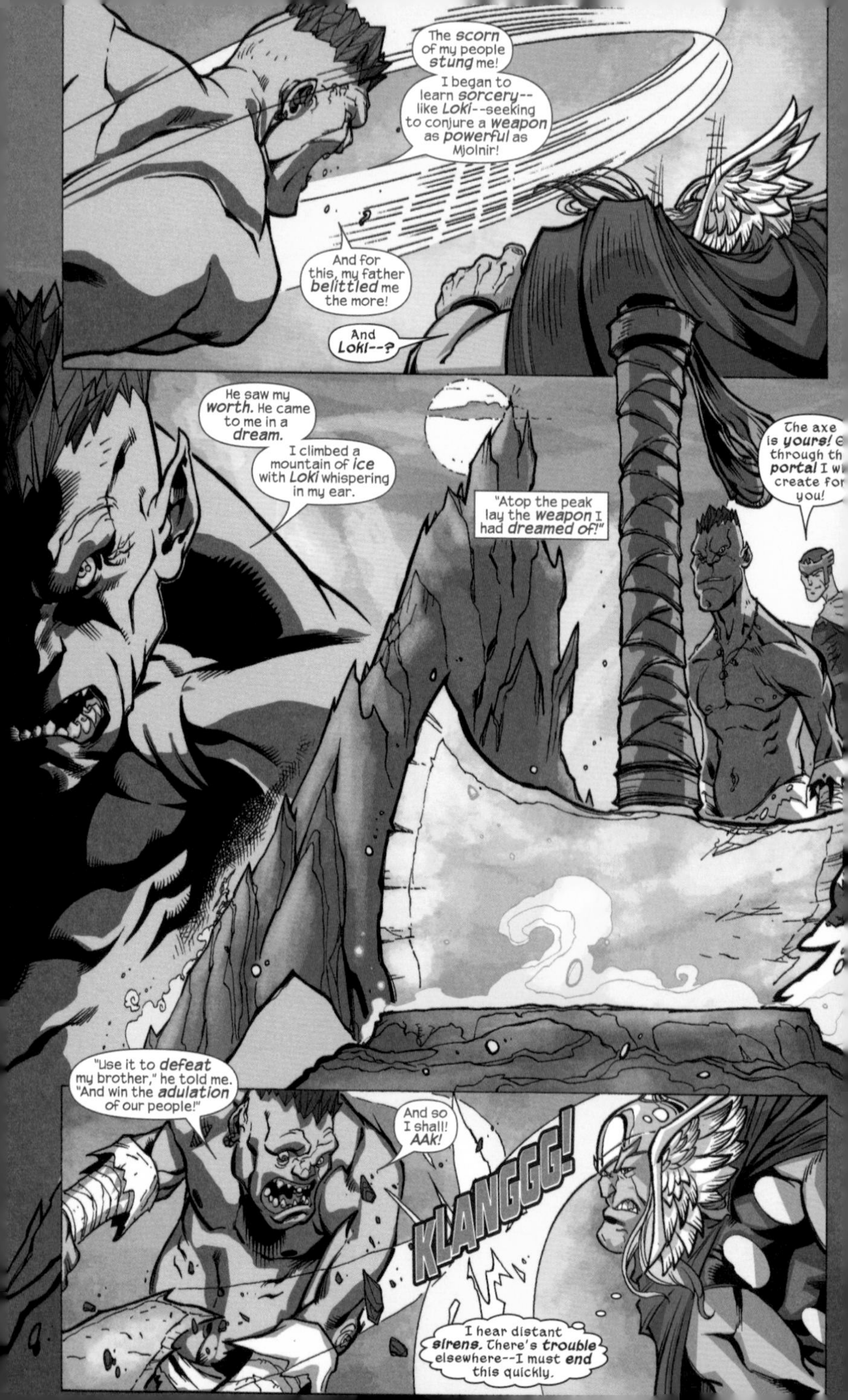
The scorn of my people stung me!
I began to learn sorcery--like Loki--seeking to conjure a weapon as powerful as Mjolnir!
And for this, my father belittled me the more!
And Loki--?
He saw my worth. He came to me in a dream.
I climbed a mountain of ice with Loki whispering in my ear.
"Atop the peak lay the weapon I had dreamed of!"
"Use it to defeat my brother," he told me. "And win the adulation of our people!"
And so I shall! AAK!
KLANGGG!
I hear distant sirens. There's trouble elsewhere--I must end this quickly.

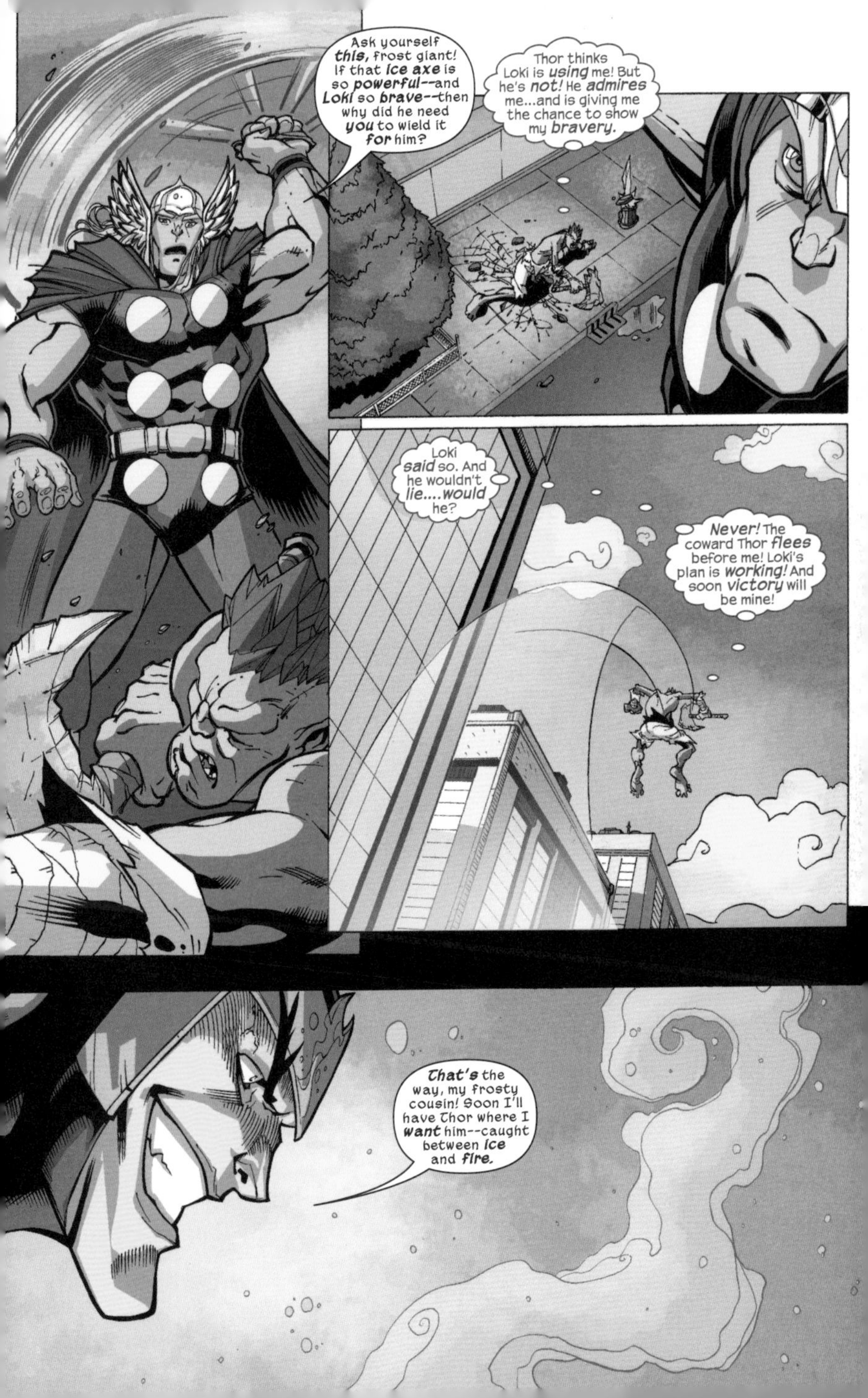
Ask yourself this, frost giant! If that ice axe is so powerful--and Loki so brave--then why did he need you to wield it for him?
Thor thinks Loki is using me! But he's not! He admires me...and is giving me the chance to show my bravery.
Loki said so. And he wouldn't lie....would he?
Never! The coward Thor flees before me! Loki's plan is working! And soon victory will be mine!
That's the way, my frosty cousin! Soon I'll have Thor where I want him--caught between ice and fire.

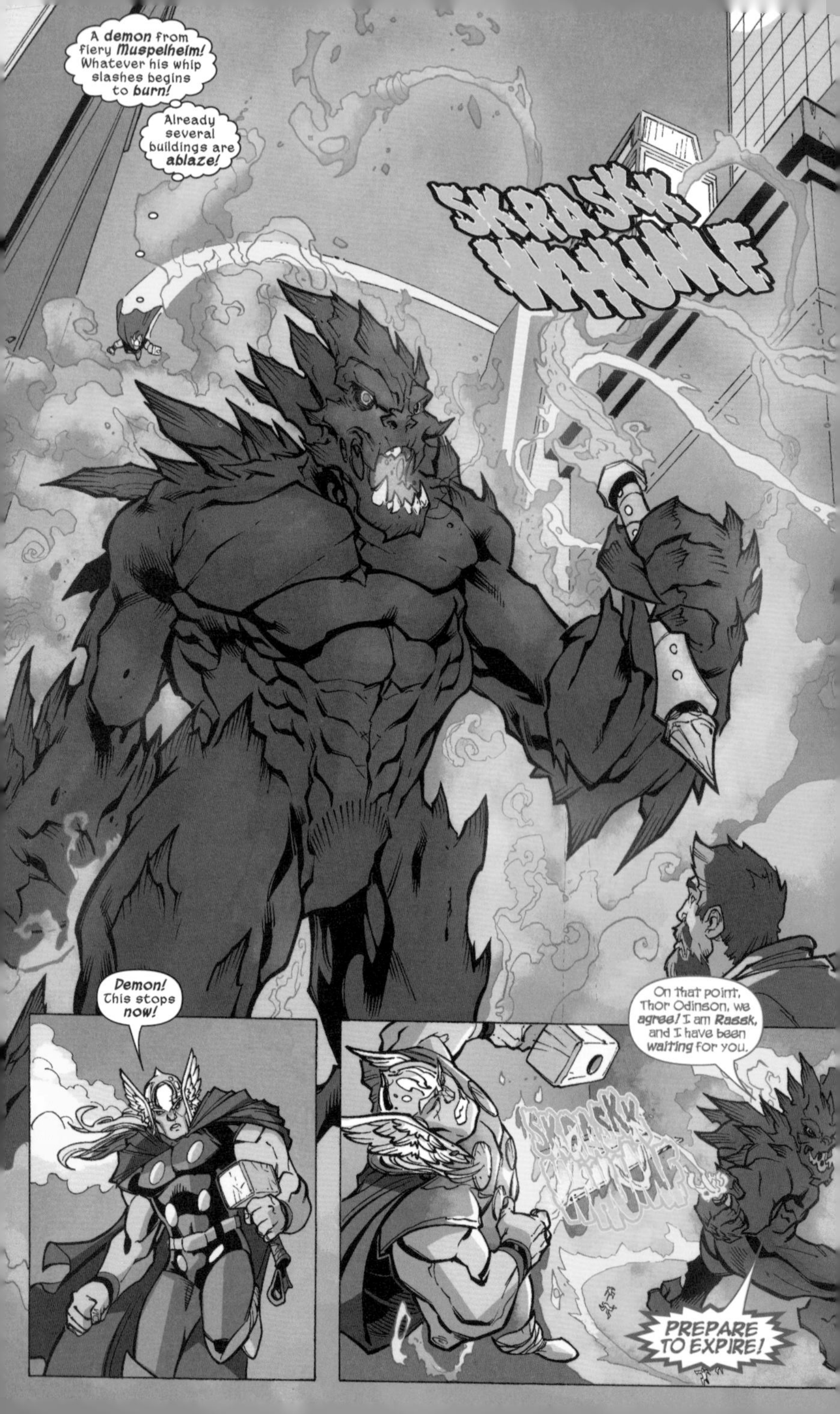

A demon from fiery Muspelheim! Whatever his whip slashes begins to burn!
Already several buildings are ablaze!
SKRASKK WHUMF
Demon! This stops now!
On that point, Thor Odinson, we agree! I am Rassk, and I have been waiting for you.
SKRASKK
PREPARE TO EXPIRE!

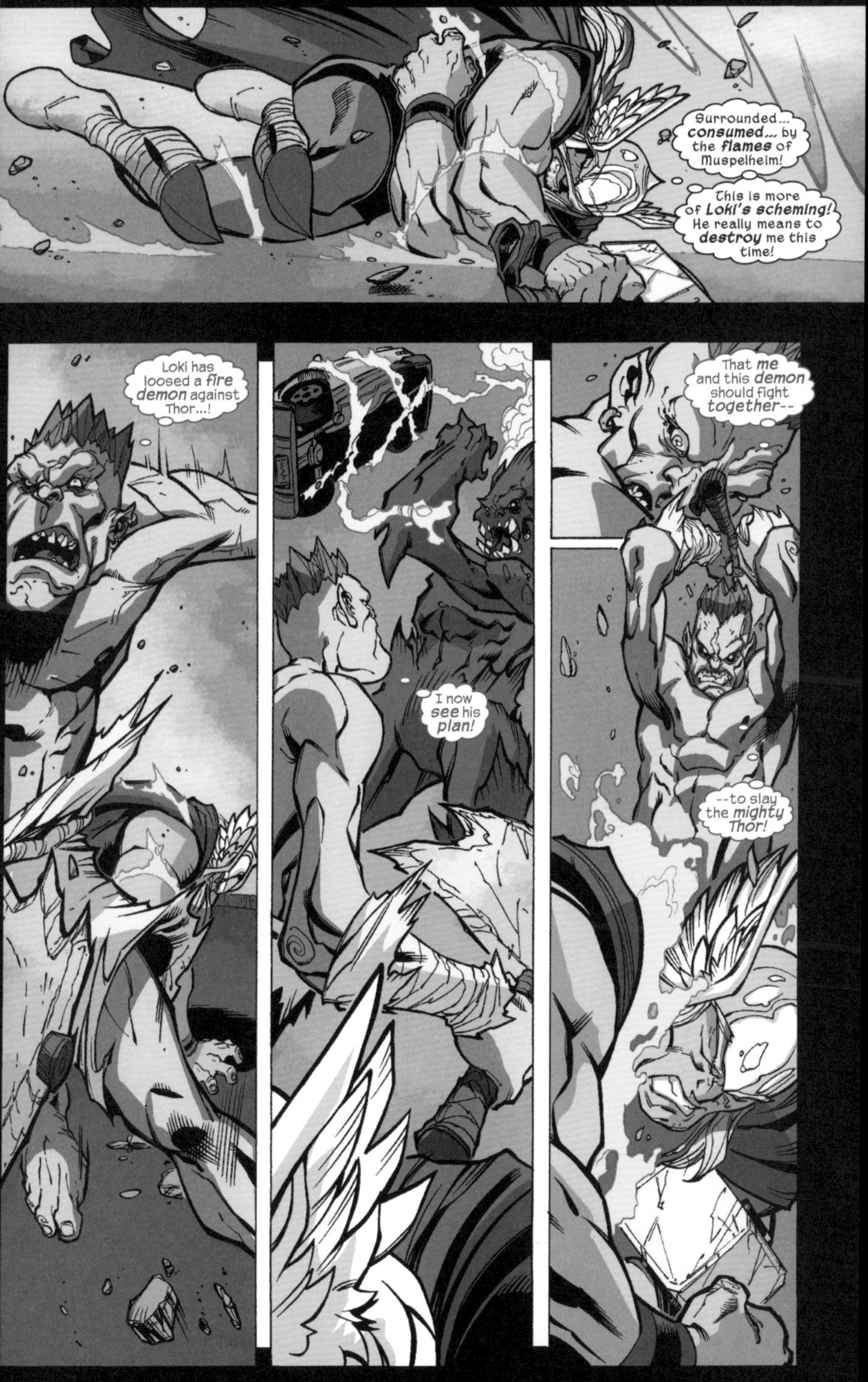
Surrounded... consumed... by the flames of Muspelheim!
This is more of Loki's scheming! He really means to destroy me this time!
Loki has loosed a fire demon against Thor...!
I now see his plan!
That me and this demon should fight together--
--to slay the mighty Thor!

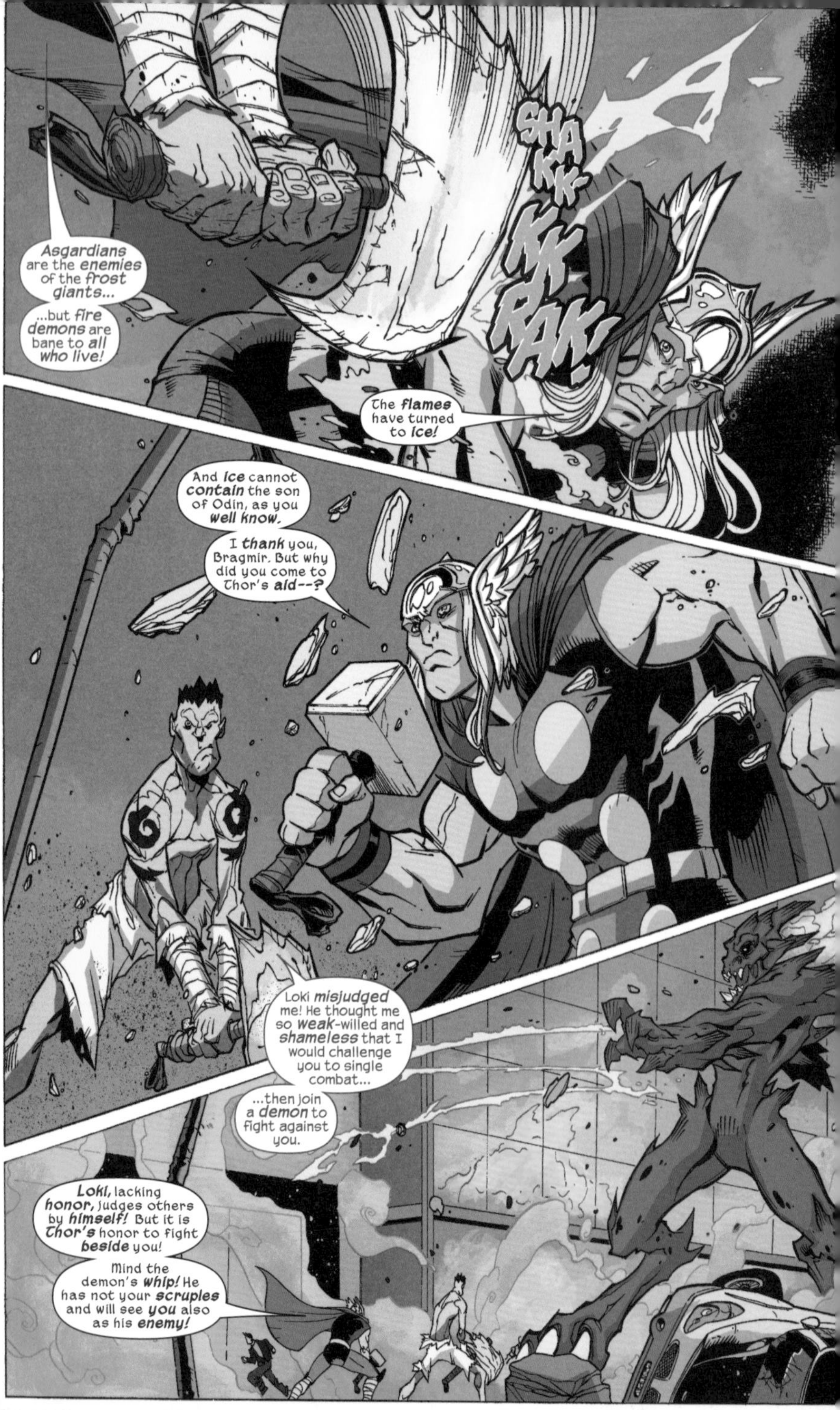

SHAKKKKKRAK!
Asgardians are the enemies of the frost giants...
...but fire demons are bane to all who live!
The flames have turned to ice!
And ice cannot contain the son of Odin, as you well know.
I thank you, Bragmir. But why did you come to Thor's aid--?
Loki misjudged me! He thought me so weak-willed and shameless that I would challenge you to single combat...
...then join a demon to fight against you.
Loki, lacking honor, judges others by himself! But it is Thor's honor to fight beside you!
Mind the demon's whip! He has not your scruples and will see you also as his enemy!

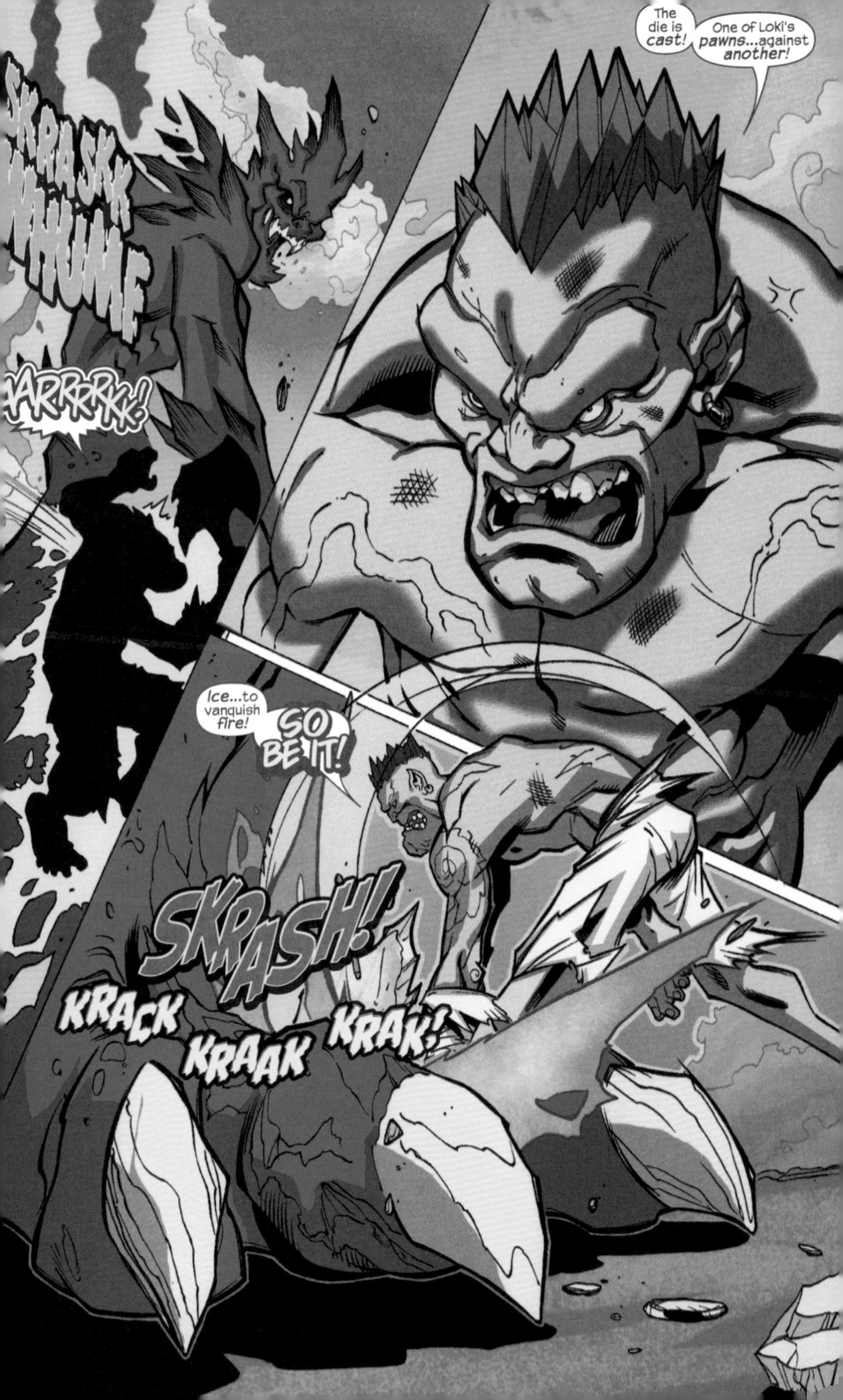

SKRASK
WHUMF
ARRRRKK!
The die is cast!
One of Loki's pawns...against another!
Ice...to vanquish fire!
SO BE IT!
SKRASH!
KRACK
KRAAK
KRAK!

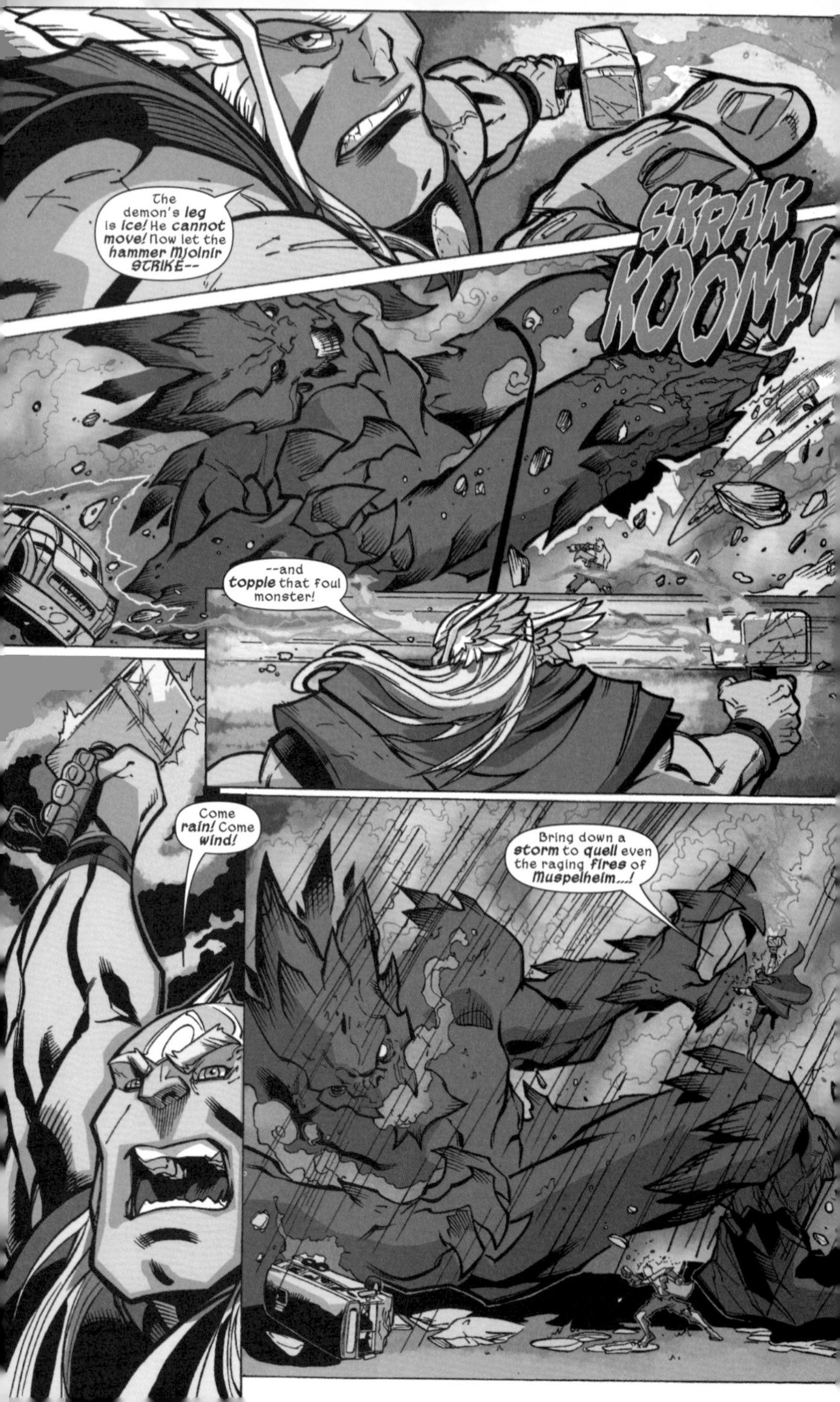
The demon's leg is ice! He cannot move! Now let the hammer Mjolnir STRIKE--
SKRAK KOOM!
--and topple that foul monster!
Come rain! Come wind!
Bring down a storm to quell even the raging fires of Muspelheim...!

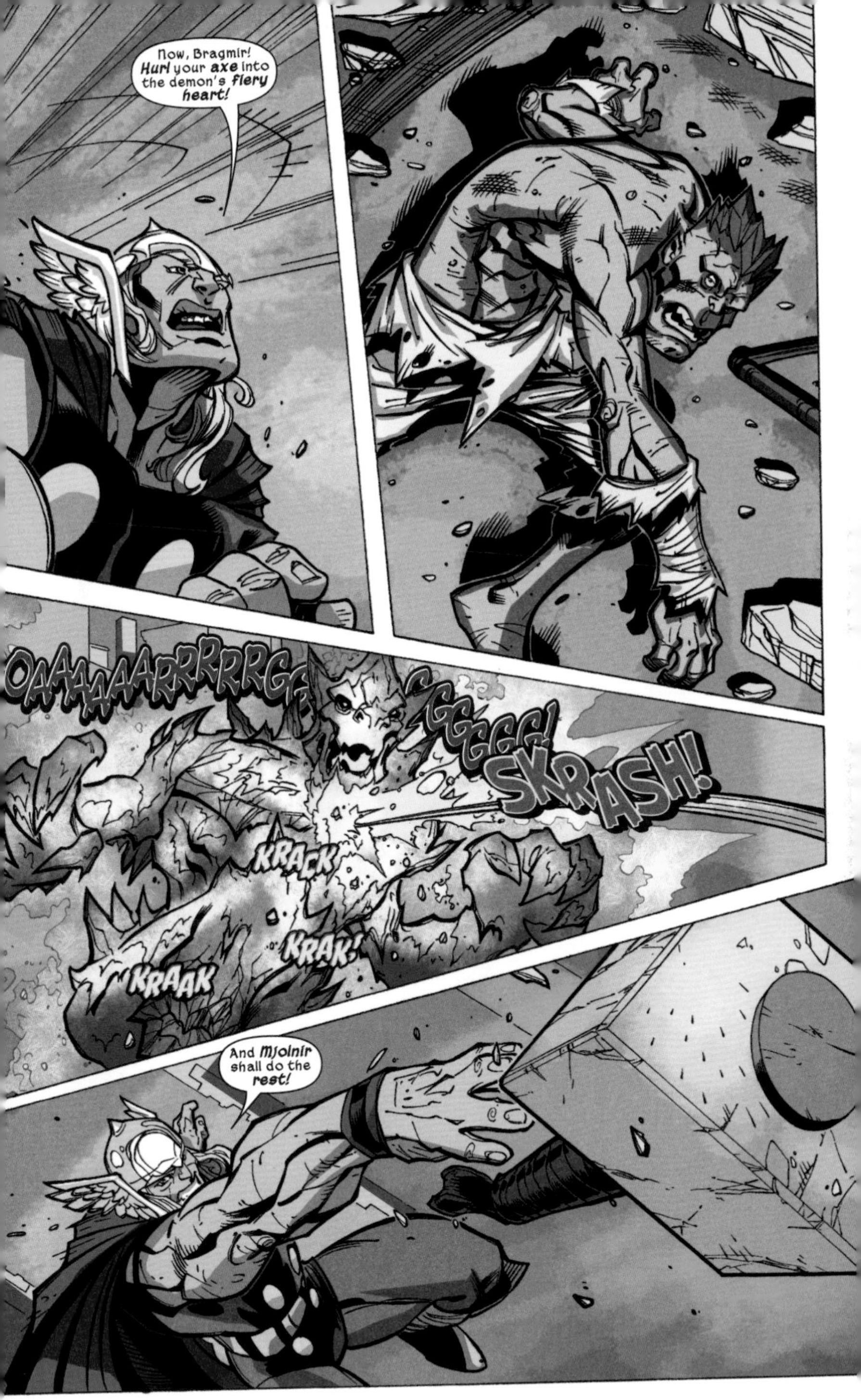
Now, Bragmir! Hurl your axe into the demon's fiery heart!
OAAAAAAARRRRRGGGGGGG!
SKRASH!
KRACK
KRAK!
KRAAK
And Mjolnir shall do the rest!

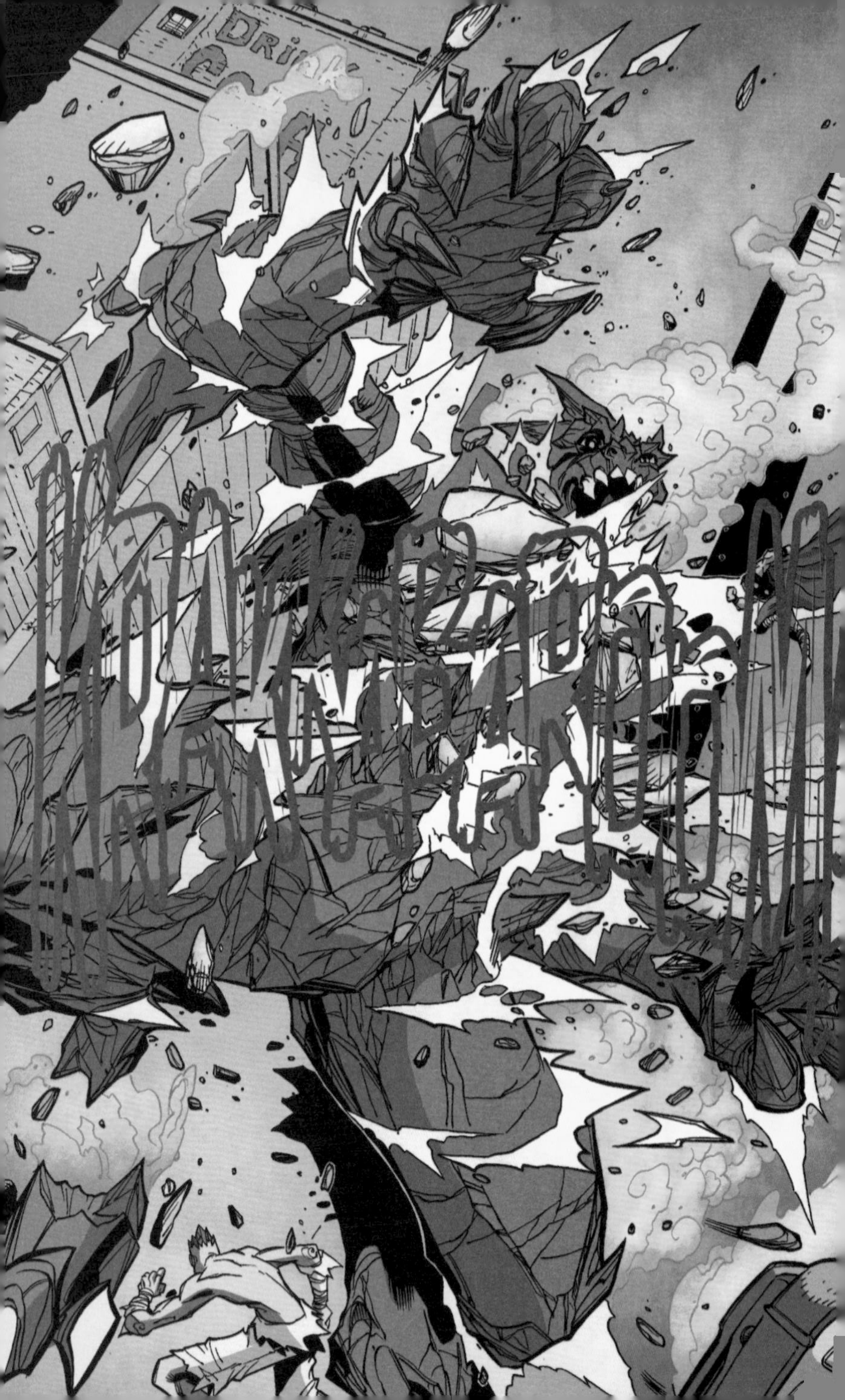

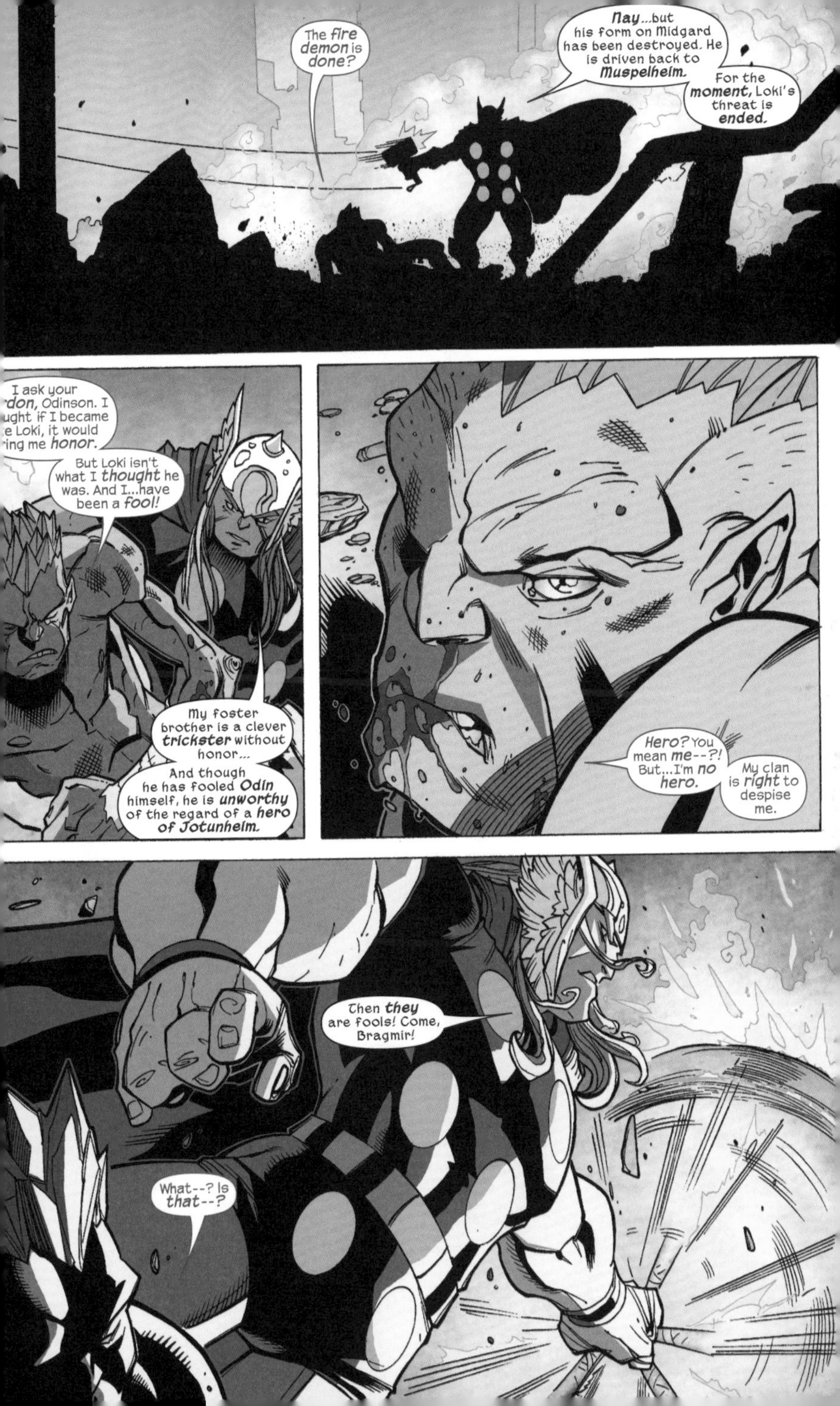

The fire demon is done?
Nay...but his form on Midgard has been destroyed. He is driven back to Muspelheim.
For the moment, Loki's threat is ended.
I ask your rdon, Odinson. I ught if I became e Loki, it would ring me honor.
But Loki isn't what I thought he was. And I...have been a fool!
My foster brother is a clever trickster without honor...
And though he has fooled Odin himself, he is unworthy of the regard of a hero of Jotunheim.
Hero? You mean me--?! But...I'm no hero.
My clan is right to despise me.
Then they are fools! Come, Bragmir!
What--? Is that--?

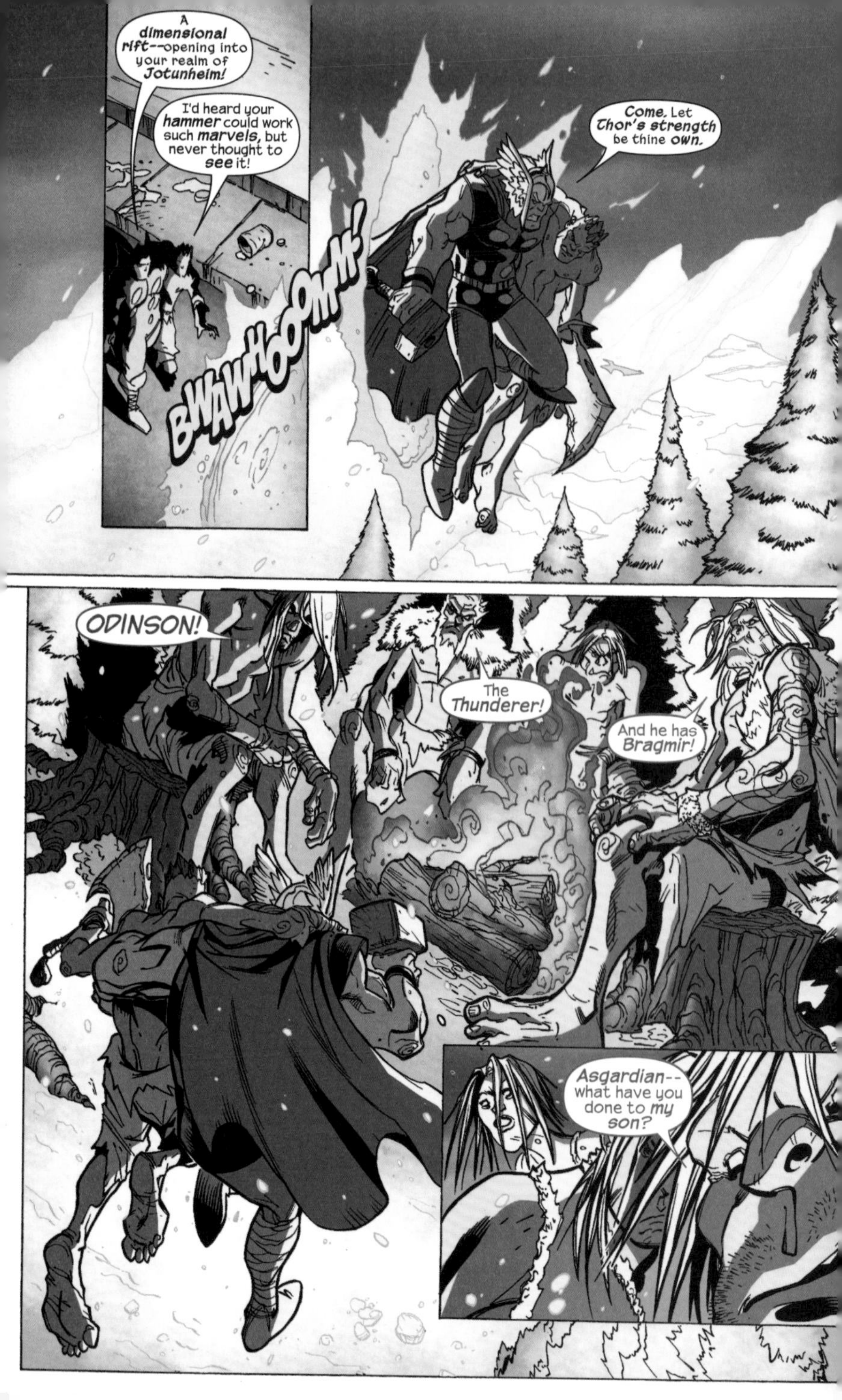
A dimensional rift--opening into your realm of Jotunheim!
I'd heard your hammer could work such marvels, but never thought to see it!
BWAWHOOOMM!
Come. Let Thor's strength be thine own.
ODINSON!
The Thunderer!
And he has Bragmir!
Asgardian--what have you done to my son?

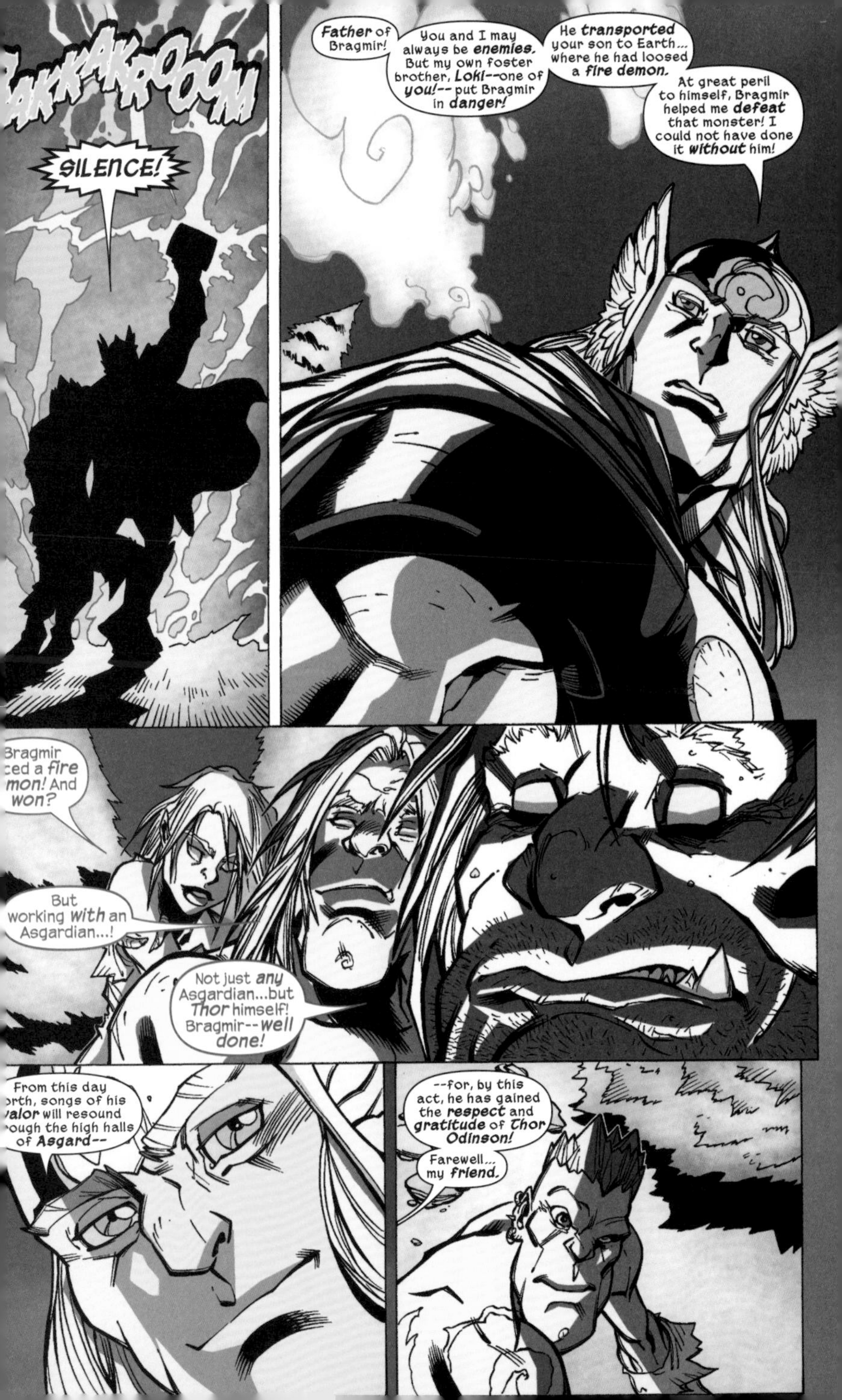

KAKKAKROOOOM
SILENCE!
Father of Bragmir!
You and I may always be enemies. But my own foster brother, Loki--one of you!--put Bragmir in danger!
He transported your son to Earth... where he had loosed a fire demon.
At great peril to himself, Bragmir helped me defeat that monster! I could not have done it without him!
Bragmir ced a fire mon! And won?
But working with an Asgardian...!
Not just any Asgardian...but Thor himself! Bragmir--well done!
From this day orth, songs of his valor will resound ough the high halls of Asgard--
--for, by this act, he has gained the respect and gratitude of Thor Odinson!
Farewell... my friend.

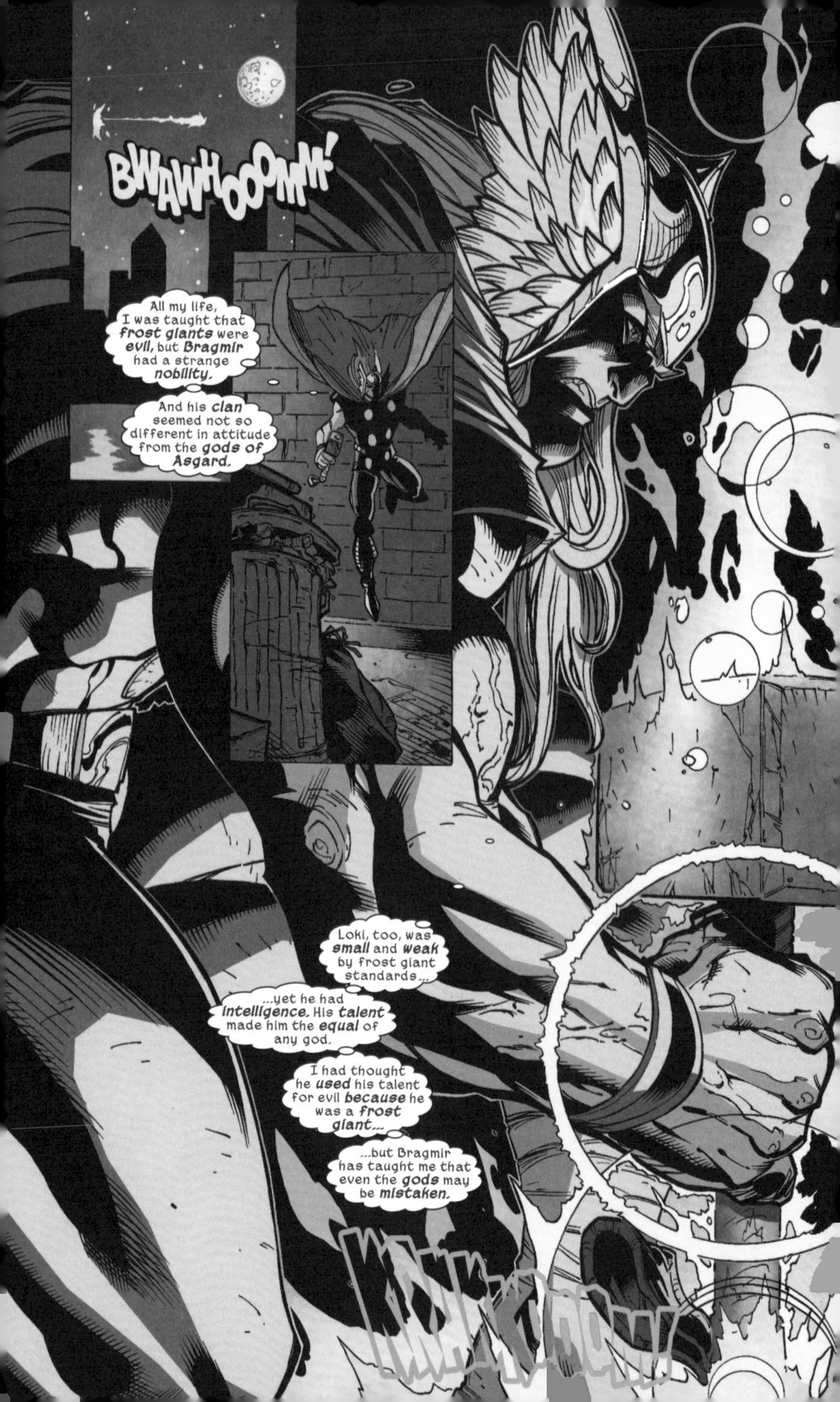
BWAWHOOOMM!
All my life, I was taught that frost giants were evil, but Bragmir had a strange nobility.
And his clan seemed not so different in attitude from the gods of Asgard.
Loki, too, was small and weak by frost giant standards...
...yet he had intelligence. His talent made him the equal of any god.
I had thought he used his talent for evil because he was a frost giant...
...but Bragmir has taught me that even the gods may be mistaken.

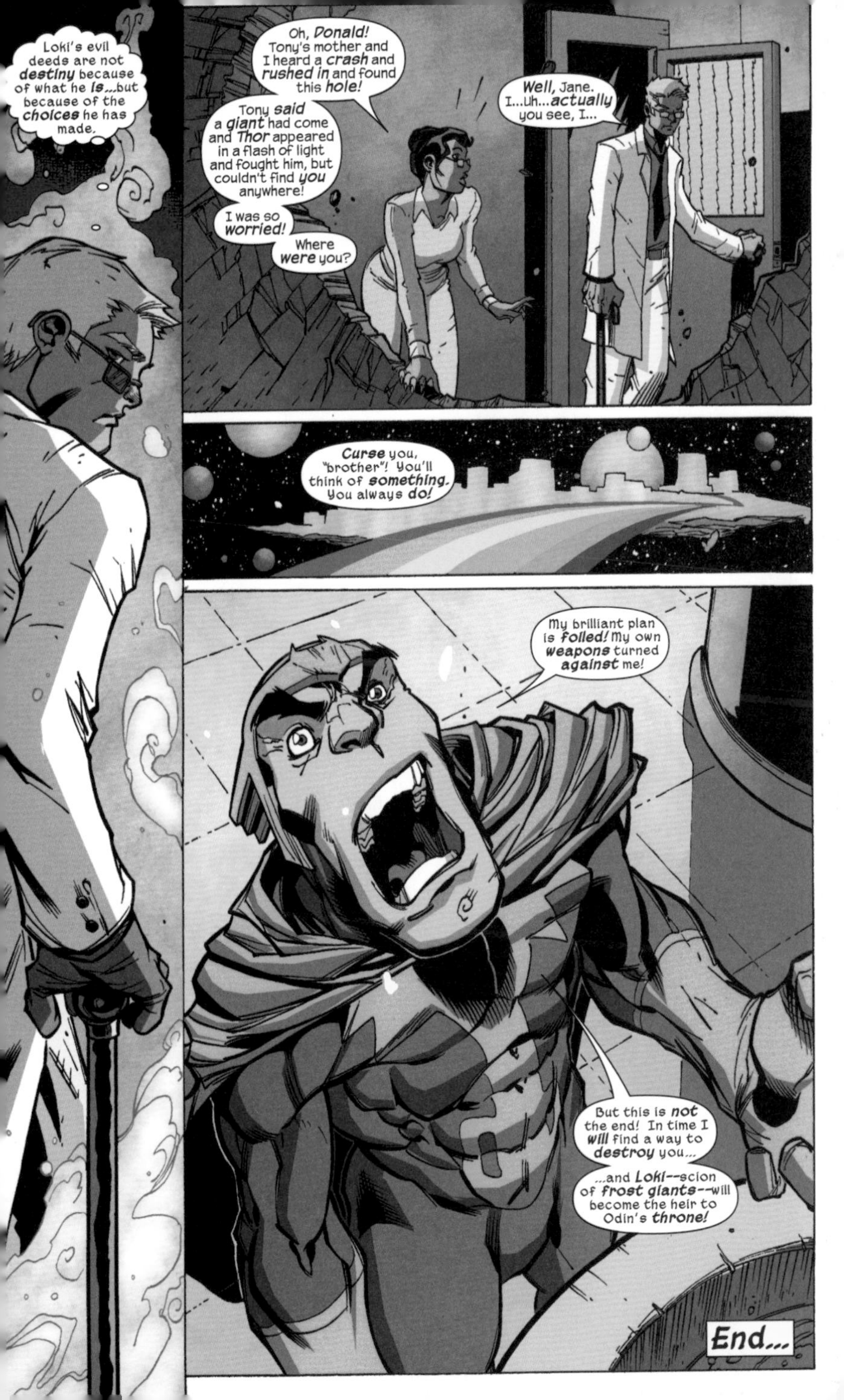
Loki's evil deeds are not destiny because of what he is...but because of the choices he has made.
Oh, Donald! Tony's mother and I heard a crash and rushed in and found this hole!
Tony said a giant had come and Thor appeared in a flash of light and fought him, but couldn't find you anywhere!
I was so worried!
Where were you?
Well, Jane. I...uh...actually you see, I...
Curse you, "brother"! You'll think of something. You always do!
My brilliant plan is foiled! My own weapons turned against me!
But this is not the end! In time I will find a way to destroy you...
...and Loki--scion of frost giants--will become the heir to Odin's throne!
End...